The Urbana Free Library

DISCARDED BY THE
URBANA FREE LIBRARY

To renew: call 217-367-4057
or go to "*urbanafreelibrary.org*"
and select "Renew/Request Items"

5-12

DATE DUE

MAY 3 1 2012
SEP 2 2 2012
JUL 01 2013

The Invitation

ALSO BY ANNE CHERIAN

A Good Indian Wife

The Invitation

A NOVEL

Anne Cherian

W. W. NORTON & COMPANY
NEW YORK • LONDON

5/12
2600

Copyright © 2012 by Anne Cherian

All rights reserved

Printed in the United States of America
First Edition

For information about permission to reproduce selections from this book, write to Permissions, W. W. Norton & Company, Inc., 500 Fifth Avenue, New York, NY 10110

For information about special discounts for bulk purchases, please contact W. W. Norton Special Sales at specialsales@wwnorton.com or 800-233-4830

Manufacturing by Courier Westford
Book design by BTDNYC
Production manager: Louise Mattarelliano

Library of Congress Cataloging-in-Publication Data

Cherian, Anne.
The invitation : a novel / Anne Cherian. — 1st ed.
p. cm.
ISBN 978-0-393-08160-2 (hardcover)
1. East Indians—United States—Fiction. 2. Immigrant families—United States—Fiction. I. Title.
PS3603.H476I58 2012
813'.6—dc23
2011044658

W. W. Norton & Company, Inc.
500 Fifth Avenue, New York, N.Y. 10110
www.wwnorton.com

W. W. Norton & Company Ltd.
Castle House, 75/76 Wells Street, London W1T 3QT

1 2 3 4 5 6 7 8 9 0

For the women who help me see the glass half-full:
Elsie, Claudia, and Selma.
Also,
Oona Aven, Anju Basu, Barbara Bundy,
Soo-Young Chin, Julie Connery, Ellie Miller,
Lady N, Mary O'Sullivan, Marie Stael von Holstein.
And always, Cole and Reid,
my two miracles.

CONTENTS

An Invitation Arrives

Frances turned around and waved to the gray-haired couple standing in the doorway. She smiled happily, her palm moving energetically through the sticky afternoon air. The elderly Millers had *finally* agreed to an offer for their home. It was her first sale in a year, and Frances was anxious to fax their acceptance and make it a done deal.

She recalled the day the Millers had walked into the office the previous July. It had been just another slow Thursday, and the two seemed a little lost. So she had offered them chairs, tea, and coffee. Houses weren't mentioned for quite a while because Mr. Miller guessed she was from India and told her he had been there during World War II.

"It was for a week only," Gene Miller acknowledged, "but I still remember the bright colors, the warm rain, and the most delicious mango I have ever eaten."

Frances had enjoyed his memories, so different from those of other Americans who revered India as "an amazing, spiritual place" she did not recognize, or, conversely, sighed about the dense crowds and spicy food that beleaguered their stomachs. She had also been relieved that she did not need to provide the usual explanation of her origins.

There were many Indians in Los Angeles, but very few lived in the San Fernando Valley, and she was constantly having to clarify: "No, I'm not Armenian, you know, and I'm also not from the Middle East. I'm Indian by way of Portugal because my ancestors came from there, hence my name, Frances Dias." Her husband, Jay, had come up with the punch line she typically finished with: "I'm from Goa, and I'm goin' to sell your house for you, so don't worry about a thing."

She had promised the Millers that she was goin' to sell their house in Burbank, but the weak market meant that it attracted very few people during the open houses she had held diligently for two months. The Millers weren't in any rush because they were planning to move into one of the units in an apartment building they owned. But after four months of no activity at all, even they grew a little anxious. She explained the down market, the difficulty of getting loans, and they nodded, though she privately continued to worry that the house might never sell.

Last month they reluctantly gave in to her recommendation to move some of the heavy furniture to the garage, making the rooms, as she had hoped, look larger and lighter. Frances brought in flowers and potted plants, and gently reminded the Millers that they would probably have to lower their asking price.

Then today at noon, on a morning that was already clammy at 9 a.m., another agent in the office, Susan Hayman, had placed the offer on her desk. The buyers were prequalified, and were putting down 30 percent.

"Any wiggle room?" Frances knew she had to fight a little, because the offer was $40,000 below list price.

"Nope," Susan said firmly. "This is the best they can do. But they're serious, and ready to sign."

So Frances called the Millers and immediately went to their house. She had expected they would make a small fuss about the lower offer, and Mr. Miller had pointed out that the house across the street had sold for more than its asking price.

"That was three years ago, you know," Frances reminded him. "This offer isn't that far off from what you want," she pressed her point, and, miraculously, a short while later, they had signed.

Now Frances started the car and decided to drive home. It was closer than her office, and she wanted to fax the letter quickly. The Millers didn't look like the sort who changed their minds, but after being in the business for fifteen years, Frances knew that anything could happen at any time, for any reason.

There was hardly any traffic—just another wonderful thing about the day, she thought happily. She hadn't had time to tell Jay, but she knew he would be very pleased that she had finally sold a house. Her mind fast-forwarded to dinner; she would order a pizza to celebrate. Her younger two, Lily and Sam, would love the unexpected treat. Amanda liked pizza too, but she was too diffident at seventeen to show enthusiasm for anything.

The air-conditioner slats blasted in cool air, while outside, a smoglike haze shimmied above the asphalt. She disliked such moist, breeze-free days. When she arrived in the office in the morning, she had grumbled that this was April, that the Valley wasn't supposed to begin boiling until later in the year. But now she didn't care. Even the slow driver in front of her didn't generate her usual curse word, *harami*. She simply changed lanes and pressed down on the accelerator.

She had just parked the car in the driveway and called out, "Hello," to their neighbor Lucy Margolis who was planting the bright red ranunculus she put in every spring, when the cell phone rang.

"You haven't sent the offer yet, have you?" Mr. Miller asked.

Frances glanced at the side of the house, at the bedroom that doubled as her office, the fax machine ready to go. "I'm just about to," she said.

"Don't. We want to stick with the original price," Mr. Miller stated.

"Are you sure about that?" Frances forced her voice to be calm.

"We're absolutely positive. We're not in any hurry, and my wife reminded me that the market is supposed to pick up in a few months."

"If you're sure, then, I'll let them know," she forced out the words through her closing throat.

"Good," Mr. Miller said, and hung up.

Frances slipped the phone into her purse, not bothering to place it in its usual pocket. The good feeling, that indisputable belief that even the traffic lights had been on her side, evaporated.

She knew from experience that it wasn't productive to wonder why the Millers had changed their mind. Once, long ago, she had even called back a client, trying to convince him. But it had backfired on her. The client had felt hounded, and she learned how easy it was for someone to switch real estate agents. She just had the one client. That client, however, had a roster of agents to choose from.

She got out of the car, her purse heavy on her shoulders, the briefcase with the signed contract clasped uselessly in her hand.

Jay would say, "Nothing always happens for a reason."

But his take on idioms no longer amused her.

The twelve months of inactivity had affected her confidence. She had been the top salesperson until three years ago, when the market took a dive, along with her income. They could not survive on Jay's middle-manager salary, and because the computer company he worked for was small, he was stuck in his position until his superior resigned, or he found another job. There were entirely too many nights that Frances lay awake, calculating the month's expenses, worrying what would happen if they used up their savings before she started doing better.

"You're home early," Lucy called out.

Frances looked at the kind face, aware that her neighbor, retired and living alone, always enjoyed a chat.

"Have to make dinner for the family, you know," she said, and walked quickly toward the front door. On most days she enjoyed catching up with Lucy, who kept Frances informed about what was happening on their street.

"A coupon for pizza was in the mail today," Lucy told her, and Frances simply said, "Thanks," before shutting the door.

She put her purse and briefcase on the buffet table and went straight to the kitchen. Mandy had made a snack for her younger brother and sister, as she was supposed to do, but she hadn't bothered to clean up. The gob of peanut butter that rimmed one corner of the sink, the bread crusts on the cutting board, the ants blackening the dollop of red jam added to the general grubbiness of the kitchen. She had just been in the Millers' renovated kitchen, and her own, with the original 1950s cabinets and dented stove, added to her despondency.

Jay and she had bought this house precisely because it was a fixer-upper. They had made grand plans to tear down one wall in the kitchen, put in an island, polish the hardwood floors. But once they moved in, they never had the money, so the kitchen drawers were rickety and uneven, and no matter how much she scrubbed the mustard-yellow linoleum floor, it always looked dirty.

Frances sighed. She picked up the sponge, then dropped it. This was Mandy's job, her only job around the house, and she should jolly well do it. Her daughter must be listening to music in her room—as usual.

As Frances walked through the living room, she heard noises in the backyard, a sure sign that Lily and Sam were playing outside. At ten and eight years of age, they didn't have much homework, and still enjoyed the jungle gym she had bought at a garage sale years earlier. Frances glanced out the sliding glass door and saw them, not on the bars as she had anticipated but bent over the exposed roots of the ficus tree.

Frances strode up to Mandy's room and opened the door, ignoring the ENTER ONLY IF INVITED sign. Her daughter was crouched over the computer, fingers traversing the keyboard, body moving to the music being piped into her ears from her iPod Touch. The pale yellow duvet was bunched up at the foot of the bed, clothes and books competed for space on the carpet, and the closet door was ajar because it was too crammed to close.

Frances tapped her daughter's bony shoulder.

"Mandy, I'm home."

Mandy closed her laptop computer quickly.

"Don't you knock?"

"Even if I did, you wouldn't be able to hear me," Frances reasoned. She looked at the computer, immediately wary. The agents in her office often anguished about finding undesirable sites on their children's computers. "What were you doing?"

"Nothing."

"Then let me see that nothing."

"Mom, this isn't India where children have no rights. I'm almost eighteen. I shouldn't have to remind you that I need my privacy."

"I pay for that privacy, you know."

"You also pay for my clothes. Do you want to wear them?"

"They're not my style," Frances said, wishing Mandy's tone weren't so nasty. She remembered her daughter's excitement the first time she fit into one of Frances's aprons. In those preteen years, Mandy enjoyed cooking with her mother and begged to wear her earrings for special occasions. But all that remained of those mother-daughter times were the videos Jay had taken. These days, anything Frances said deteriorated into just another argument.

Frances recalled the sticky mess in the kitchen.

"You didn't clean up, and now there are ants."

"I was going to get to it, but I thought you'd want me to finish this paper that's due tomorrow."

This was another Mandy maneuver. She knew Frances put schoolwork above everything else.

"Let me see it, then."

"It's not done yet."

"Now."

With a great sigh, Mandy slowly flipped open the computer. A few clicks later, the screen was filled with the heading "The Good Earth," followed by paragraphs. Except that Frances wasn't sure if Mandy had, in a few strikes from her fingers, exited a site she wasn't supposed to be on, to the Word document containing her paper. Jay had meant to put in one of those parental-control programs when they bought Mandy the computer at the start of high school, but, like so many things around the house, that, too, hadn't happened. She opened her mouth to confront Mandy but knew that this time she was partially responsible. She should have insisted that Jay do it. Besides, she already knew how Mandy would react, and was too out of sorts to add a squabble to her day.

"I've told you a hundred times that ants are hard to get rid of, you know."

Mandy rolled her eyes. "Bad day at work?"

Frances immediately shook her head.

She had never wanted to be one of those mothers who got angry at her children because of work problems. But an upsetting day like this took her right back to the early years when she had felt so vulnerable, unsure how to succeed as breadwinner and breadmaker—while keeping both lives separate.

She had been raised by Mama, who, like other women of her generation, had stopped working as a nurse when she married.

Even housework was easier in India, because everyone, including middle-class families like theirs, had a servant. Mama never had to leave in the morning for the office, then return home to a teenage daughter who believed in having rights, and two small children who thought that dinners magically appeared on the table.

The first time Frances encountered working mothers was in the Anthropology Department at UCLA. The graduate students never complained; they simply dropped off their children at day care. She was too new to the workings of an American university, where she had to write papers (instead of take exams) and teach undergraduates (some of whom were older than she), to look beneath their easy smiles. Back then, it never occurred to her that she would end up like them.

After all, her sisters were married, had children, and were not doing anything different from what Mama did. The only woman in their small town in Goa who had a job was the one with the sickly husband. But everyone was aware that the poor fellow could not keep a full-time job, which was why the nuns had taken pity and given his wife a position in the school office.

When Frances married Jay, she was midway through a PhD in anthropology, and a job was a faraway notion, something the older students obsessed about. She still had course work to complete, PhD exams to take, the long and painful process of a dissertation to embark upon, and even though Jay joked that he was a portable husband, that MBAs could get jobs anywhere, she wasn't close to giving job talks.

Then she got pregnant, and they both agreed that she needed to stay home the first year with Mandy. They bought a house in Sherman Oaks, and the distance from UCLA, along with the constant demands of the baby, kept her from doing any schoolwork. She didn't miss the university, and one morning woke up with the knowledge that she no longer had the ambition to keep going. It made her a little sad that she wasn't going to be the first PhD in her family, the one Jay said was "a Fud, a nonmedical doctor who will soothe me with stories instead of pills." As she and Jay discussed, the degree would take at least another five years to complete, and his salary wasn't enough if they wanted to have more children, move to a bigger house, drive nice cars.

She *had* to get a job, so she was delighted when she came up with the idea of becoming a real estate agent.

"It's perfect, you know," she told Jay. "I can work weekends while you're home with Mandy, I'll still have flexible hours during the week, and best of all, I have the potential of making tons of money."

"Too bad we already bought our house," Jay said. "We could have saved on the agent's fees."

She studied for the real estate exams while Mandy napped, and, once she started working, explained her change in career by saying, "I'm using my anthropology studies in a real way, the real estate way." It always generated appreciative laughter, and at the same time neatly highlighted her almost-degree, letting people know she had an academic pedigree.

It was only after she entered the world of buying and selling houses that she realized the immense costs attached to having her name on people's lawns, with the SOLD OF IN ESCROW sign touting her success. It was entirely different from her previous—and only—job as a teaching assistant in the Anthropology Department. Then she had been in charge, and her students had looked up to her as the authority on Indian churches. But real estate agents, she quickly learned, were a little like servants back home, dependent on the kindness, and cruelty, of the *memsahib*. Though most of the people she worked with were nice, she had acquiesced to ridiculous demands and listened to long, unfair diatribes, just to keep a listing.

The flexible hours she had counted on turned out to be unyielding. She still felt guilty, still could not believe that she had once left a bronchitis-weakened Mandy home, alone, because a client insisted on meeting her, and Jay was out of town. Then there were the many Tuesdays she had sent the children to school with low-grade fevers because she could not miss "tour days." She had lived in fear of the phone ringing and the school telling her that she had to come right away and pick up the children, code for being a bad mother.

The other mothers in the office just accepted such decisions as a way of life. They had grown up expecting to be a two-income family, and they often said, "It's easier to come to work than cater to the children's every need."

Frances, however, had loved being at home with her children. It was one of the reasons she had agreed to have Sam. Jay had wanted to try for a boy; she had looked forward to taking time from work, cradling her son as he fell asleep at her breast.

Things got a little easier when Mandy became a teenager and was able to look after her younger siblings. But Frances had never gotten used to this unexpected life, what she regarded as the only negative side effect of living in America.

But she never burdened her children by telling them how she truly felt about her job, just as she never, ever let them know the many bad moments she encountered in her workday.

Now, instead of telling Mandy about the Millers' last-minute change, she told the other truth, "Busy day at the office."

"I need to finish my paper," Mandy said, turning back to her computer.

Frances gazed at her daughter's taut back, head tilted to the left. Was Mandy really concentrating?

She mentally flipped through hundreds of "Mandy studying" images. Nine-year-old Mandy curled into the sofa, giving the answers even before Frances finished asking the questions. Mandy in middle school, not requiring any help with homework except for some big projects. Once Mandy got her computer, she stayed in her room, her drive to become a neurologist keeping her up late at night.

Frances had no idea where her kindergartner daughter had come up with that ambition, announcing at the same time that she was going to Harvard. Both Jay and she marveled that Mandy even knew about Harvard, and they were amused when she got annoyed because their neighbor, a Yalie, teased her, saying, "There *are* other schools out there."

They were long accustomed to her straight-A report card, until this year, when it was C's and D's. Mandy provided no apology, just a shrug followed by, "It's better than failing."

Frances immediately worried that another student was being mean to her, that she didn't understand her teachers, but Mandy insisted school was the same. "I guess I didn't know the answers," she always claimed.

After that, every time she saw her daughter studying, Frances desperately hoped that it would translate into the old A grade. But it never did.

She wasn't going to let Mandy use school to get out of her only chore.

"The kitchen," she said, just as she heard Lily's voice.

"Mom, you're home!" Lily yelled loudly from the living room. "Something bright red came for you."

"What is it?" Frances hurried toward the high, reedy voice.

Lily was still young enough to get excited when she came home, still could not sleep unless Frances kissed her goodnight. Now she rushed up to Frances and gave her a hug. Frances held the thin body, knowing that soon Lily, like Mandy, would ignore her. Sam had never felt the need to hug or kiss, which Jay, approvingly, said was manly.

"It's a very pretty red envelope with gold all over it," Lily said. "I put it on the dining room table. I know you don't like it when the mail is on the carpet."

"Lily's the good daughter," Mandy noted as she walked past Frances to the kitchen.

"Is Sam still outside?" Frances ignored her older daughter's comment.

"He's looking for crystals. They found a few in the yard at school, and he's sure we have some too. He wants to sell them on eBay. Look, Mom, this is so pretty," Lily held up the oversize envelope.

Frances guessed it was probably another wedding invitation. These days many Indians were taking advantage of the Internet to have their invitations designed and printed back home. Their circle of Indian friends had been steadily shrinking, because new ones were hard to find, and they were too busy to keep in regular touch with the old set. But people invariably found their much-crossed-out address books for weddings, and in the past few years, she and Jay had been receiving invitations for children they had last seen as toddlers. Both agreed that they could send their regrets to most, and she usually tossed away the invitations, though Lily had cut one up for a school project.

"It's from Vic and Priya Jha," Frances said, reading the address on the upper-left corner and starting to open the envelope. "Their son must be getting married." Nikhil was only four years older than Mandy. It was a little young for a boy to marry, but perhaps Vic had gone the traditional route and arranged a bride for his son, the way his parents had for him.

She looked down at one of the most garish cards she had ever seen. Bright yellow mango-and-flower patterns were embossed on a red background meant to represent doors. The two leaves were held together with gold thread, and when she pulled it open, the pale gold inside had a pocket containing the invitation.

"Oh, he's not getting married."

"Maybe he's getting divorced," Mandy remarked archly as she headed back to her room, then added, "The ants are gone."

"It's a party for Nikhil. He's graduating from MIT."

Frances stared at the red paper in her hands, for one second imagining her daughter's name on the invitation: *Please join us as we celebrate Amanda's graduation from Harvard.*

Frances wanted to be happy, purely happy, for Vic, but her insides whirled with resentment, sadness, and jealousy that she would never be able to send out such a triumphant card.

Mandy, the little girl who knew how to use the phrase "It's my mandate" correctly at the age of three, was supposed to do better than Nikhil.

But Mandy had shut the door to her room, closed herself off from any such chance when she started doing badly in eleventh grade, the very year that was important for college applications.

"Mighty Indian Triumph," Mandy rolled her eyes.

Her daughter's indifference, her brazen insolence, incensed Frances.

And with that rage came the familiar, sickly feeling that while she always got close to her wishes, they were invariably whisked away at the last minute.

Her entire life, Frances felt, was a series of good beginnings and bad endings, starting with her birth. Dada had been so optimistic when he took Mama to the hospital, sure that after four daughters, he was finally going to get the son he longed for, and for whom he had already chosen the name Francis. Then the doctor announced, "It's another girl," and Dada changed the *i* to *e*, and turned it into a nice story.

She knew she should be used to reversals. Instead, the blank white door to Mandy's room mocked her, reminding her of the many other doors that had been slammed in her face at the final moment.

If only Mr. Miller had called a few minutes later.

If only Mandy had continued doing well in school.

"You think graduating from MIT is a joke?" Discontent and anger added decibels to her words. "You can barely get C's, you know, and you have the nerve to make fun of someone who has done so well?"

Frances knew her daughter was already plugged into her electronic world, but she could not stop herself. "He's graduating summa cum laude. That means he's a 4.0. Something else you want to make fun of, huh?"

"What's going on?" Jay opened the front door. "I could hear you from the driveway."

It wasn't like Frances to shout, and Jay was relieved that no one was passing by their house. At work, when the other men grumbled about middle age, mortgages, and falling stocks, Jay liked to add, "What about a menopausal wife and a teenage daughter?" But as with so many witticisms, it wasn't really funny.

"Nikhil is graduating from MIT, and your daughter thinks it's hilarious," Frances handed him the invitation.

"Daddy, isn't the invitation pretty?" Lily asked.

"It's very pretty," he said overenthusiastically, grateful for the distraction.

"You don't have your glasses on," Lily remonstrated. "You can't even see it."

"I can now," Jay held the invitation at arm's length. "It's yellow and red and pretty and see here at the very bottom?" he pointed with his finger. "We have been instructed to wear 'elegant attire.'"

"What does that mean?" Lily asked.

"It means the men have to wear tails."

"Like peacocks?" Lily wondered.

"Not quite," Jay patted at the velvet bow that held her ponytail together. "Tails are a certain kind of suit."

Frances knew that Jay was, as he would say, seeing the brighter side of this unexpected, unwanted invitation. She wished she had the same ability.

"Vic will act like a peacock, that's for sure," Frances said. "Why the elegant attire?" she asked, finding fault with yet another part of the invitation.

"Oh, Vic probably picked up the phrase from bar mitzvah invitations. The Jews in Newport Beach must be as swanky as the ones in Studio City."

"Everyone in Newport Beach is rich-tzy," Frances quickly changed her word choice, because Lily looked too interested. She had recently taken to asking disturbing questions like, "Why don't we have a pool?" and "Why did Daddy change his job?"

Sam came running in, shouting, "Look at this sapphire I found!"

"Let me see, let me see," Lily begged.

"Dad, how much do you think I can sell this for?"

"Hmmm," Jay considered the stone. "Nothing?" he raised his eyebrows.

"No way!" Sam protested. "Sapphires are expensive."

"That's right, Sam, *sapphires* are expensive. This, I'm afraid, is just a plain old blue stone."

"Go do your homework, Sam, Lily," Frances instructed, putting the invitation facedown on the piano so that she knew it was there but didn't have to see it glaring at her all the time.

But the bright red invitation kept popping into her head, taunting her. Vic, who, like them, had come to UCLA to study, had truly achieved the immigrant dream of having it all. She was used to thinking of him as the rich CEO of his own computer company. Now she had to add a son who was graduating from one of the best universities in the world. Vic was holding the party at what Jay called his "big man-sion," while the 1,500 square feet they called home could only accommodate a small number of people.

Later that night, when Lily and Sam were asleep, and a strip of light under the door indicated that Mandy was still awake but probably engrossed in her beloved computer, Frances brought up the invitation.

"We have to go, you know," she stated. "We didn't attend his high school graduation because Mandy was having her wisdom teeth pulled that day. We can't stay away twice."

"I agree. Anything we say now will seem like an excuse, like we just don't want to go."

"I guess we should treat it like a wedding and give a hundred bucks," Frances sighed, thinking of their bank balance. "Don't forget to mark June eleventh on your calendar."

They lay in bed, bodies parallel, faces staring up at the ceiling.

She opened her mouth, then closed it. It had been a while since she had turned to Jay for comfort.

When had this abyss first appeared between them? She remembered, clearly, nostalgically, the chatter-filled beginnings of their marriage, when they preferred dinner dates to movies because they needed to tell each other about their days. Then Mandy came, and Frances felt pulled apart as she drove daily between work and day care. Evenings were a rush to get dinner cooked and Mandy to bed, and weekends became the time to finish chores, not relax. She had just started thinking she had made peace with being a mother, wife, and working woman, had achieved a livable balance, when they had Lily and Sam in quick succession. She became a time-bound dervish, whirling from appointment to appointment, and hadn't noticed that Jay and she no longer talked.

"Everything's fine," she always told the other agents when they sat around grumbling about their marriages. "I have a wonderful, supportive husband."

Mama had taught her children to keep problems to themselves. Mama always pretended that they were doing fine, would not dream of confessing, even to the priest, that her family often had to eat plain rice and dal at the end of the month, because there was no money for meat or vegetables.

Besides, she wasn't lying to her officemates. Frances and Jay had the usual problems associated with having a house and children, but nothing traumatic, like a foreclosure, cancer, or a third person ready to step in and ruin their family, she always thanked God. Had she not noticed the silence because it had grown gradually, the way one looks at a puppy and suddenly realizes it is a full-size dog?

Then the Mandy situation erupted, and for a brief time they had talked every night. Perhaps that was when the great gap between them cemented, for though they spoke together in the same room, their responses put them in different countries.

"I can't believe how American you've become, you know," Frances had told Jay. "You really think Mandy's just going through a rebellious stage?"

"I think *you* are being ridiculously Indian," Jay punched back. "What do you suggest we do? Lock her in her room, force her to study twenty-four hours a day? Parents can do that sort of stuff back home, but here they realize that children make mistakes. I'm sure Mandy will straighten up eventually."

She had hoped Jay was right, that their American daughter was going through something no one in India had the luxury to experience. As Jay said, "This is a forgiving country. People are always given second chances."

But the miracle Frances prayed for never came.

Instead, they received the invitation to celebrate Nikhil's grand achievement.

Frances turned her head and eyed Jay. She knew that there was no one else who would understand how she felt about Nikhil's success when her own daughter was slaloming down the failure slope. The agents at work always acted happy at other people's good fortune. Frances had long wondered if it was genuine, if Americans did not feel jealousy because they lived in a land of plenty and didn't have to fight for anything, from a place on a bus to a good job. Or, as Jay had told her, she was too much the immigrant to pick up their green-eyed signals.

Did Jay feel the same way that she did about the invitation? She used to be able to read him so well in the old days. Now all she could sense was his rigid body.

She thought back to that tableau in the living room. Jay had shrugged off the party, made a joke of the small print. But that was typical Jay. Jay the Joker, they had called him at UCLA.

Jay watched the blades of the fan turn in the dark. When they first switched off the light, he had not been able to see anything. Now each blade was clearly visible. If only life were like that. If he stared enough at Mandy, would he be able to figure her out?

Everyone told him that Mandy looked just like him. She had his eyes, his hair, the shape of his head. But for quite a while now, he had worried that she had inherited more than his physical features.

Was she becoming like him?

He, too, had been an excellent student, hardly needing to study in order to ace exams. His abilities had gone beyond books, and the blokes in school had admired how easily he jammed on the guitar, wielded the épée, hit a tennis ball. He had enjoyed that idolization, and, perhaps because of it, had kept darting from interest to interest. So what if he could strum but not pluck the guitar, and could not read music—which was the reverse of French, which he learned to read but not speak? Papa used to yell and tell him to learn one thing to completion, but in those days Jay had thought his father was too much the stick-with-it sort, a man who could not possibly understand an eclectic son.

But he knew why he never became an expert. He always stopped at the very moment things got difficult enough for him to have to really try. "It's a bore," he would lie with a shrug. It was just luck that schoolwork was so easy, and of course, his teachers would have contacted his parents if he slacked off.

Mandy's American teachers just left her alone. Students here did not suffer from the same sense of shame that failures endured back home, where the blokes who got a Third Class were scorned. Never mind if they were excellent cricket players; they were academic zeros, and in India, that mattered the most.

Had Mandy given up doing well because her classes suddenly got difficult? When she started high school, she was in every honors class and finished her homework so quickly she always had time to read the piles of books she brought back from the library. Frances had said that recently Mandy had even stopped reading. These days, she just listened to music.

"She gets it from me," Jay had informed Frances when she told him of Mandy's latest love. "I was the music guru in my school." He had made the same claim whenever Mandy dazzled in something new. She had played the piano, then moved onto swimming, winning a few cups before deciding she no longer enjoyed it. Then she gave dance a try. She won the main role in the school's yearly performance but didn't take it. "Too many practice hours," she had said, shrugging off the coup, and because this was America, they could not force her.

Now he worried whether incompletion was a gene one could pass on.

Jay heard his wife's uneven breathing, knew that she was awake.

"How is Mandy doing in school these days?" he asked softly, not sure why he was venturing into fractious territory. When they had discussed and dissected Mandy's unexpected, unacceptable grades, Frances had insisted that they be stricter, force her to study more, while he had advocated a "wait and she'll go back to her old self" approach.

"The same," Frances responded flatly. She had made many novenas, had prayed every night, and had resisted believing that *this* was God's answer to her.

"Perhaps we should get her a tutor."

Frances realized that Jay was taking a step toward acknowledging that she was right in her assessment of Mandy.

"I already asked her, you know. She acted as if I was forcing her to get married."

"Is she handing in her homework at least?"

One of the frustrating things about Mandy was that she would "forget" to give the teachers her homework. She would get an A in a test, which always got them excited, then deflate them with a final C grade because of all the incompletes she received for homework.

"I ask her," Frances said.

"But do you remind her?"

"Of course I do." Anger flared in her, and she wanted to tell Jay that it was easy to ask questions about Mandy rather than speak to her directly. But it was no use to think like that. They had decided that because he had the nine-to-whenever job, she was in charge of schoolwork. Jay helped when he could, but it was an exception, not an expectation.

Was he blaming her for Mandy?

Years ago, Frances had been furious when he suggested that she should have noticed Lily could not say her *r*'s before the teacher had to call them in to recommend speech therapy. "What, you don't have ears?" Frances had demanded. "Why is it that every time something goes wrong with the children you turn to me, but when they do well, you think it comes from your side?"

But this time she *did* blame herself, wondered whether Mandy would be a different student if she had been a more present mother. Had Mandy stopped asking to be quizzed before tests because there were too many evenings when Frances simply hadn't been able to do it between client calls, dinner, and bedtime for Lily and Sam?

Julia Carnahan, the agent who had the desk behind her, had only started working when her youngest went to college, because she believed children most needed their parents during high school. "People think stay-at-home kids fare better than the ones dropped off at day care," Julia had told Frances. "But think about it: kids love playing with other kids and the worst that can happen is they get colds and fevers from each other. The silver lining is that they build up immunities, get stronger. Teenagers are the ones who really need their parents around. I was always at home, listening in to conversations, checking backpacks, snooping around their rooms."

It made sense to Frances, and she wished, again, that she could finish her work by the early afternoon. But since most of her clients worked, she often had to meet with them in the evenings, which meant she relied on Mandy to look after her siblings. She had long lost count of the number of evenings when she only had time to kiss her children goodnight, hoping they had done their homework.

"I know you remind her about her homework," Jay said. He sighed. "She isn't depressed, is she?"

This was something else they had fought about. The school counselor thought that Mandy's poor grades might be the result of depression, and she had recommended a therapist. They had made an appointment right away and had taken Mandy out of school for the first session. The therapist, citing patient confidentiality, had refused to tell them about the session, which had agitated Frances. He did, however, inform them that Mandy was acting like a typical teenager and refusing to cooperate.

"What does that mean?" Frances and Jay had asked at the same time. They both felt like illegal immigrants in the book-lined room with no couch. This was not a place where they had ever expected to end up. The therapy was not covered by their insurance, and they hoped that Mandy wouldn't need too many sessions.

"It means it's going to take a little longer to get to why she is suddenly getting bad grades," the therapist had said.

After three appointments, Frances decided it wasn't working.

"We've spent $300 and there's been no change," she told Jay. "And Mandy makes a great fuss before every session. I'm going to tell the therapist we're taking a break for a while."

Jay knew that she wasn't talking about a temporary break, and he told her she was wrong, that Mandy should keep going.

"It's about the money, isn't it?" he accused her. "How can that be more important than our daughter?"

"I spend more time with her than you do, you know," Frances had pointed out, her voice singed with hurt. "Mandy doesn't have any of the symptoms. She eats, she doesn't cry all the time."

Even Jay could not deny that the only visible difference in Mandy was her grades. The keeping to her room and rudeness had been going on since tenth grade. So Frances had stuck with her decision and kept vigilant watch over Mandy to see if there were any changes.

"Like I said," Frances responded now, "she's the same."

Silence.

Outside a cat yeowled, and they heard the sound of something scurrying along the ground. It was probably the opossum that lived in their yard. Frances had seen it just once, though it left little piles of black poop all over the garden.

Frances could not stop herself from saying, "I wonder if Vic went through any of this with Nikhil."

"I doubt he'll tell us. Maybe Nikhil is like his father, totally self-motivated."

"Well, Vic certainly did something right. Nikhil is an MIT graduate, and even Lali's son just started Harvard." Frances always thought of Lali in connection with Vic. The four had met as graduate students at UCLA, and though they kept in sporadic contact with each other, the old relationships always surfaced for important events.

"I guess we have to make the best of what we have," Jay sighed.

Was this Jay's way of giving up? "We didn't come to this country to make the best of what we have, you know," Frances said sharply. "We came here to excel, to give our children opportunities they would never have in India."

"You can lead the child to class, but you can't make her top brass."

"Please, please stop with all those sayings. They really annoy me."

Jay moved closer to the edge of the bed. She used to enjoy his rearranged aphorisms, used to be proud when he'd proffer them at parties.

Frances felt the mattress quiver.

"I'm sorry. I guess I'm tired," Frances said. "And disappointed. There was a great offer for the Millers, but they pulled out at the last minute."

"That's too bad."

"I really wanted this sale, thought it might be the start of more, you know."

"Do you think you should change jobs?"

"In this economy?"

This wasn't the first time Jay had suggested she find another job. It felt as if he was telling her she wasn't doing anything well. But she knew that he, too, was concerned about their finances, that he always took his lunch to work to save money, and he hadn't bought a new suit in years.

She circled back to the red card, the equally bright RSVP envelope.

"Vic's still the old cheapo, you know. The invitation had more gold than a wedding saree, but he didn't put a stamp on the RSVP." Frances knew that they always agreed about their friend's stingy nature.

"If it was someone else, I'd say he forgot, but Vic never believed in paying when someone else could," Jay smiled into the dark.

"Remember how he'd come empty-handed to those parties? I can't tell you how many times I'd call and suggest he buy the $4 Gallo wine, but he never listened."

"He'd act like this was India, that bringing something would insult the hosts, make them feel they could not provide stuff for their guests. It was a cop-out, but I have a feeling he really believed it."

"He never cared about fitting in. Remember his thick glasses, rubber flip-flops, and those ratty kurtas he kept recycling?"

Vic was probably the first member of his family to be educated, to speak English. It was precisely because he was lower middle class, with parents who said "Yumrica" instead of "America," that she hadn't been intimidated by his brains. Oddly enough, he never hid the fact that he was on a scholarship. He worked every summer at jobs that paid well, but continued to radiate the village air he had brought with him.

She would never have gone out with someone like that.

Jay was the total opposite of Vic. She had liked everything about him, even his name, Jayant, the two syllables so different from the more common Mohan, Prakash, Ram—boys' names she was used to hearing. His family owned a large estate in northern India, and he had attended a boarding school in Darjeeling. He had done his BA in his father's alma mater, St. Stephen's College in New Delhi, before heading out to UCLA for his MBA—funded by his parents.

Jay's father had inherited vast holdings, and Jay had told her that part of his mother's dowry had been a couple of racehorses. His father had tried to breed the horses, but they hadn't taken. "I guess Papa should have looked the gift horses in the mouth," he had laughed, and she had marveled at how easily he spoke of things she had only seen in films and read about in books.

Jay's trajectory, as well as his family, had set him apart from—and above—her. Like all her friends back home, she had walked up the road to the local convent school run by the brown-garbed Carmelite nuns. Then she had gone to college in dinky Hyderabad, a town that was no comparison to cosmopolitan New Delhi. Her parents barely had enough money to send her there. Dada taught math and science at the local Jesuit school for boys, supplementing his income by tutoring.

She had been very nervous when she finally met Jay's parents three years after they were married. She had never met upper-class Indians before. For the first time she was actually embarrassed by being Goan. And Catholic. Jay's family had been Brahmin for centuries, wealthy for generations. Their name had a significance she had always claimed hers had. Frances Dias, she used to believe, was far better than plain and simple Sita Gopal, Rani Choudhry,

Malini Nair. That changed when she walked into Jay's large house, where his mother served her sweets from a silver platter ("It wasn't that I was born with a silver spoon," she recalled Jay telling her, "it was just that my family preferred silver to other metals for all our dishes and flatware"), and numerous servants bowed and salaamed the prodigal son.

She, of course, was the reason he was a prodigal. Jay hadn't asked his parents' permission before marrying her. He had known they would say, "No." She had worried that, like some Indians, his parents might look down on Goans as upstarts who had given up their religion and names to join forces with the Portuguese. Jay's parents only had to see her name to know that she was the wrong sort.

Then there was the sticky issue of her career. She was studying anthropology, with an emphasis on India. "Why would you need to go to America to study how the services in the Catholic churches in India have changed in the last two hundred years?" her father-in-law, who had read philosophy at Oxford, had raised his palms in surprise.

She had been asked the same question when she came to UCLA. Her roommates had shrieked with laughter when she told them that she had always wanted to come to the United States, so what better way to ensure herself a spot in a university than to apply fully prepared with language, culture, and a project? She was aware the rationale that had made her sound so canny to her friends would make her father-in-law think she was too stupid to study anything else. She had looked at Jay, who quickly started asking about his younger brother's plans after college—a sore subject in the house. But she knew that Jay's parents were disappointed in every way that he had chosen to marry her.

But choose her he did, proposing two years after they met at an orientation party.

She had gone to the party only because her roommate Katrina had dragged her there. She had clung to Katrina until Jay approached, outstretched hand holding a glass of wine for her, his worldliness a contrast to how mousy and out of place she felt. Vic had been slouching in one corner, and the president of the university, who had visited India while he was a student, brought him over to them. Lali was the last member of the "Gang of Four," as they took to calling themselves. Lali told them that she had come to the party because her adviser assured her she would meet all sorts of new graduate students. "And what did I find there? A bunch of other Indians whom I could have met if I had never left Bangalore!"

Though they were in different disciplines, the four kept in contact with each other, because there weren't many Indians on campus in the early eighties. When Frances told that to her clients, the younger ones looked shocked, saying that these days it was impossible to go anywhere at UCLA without finding an Indian. "I guess the Indian is out of the cupboard, you know," she'd laughingly agree, referring to the book *The Indian in the Cupboard*, which Mandy had read in first grade.

The last time the four had been together was at the dinner celebrating Jay's graduation. Vic and Lali, too, had walked in their caps and gowns, but it was Jay, naturally, who put on the dinner.

Frances had been especially happy because Jay had asked her to marry him a week earlier. She could not stop looking at her ring, which felt bumpy—but so right—on her finger.

Sitting next to Jay, holding hands, Frances had felt that her life was finally perfect, with no last-minute setbacks. Jay already had a job, and they had just signed the lease on an apartment they would move into after they got married. There was no hurry for her to finish her PhD, Jay had assured her. She could take her time to do research, write the best dissertation. Jay told people that they were going to be a power couple—he in the business world, she in academia.

Lali was going off to San Francisco—alone—to begin work as a copywriter. Vic wasn't sure whether he was going to stay in LA, move north to the Bay Area, or go farther south toward San Diego. Vic didn't have a business plan, or seed money, and he mentioned vaguely that a few people were interested in his idea for a start-up computer company. "The poor bloke is going to fail miserably," Jay had prophesied. Frances had believed him and had secretly worried that Vic might come asking them for money.

Instead, Vic had started VikRAM Computers at just the right moment. The next time they met him was at a dinner in his Newport Beach house. He wanted to introduce them to Priya, the woman his parents had arranged for him to marry. Priya spoke English as though she were allergic to the language, but she was wearing a Rolex watch that matched the one glinting on Vic's wrist. It was clear that he was already doing well and had money to spend.

Frances still could not believe that Vic, who said "COM-puter," instead of the American-accented "com-PUTE-r," would end up living in a huge house with a master bath with his-and-her showers, as well as a specially designed pool with a lap lane so his son could swim his way to many championships—and MIT. Vic, the bumbler who told everyone he had almost missed his flight to Los Angeles because he had been riveted by the escalator in the Amsterdam airport, had become the most successful member of the Gang of Four.

But she didn't want to think about Vic anymore. All the ascendancy she used to feel in the old days was gone, and she was left wondering how it was that she and Jay, the golden couple, were struggling.

"It's 11 p.m.," Frances looked at the scratched face of the

alarm clock they kept meaning to replace, but, as Jay said, it still worked, and wasn't nearly as important as a new kitchen, roof, and paint job. "I'll check on Mandy."

"No, I'll do that," Jay said quickly. He had sensed her irritation when he asked about Mandy and wanted to show that he, too, worried, cared about their daughter.

In another second he returned and said, "The light's off. She must be asleep."

"Did you look into her room? Sometimes she turns off the light and sits at the computer in the dark."

"It's all good," Jay said obliquely. He didn't want to tell an outright lie but at the same time didn't want to nag Mandy to go to bed when she was about to do so anyway.

"Goodnight, then," Frances yawned, pulling up the covers.

Jay closed his eyes and tried to sleep. But the invitation refused to let him rest. It was, as his buddies back in India would scornfully agree, *jaal*, the gold as tacky as wearing too much aftershave, the ornateness a pathetic show of new money and tastelessness. Yet the irony was that Vic, whom Jay had always thought of as out of sync with America, had chosen an over-the-top invitation that was, in today's market, very in. Along with the son graduating from MIT.

Jay considered the labyrinthine passages of his life, the twists and turns that had brought him to this bed, in this house. He had been born into the expectation that his every step would bring him closer to bigger and better successes. Instead, it was Vic who had chosen wisely.

He had started out feeling sorry for Vic but after a while realized that his friend did very well on his own, in his own way.

Vic had asked for help in buying a suit before going on "money-asking" junkets, because he knew that Jay was more familiar with everything in the west. He liked the one Jay selected but thought it was too expensive, and wanted to bargain with the salesman at Macy's.

"You can't do that in America," Jay told him quickly in Hindi. "Besides, it's on sale, so it's marked down anyway."

"Let me handle this," Vic said, and Jay had stood by, uncomfortable, worried that he would also be viewed as a cheap immigrant.

Vic hadn't haggled the way people go back and forth in India, the price a tennis ball that stops being hit only when one person gets the point. He had simply shown the salesman an irregularity in the material, and Jay had watched in amazement as 10 percent was taken off the sale price.

"See, you never know until you try," Vic had shrugged his shoulders as they waited for the suit to be wrapped.

Jay had gotten used to Vic's odd habits, and, as with the Macy's experience, even learned from them.

He had never encountered anyone like Vic at St. Stephen's, where all his friends were city raised and city smart. He wrote them amusing letters about the *dehati* he had met. They, in turn, marveled that a country boy was living so close to Hollywood. But in spite of what he told his friends, Jay found himself bonding with Vic as two Indian males in a country where people saw them as more alike than different.

Which was why, late one night over drinks, he had told Vic he was uncertain about Frances. He had been dating Frances the entire two years it had taken him to get his MBA, and in true Indian fashion, they had held hands and kissed but never slept with each other. But he knew that as the months kept moving toward June, and graduation, Frances would be wondering why he wasn't proposing marriage.

"It's make-or-break time," he had confessed to Vic as he

ordered yet another beer from the bartender. "And the problem is, I don't know which one to choose."

"No, the problem is that you went out with her, and now you do not want to do the right thing."

"Easy for you to say, Mr. *Seedha Rasta*."

"I know you think of me as a straight road. But you see, that is how I arranged my life, because I did not want any complications."

"I guess you didn't get lonely, then."

"Not too much. It's always easy to find someone in America to make you less lonely."

"Wait a minute. Are you telling me you have girlfriends?"

"Not girlfriends. Never a single girlfriend. But I did have some girls."

"You?" Jay had been disbelieving. Vic had always deferred to him when there were girls around, and Jay would joke and ask him, what exactly was it about the opposite sex that rendered him mute? "How come I never saw you with anyone?"

"I always told them I was only available for our mutual comfort. I was very upfront with them."

"You were never tempted, then, to stick it out with one of them?"

"No. Never. My parents made me promise I would return home and get married. I cannot disappoint them."

"My parents think that I am going to marry their best friends' daughter. It's one of the unsaid expectations, like getting a First Class in every exam. They would yank me home right away if they knew about Frances. I mean, she's a Catholic. Not to mention a Goan." Jay knew that Vic would understand what he was saying. Though Vic hadn't said much about his own family, it was obvious they were Hindus, from a small village, which meant they saw Catholics as outsiders. And even illiterate villagers would find something laughable about Goans. Like Anglo Indians, who touted their English connections, Goans were ridiculed for hanging onto a Portuguese lineage that had taken place centuries ago and was no longer relevant.

"So either way, one girl will be disappointed."

"What would you do if you were in my place?" Jay had been confused enough to ask. He had not spoken about Frances to anyone. His friends back home kept asking whether he was dating blonde chicks. His parents believed he was studying hard all the time. His American friends thought his relationship with Frances was like the ones they had. He had never told them that he hadn't gone all the way with her, because he feared their ridicule. How could he expect them to understand that Frances, without having sex, or moving in together, or even discussing marriage, expected him to propose? But he could feel her anxiety, her sadness, every time they met. He didn't know why he felt weighed down at the thought of marrying her.

Vic rested his chin on his fingers and looked around the smoky, student-filled room.

Finally, he said, "Maybe I am not the right person for you to ask. I am not like these people around us."

"And you think I am?" Jay had always felt more American, more modern than Vic. Yet he wasn't like the others in the bar who had probably slept with at least six partners, and who would not feel obligated to marry someone just because they were dating.

"For sure you are like them. When you were in Delhi, you, too, were a *seedha rasta* and did not go out with any girls. We both know that any *hera pheri* in India leads straight to marriage. But when you came over here, you asked Frances to see films and other such things. I did not change just because I had dollars in my pocket instead of rupees."

For the first time, Jay had envied Vic. Vic knew himself so well. And Vic had stuck to the *seedha rasta*, to the plan he must have formulated when he was in Kharagpur, attending the Indian Institute of Technology.

Vic had started his own company, and, based on what Jay had read about computer firms, he was probably a millionaire many times over.

Jay had asked Frances to marry him as they were walking back to her apartment after seeing a movie. He hadn't gone down on one knee, he didn't flip open a small box containing a diamond, he simply articulated, "How about we get married?"

He knew that Frances accepted his proposal as the expected finale to their years together. She had no idea about the earlier phone call from his father that had propelled him to say those words.

Papa had quickly done away with the obligatory "How are you?" and asked him outright if he had a 4.0 GPA.

"Papa," Jay had laughed, glad that years of dealing with his father had left him prepared for such questions, "no one asks a graduate student for his GPA. It's only relevant for undergraduates."

"Sheer nonsense," Papa had dismissed him. "You did not go to Oxford as I told you, and since American universities are easier, I expect you to get that 4.0."

Papa was never going to forgive Jay for breaking family tradition by choosing UCLA over Oxford. From the time he was young, he had been groomed to attend Oxford's Balliol College. Papa had even taken him to Oxford one year, walking the grounds as though the entire place were a church. Jay admired the old buildings but was more aware of the rude waitress who had to be asked three times for water, the sudden silence when they entered a pub. He never knew if it was real or imagined, if the waitress did that to all her customers, if the men in the pub were pausing before carrying on in their conversation. But he sensed the same dislike he had picked up on the roads of London, where a passerby called them Pakis.

Jay decided that he would be the pioneer in his family and keep going west. The farthest place was Los Angeles, and UCLA had a good business department. He didn't tell Papa, just as he didn't tell him that he hadn't sat for the Oxford exam. Papa's eyes got hard, his veins bulged, but Jay refused to stay home another year in order to try for Oxford.

Papa had reluctantly agreed to fund "the foolish endeavor," but created all sorts of opportunities to remind Jay of where he *should* have gone.

"No matter," Papa waved away his earlier question. "I have arranged a good job for you when you return. It is in Delhi, and your mother and I have decided that December is a good time for you to marry. Geet's parents are also in agreement. So get that degree and get on the first plane home."

Jay imagined arriving home—Papa asking to see his MBA diploma, Mama telling him that Geet had grown even more accomplished since he had been in the United States. Papa hadn't just gotten him a job; he had also found a room in another friend's house where Jay could live until he was "on his feet." Jay knew exactly what that meant. He was meant to rise quickly, like yeast. When Jay heard Papa's "yeast" explanation of success, he had laughed and asked, "But doesn't that mean getting into hot water?" Papa had been furious and told Jay to "stop being ridiculous. I want my son to rise higher than me." Papa would call weekly, Mama would want to know how things were going with Geet—in other words, when was she going to become a grandmother? He had no idea whether Geet wanted to marry him or whether she, too, was appeasing her parents.

That evening he had proposed to Frances. His parents had

been furious when he phoned them to announce the fait accompli. He had angered them even more when he said he was going to stay in America.

"How can I tell my friend that you don't want the job he has arranged?" Papa demanded, then asked, "What about Geet's parents? They have wanted an alliance with our family ever since she was born."

"She can marry my brother," Jay suggested.

"Shall I also give the land to your brother?"

"Why not," Jay had reacted magnanimously to Papa's threat. This would get Papa off his case, and he was sure that he was going to be among the successful immigrants in the United States. His brother's future wasn't exactly promising. He had got a Third Class in school and consequently was doing his BA in a small, unknown college, still getting poor grades, which meant that there was no way he could get into Oxford. It was one of the many reasons Papa had put such pressure, such hope, on Jay.

Frances's parents too, had been upset, not because she had chosen her own husband—normal for Goans—but because he was a Hindu and they had had a civil marriage. They calmed down, however, after she promised on the Bible that the children would be raised Catholic.

The collective anger from across the ocean had made them closer. Jay and Frances assured each other that this was the right decision. "Most people say marriage is hard," Jay told their friends, "but for us, *getting* married was the difficult part. The rest is going to be child's play." Having already gone against their parents' wishes, they planned to sculpt their own lives, unfettered by tradition and continuous expectations.

They began the process of becoming Americans long before they changed their passports. They didn't want to be like other Indians who were already worried about their retirement portfolio and refused to spend money on fun activities because they were saving for a house.

"We're too young to think that far into the future," Jay had dismissed such thrifty foresightedness. He came from wealth, and, given his MBA degree, expected to make money. So they took advantage of every three-day weekend to drive up to Napa for mud baths, or to go down to Baja to take parasailing lessons. They even considered investing in a timeshare in Mammoth but changed their minds when Frances became pregnant. Suddenly a house was essential.

Frances didn't need to convince him to give their daughter a Western name. Amanda was going to grow up in this country, and he didn't want her to have a name that she would either change or shorten, as he had done, to make it easier for Americans to pronounce. Lily came along seven years later, and he convinced Frances to try for a son. He knew that Papa was probably regarding the two daughters as punishment for his marrying out of their faith and community. Jay himself was Indian enough to want a son to continue his name, and he had been thrilled when the ultrasound showed a penis.

"See that?" the doctor had pointed to a section of the moving mass in Frances's uterus. "That's definitely a boy."

Sam was born the same year they stood in a large room with all sorts of other immigrants and pledged allegiance to the American flag. Frances suggested they name the baby after Uncle Sam, and Jay agreed, though he insisted the middle name be Suresh, after his father. Papa had been quiet over the phone, but he sent Sam a silver plate and spoon.

They had a wide assortment of friends—American, English, Turkish—and continued to keep in loose contact with the burgeoning Indian community in Los Angeles. Most Indians were engineers or computer programmers, and Jay enjoyed being the anomaly. But the varied professions created differences, compounded by the fact that Frances did not have much in common with the other wives, all of whom had come from India as arranged brides. Many, like Vic's wife, Priya, preferred speaking in Hindi, a language Jay spoke well but Frances had barely passed in school. It always amused him when she cursed in Hindi, because she never used that language for anything else. The wives were equally uncomfortable with Frances, not sure what to make of her short hair and jeans. The social disparity was cemented by physical distance when they decided to buy a house in Sherman Oaks, which was filled with Jews, not Indians.

"The Jews are like us," Jay rationalized. "We both believe in family and education." It also suited them not to live in an Indian ghetto, for why come to America if they were to live among their countrymen?

Jay got a kick out of shocking Indian men by announcing that of course he would allow Mandy to date. "I, myself, had a love marriage," he reminded them. "My daughter can marry whomever she chooses. And the added benefit is that unlike you bozos, I won't have to save money for a dowry."

He had said that to Vic the day they met for their yearly lunch, expecting to get the usual lecture on how Indians must not give up their traditions. Instead, Vic had warned him that girls can get pregnant.

"I think that is what God intended when He gave them uteruses," Jay had joked.

"It's better to be strict," Vic had advised. "Soon our children will want to pull away, so we as parents must ensure that we exert control over them while they are still young."

But he had been so sure that he and Frances, not the Vics of the world, were doing the right thing as parents. Especially when Mandy was able to hold her own in conversation with adults, and

Nikhil, older than she, squirmed with discomfort when asked about his swimming medals and grades.

Yet Nikhil was graduating from MIT, and Mandy was—still not doing well in school.

He had assured Frances that Mandy was just going through a phase. He wanted to believe that, didn't want to jump all over his daughter the way Papa did to him the one time he got 59 percent in Hindi. Papa expected him to get above 60 percent in all his subjects. Jay wanted to be like the fathers in his office who shrugged off their children's peccadilloes, sure that things would turn around as soon as their teenage years were behind them.

Perhaps Vic was right; they ought to have been stricter with Mandy.

He suddenly worried that he *should* have gone into her room to check up on her. What if she was signed on to one of those chat rooms, conversing with a strange man, planning to meet him in some motel? This was a fear shared by many fathers.

He slipped out of bed and padded quietly down the corridor. Sam was making soft noises, a sure sign that he was asleep. His baseball trophies were neatly arranged on the chest of drawers. A huge poster of Kobe Bryant, Sam's favorite Lakers player, was barely visible in the moonlight that slipped through the blinds.

Jay peeked into Lily's room. Her bed was against the wall, and there was just enough space for a bookcase. It was small for a bedroom, but Mandy had pointed out that all her friends had their own rooms, so they had acquiesced. As compensation, Frances had allowed Lily to choose a deep purple duvet, a color she disliked and that she claimed made the room look smaller.

Jay stood outside the closed door of Mandy's room. He had started calling it the Greta Garbo room after Mandy put up the ENTER ONLY IF INVITED sign in ninth grade. "Leave me alone," he had said, imitating Garbo, and Mandy had smirked. The younger children wanted to know what was funny, so he had explained that the famous Swedish actress had stopped making films at the height of her career and lived like a recluse in New York, hiding from the media.

"Why did she do that?" Lily had asked.

"I don't know," Jay had answered in his fake Swedish accent, while Mandy said at the same time, "Because she was gay," and he was glad that the children had not heard her.

For a short time after that, whenever Mandy went to her room, Jay would tell his younger children that their sister was channeling Greta Garbo.

When he had held her fragile, newborn body, he had rejoiced in imagining all the opportunities she would have because he had decided to stay in America. But these days she had forgotten about being a neurologist, and she only left her room for meals and school.

Was Mandy on the computer? Had she been in a chat room all this time?

He turned the brass knob and heard shuffling, movement.

Prepared to begin a lecture, Jay was stunned to see his daughter in bed, struggling to sit up.

"What are you doing?"

"I was reading."

"Without the light?"

Mandy raised the blue flashlight they had given her for her twelfth birthday. She had gone through a phase of reading spy novels and had briefly considered giving up being a neurologist to work for the FBI. He wasn't surprised that she still had the flashlight. "The one benefit to her not cleaning up her room is that she will have everything we ever gave her," he used to tell Frances.

"Why?"

Mandy didn't answer. He waited. He wasn't like Frances, who rushed in to fill the gaps.

Then Mandy yawned and said, "It reminds me of when I was younger."

His heart broke. He had just been regretting how much she had changed from the young girl who got straight A's. Was she, too, wishing the same thing?

"Want me to set up the tent in the backyard?"

"Oh, Dad, that would be too ridiculous. I'm tired. Goodnight."

Had the invitation made her go back in time to when she was clearly better than Nikhil?

"Did Uncle Vic's invitation upset you?" Jay asked.

"Why would it do that?"

"Nikhil is graduating from MIT," he said, stating the obvious.

"So? Why should I care about that? I'm not even going to the party," she said, pulling up the covers.

"Of course you have to go."

"I'm not going, Dad," she yawned again, and Jay wondered whether it was to get rid of him or because she was truly tired. It could also be a sign that she was anxious. When the school counselor had told them that Mandy seemed depressed, he had read a few books on the subject. Yawning, one author asserted, was a great way to relieve tension.

Jay understood well the tension that came from comparing oneself to another person who is more successful.

"We're going as a family," Jay said firmly.

"Why? I don't know him."

"You knew him when you were younger. His parents are our friends."

"God, you and Mom are such hypocrites. You hardly see

them anymore, and yet when we receive an invitation, you suddenly say they are your friends."

"Why don't you want to go?" Was she, too, embarrassed about her grades? Did her "I don't care" attitude hide her shame?

"Because I don't know him. I won't know anyone there. How can I have a good time? I'll have more fun just sitting at home."

"You can stay close to us," Jay offered, a little taken aback that her refusal was so—banal.

"God, Dad, you are so lame. Indian parties are the worst ever. People I don't know will come up and ask me questions, *personal* questions. I just hate that," Mandy asserted.

"They're interested—," Jay started, then stopped as Mandy interrupted loudly.

"Come on, Dad, they don't even know me. They don't even know *you*," she said. "Mom and you hardly ever go to Indian events."

"We used to go all the time," Jay fudged the truth. "Now it's inconvenient because we live so far from everyone."

"I wish this party were inconvenient, but no, you *have* to go."

"Yes, we do. I met your Uncle Vic when I first came to America. Don't you remember we used to visit them when you were younger? You thought their pool was very strange."

"Oh, yes, they had the lap lane," Mandy remembered. "Their son was very quiet."

"Sons," Jay corrected. "Yes, Nikhil seemed to have taken after his mother more than his father. Though perhaps he is like his father. Vic talks, but only when he's comfortable."

"Wasn't he the one who kept asking me about my grades?"

"That's Vic's way of showing an interest in you. So you'd better be prepared."

"There was some old woman we once met who got very angry that I had a higher GPA than her son."

"You don't have to worry about that now," Jay said lightly.

"Dad, Mom's already been on my case today, okay?" She turned her back to Jay and said, "Goodnight."

"Goodnight," Jay said, closing the door.

Too overwrought to sleep, he went to find the pack of cigarettes in the glove compartment. He didn't want to risk opening the noisy garage door, so went back into the house. He pushed open the front door carefully and then walked to the edge of the lawn, away from the bedroom windows, before lighting his Marlboro.

It was a cool night, and the scent of jasmine drifted from across the street. Every now and then, Sherman Oaks felt like India. Lucy Margolis had a guava tree, and she allowed Jay to eat as much fruit as he wanted.

"I didn't know what they were until you came along," Lucy said. "I'm glad the fruit isn't going to waste."

Jay took a deep drag, then held the glowing red tip away from him. He had come halfway around the world and was still sneaking cigarettes like a schoolboy. He had started the habit in boarding school because it was the cool thing to do. His best friend, whose parents lived in Washington, DC, always brought back a few cartons of cigarettes, and they would wait till lights out before sitting by the window, puffing away. Frances had asked him to stop smoking shortly after Mandy was born, and the doctor warned him that he was too old to play around with his lungs.

These days, he smoked when he didn't know what to do about his anxieties.

Mandy.

He wished she would just go back to being a good student. Perhaps all she needed was something positive, something wonderful happening to her that would plug the desire to do well back into her.

Footsteps intruded into his worries.

He quickly ground down the cigarette and waved away the smoke. He didn't want anyone to tell Frances, however jokingly, that he smoked.

Griffin Zlotnick, the tall boy who lived three houses away, came into view. He was staring at their house and slowed down as he approached it.

Jay coughed. He didn't want to startle the boy.

"Hey, Mr. Bakshi," Griffin nodded.

"I'm not sure whether to wish you goodnight or good morning," Jay smiled.

Griffin shuffled his feet and glanced again at the house.

"Are you looking for Mandy?" The question burst out before he could contain it. He had always promised himself he would never act like the stereotypical Indian father.

"Mandy? No, no. I was out jamming with my friends, and we forgot the time."

His answer—complete with the guitar slung over his back—was honest. But the boy's forlorn air, the snap of the eyes when he said, "Mandy," took Jay back to his own youth.

This boy, with his long blond hair and torn jeans, liked his daughter!

Jay almost laughed out loud. Who would have thought that? He used to see Griffin daily when the kids were young and routinely played together. But it had been years since he had spoken to Griffin, and Jay only knew that he was going to the same high school as Mandy.

Did Mandy also like Griffin? Had she faked being tired so Jay would leave her room and she could sneak out of the house?

He recalled their interaction. Mandy had been wearing pajamas. Girls don't meet boys they like in old flannel nightwear.

Besides, Mandy showed no interest in boys. She never brought them up, and didn't ask to go out on dates. When he and Frances talked about it, they were relieved that Mandy wasn't in any danger of getting pregnant, but worried that she might be a social outcast. "She'll go out when she's ready," Jay had assuaged his concern. "We will never stop her."

"Tell Mandy I said, 'Hi,'" Griffin said.

He definitely liked Mandy.

"Why don't you come by sometime and tell her that yourself?" Jay suggested.

Griffin grinned. "Right," he said, and saluted Jay as he walked away.

Jay was surprised at how happy he was that Griffin seemed to have a crush on Mandy. He had wondered who his children would go out with, and he had always told them they were Caucasians, the same as everyone else on their street, except that God had left them in the oven a little longer, so they were brown. That was his way of informing them that though they were minorities like the African Americans, they were more white than anything else. He knew that he should feel a kinship with the other groups who are marginalized in white America, but he could not help his prejudice. It had come with him from India, where, being rich, and with skin paler than the others, he was considered superior.

He sighed. As he looked at Griffin's retreating figure, he suddenly remembered Griffin's mother saying that her son was taking math classes at the community college because he was so advanced. He'd been tagged as highly gifted in math ever since first grade, and teachers had always had a difficult time keeping him challenged.

If Griffin came back into Mandy's sphere, it might improve her grades and her social life. He'd mention this encounter to Mandy tomorrow, ask her if she wanted to invite Griffin for a barbecue.

Jay rubbed his hands together and looked up at the dark sky.

There was a ring around the moon. He sniffed the air but did not smell rain. Not everything is what it seems, he thought.

That was true also for Mandy.

Who knew what might happen by June eleventh, when they had to drive down to Newport Beach?

LALI PULLED INTO the last parking space and slung her computer case and handbag over her shoulder before heading for the glass door. She did not like staying in the house while it was being cleaned, so she left for Starbucks as soon as she reminded Rosa that the fridge and the freezer needed a thorough wipe-down.

"Hi, Mrs. Feinstein, the usual?" Ellen called out as she approached the counter. Ellen Krueger had been in her son Aaron's class in high school and now worked weekends to pay for college. Lali remembered her because she was the only girl who had worn shorts even in the cold.

"It's to show off her genetically modified legs," Aaron had commented, and Lali had laughed and said, "It's a good thing your father didn't think that way. Otherwise he would have thought I wore a saree just to display my genetically unmodified midriff."

Lali glanced up to see if the chalkboard would tempt her, then said, "Yes, my usual boring chai, Ellen."

She used to feel awkward coming here on her own, but after four months, it was almost normal. The other patrons didn't notice or care that she was solo. Cafés had changed so much since her UCLA days. Back then, students spread their books on tables and cappuccino was the most exciting option on the menu. Now no one had books. Old and young carried laptops, taking advantage of the free Wi-Fi to read the news or check e-mail.

The corner table she preferred was unoccupied, so she booted up the computer and went into her Yahoo account.

One new message.

She waited impatiently for the page to open and then was immediately nervous to see Aaron's name. He hardly wrote, and when she called him, he only stayed on the phone long enough to assure her that he was fine. "I'm eating and studying and behaving," he repeated the same sentence every time they spoke, and Lali knew he was just placating her.

Something must have happened for him to write.

"Mom, I'm going to Vermont for the weekend with my roommate. He says there's no cell reception in their cabin because it's in the woods. I'll call on Sunday or Monday."

She reread the message to make sure she wasn't making it up. Aaron was fine! She imagined him in his dorm at Harvard, sitting at a desk that had served thousands of students before him. He was making friends and having fun. And now he was off on a trip. This was the first time he was going away for the weekend, and Lali was thrilled.

His college experience was so different from the nun-run establishment she had suffered through in Bangalore for the three years it took to get a BA degree.

"The dorm, or hostel as we called it, was right next to the college buildings, and the campus was encircled by a thick, high wall," she had told him when they strolled through Harvard Square. "We were only allowed to walk through the gates on weekends, from nine to five. And any male visitor had to ring a bell, wait for the maid to answer it, and write down his name, which was checked against a list every parent gave the school. Only then was the girl called."

Aaron had narrowed his eyes and asked, "You aren't going to turn this into one of your 'India is wonderful' stories, are you?"

Lali had laughed and said, "No, not this time. My poor cousin once waited a whole hour for me! I just think it's wonderful that you can have such a different experience. You're not just going to a fabulous university; you have the freedom to enjoy everything, from a late-night coffee to weekends away."

She looked at her mailbox again. She had been expecting another e-mail.

Aakash hadn't written. He usually sent her an e-mail early on Saturday mornings, reminding her that he would be available for instant messaging at ten, which was right now.

He must be busy.

She, too, used to be busy on Saturdays, and never dreamed that one day she would while away the morning in a café.

For years she had waited for Rosa's 9:30 a.m. arrival, because she and her husband, Jonathan, always went out for breakfast, except when he was called into the hospital, or Aaron had a game. She used to jokingly call it a "forced date," though Jonathan knew that she looked forward to it—starting from Wednesday, when she flipped through the food section of the *San Francisco Chronicle*, hoping a restaurant in Marin County had been reviewed. Jonathan refused to drive across the Golden Gate Bridge on the weekends, because he said it was crowded with tourists so busy looking at the scenery they forgot to stay in their lanes.

Aaron used to join them until he reached the age when he preferred sleeping in, and brunching with one's parents was just weird.

Lali took a sip of tea and gazed through the glass wall. If she tilted her head, she could see the Golden Gate Bridge. As always at this time of the morning, the bridge was a giant orange divider, silhouetted against the fog that hadn't lifted from the ocean side, while rising magnificently over the blue waters of the bay where the sun had burned off the haze.

It was as if she were looking at her life. One side reflected the halcyon days she used to spend with Jonathan. They had season tickets to the symphony and ballet, and when they married twenty-two years ago, she was usually the only Indian in attendance, her sarees garnering lots of attention. She and Jonathan often took bets on how many people would come up and compliment her. They went to plays, packing a picnic when they drove across the bridge to see the Berkeley Shakespeare Company's production of *Romeo and Juliet*, and watched movies the first weekend they were released.

She became pregnant with Aaron, and they both marveled as slowly, over the forty weeks, her stomach rose above the bath waters. He didn't object when she moved the crib into their bedroom, and laughed when she told him that the Swedes had gotten the idea of a family bed from the Indians. Though Jonathan's job as a cardiologist in a San Francisco hospital kept him busy, he tried to keep his weekends free for family-centered activities. They went to parks, fairs, and museums, and Lali was always trying to find interesting, out-of-the-ordinary things to do.

Lali had gloried in their family togetherness, which was so different from the way she had been raised. Appa had been the typical Indian father, more absent than present, and though she loved him, she had never felt comfortable around him. Amma, like the other mothers, spent more time in the kitchen and visiting her women friends than with Lali. Every day after school, Lali would finish her homework, race outside, and return only in time for dinner. The weekends meant endless hours of playing badminton, seven sisters, hide-and-seek with the neighborhood children. The only times her parents took her anywhere were to Sunday church, and events like weddings and funerals, where she had to behave. Her friends had similar experiences, and until she married Jonathan, Lali had thought that only books and movies portrayed families where people spent fun time together and parents were interested in more than report cards.

She and Jonathan kept pace with all of Aaron's changing interests. They attended his music recitals, clapped loudly when he played a turkey in the school play, and when he entered the talent contest, they bought extra strings for his guitar in case his broke. When Aaron became sports-crazy, Jonathan coached, and she turned into a team mom. She learned to wrap hot dogs in foil to keep them warm, and bought a wheeled Igloo that was easy to maneuver on bumpy grounds. The quantity of the snacks grew to accommodate the teenagers' vacuumlike stomachs, and there were days when they stayed out till late evening, because Aaron had two games back-to-back.

Then, just like that, the previous September, the fog had set in.

Aaron started his freshman year at Harvard, and suddenly the house was too big. Lali had anticipated the empty-nest syndrome everyone warned her about, but had not realized how much she would miss picking up his dirty clothes from the floor, taking him for burgers after an evening game, sitting in the theater with her eyes closed, fingers clutching Jonathan's hand, because Aaron wanted to see a scary movie.

Once she realized those "what shall I do with my mothering ways?" days were going to stay, she thought it was the perfect opportunity to return to the early years of her marriage.

Jonathan still worked at the same hospital, and was as busy as he had ever been, but his weekends remained open, and she began planning things for them to do. She started by buying a book on the trails around Marin County. "I know you dislike gyms," she explained, "but you keep saying we are past the age when our bodies take care of themselves, so let's hike." They went to

Sonoma and Mendocino, and liked the latter so much they considered buying a cottage—until Jonathan looked at their finances and said they could afford nothing extra while Aaron was going to Harvard. Saturday became their hiking day, and they walked the bluffs, trekked up to Mount Tamalpais, and one time crossed the Golden Gate Bridge on foot. When they were standing in the middle of the slightly swaying bridge, Jonathan had spread his legs apart and said, "Look, I'm in two places at one time: Marin and San Francisco." A tourist heard him and did the same thing, and Lali had felt as happy and carefree as when they first started going out together and Jonathan had done cartwheels in Golden Gate Park. Once he had even rolled down the window of his car and shouted out, "I love this girl!"

"It's like a second honeymoon, only better," Lali told Mary Kibrick, her coworker at Marin College. She had taken the job as secretary of the English Department when Aaron started his senior year in high school and didn't need her to drive him anywhere. She had hoped to get back into advertising, but no firm wanted a woman who had stayed home for sixteen years to take care of her son. She was overqualified for the secretary position but enjoyed the simplicity, the fact that she could leave the office on Friday evening and not think about work the entire weekend. She liked the people in her department, especially Mary, and often got recommendations for hikes and restaurants from them.

Then, on a day she thought they would go hiking, Jonathan said he was tired. He wanted to stay home and read. A few days later, she picked up one of his books and saw that it was on Judaism.

When they started dating, he had told her that the only thing Jewish about him was his name. "My parents don't go to synagogue," he said, "and the first time I tasted matzo-ball soup was at a friend's place." Their decision to have a civil wedding was mutual, because neither of them was affiliated with a religious organization.

When they moved into their first apartment together, he had seen her two cutting boards—one for meat, the other for vegetables—and assured her that she didn't need to keep a kosher household.

"It's not kosher," Lali had explained. "My mother does the same thing."

Jonathan had been curious about why a Christian woman in India would keep food separate, and Lali said that almost all her friends' mothers, including the Hindus, did the same thing. "I told you that India is a highly cultured country," she reminded him.

Jonathan had laughed and said, "So you keep saying—and yes, yes, I do remember the Gandhi quotation you are always throwing my way—that Western civilization is a good idea. You're probably going to tell me that the Jews got their kosher notion from the Indians."

They celebrated Christmas, not Chanukah, and Aaron grew up knowing his parents' religious backgrounds but never wanting instruction in either one.

The book with the Star of David emblazoned on it felt like an intruder. Then every week, it seemed to Lali, there was another Amazon delivery. She knew that when Jonathan got interested in something, he bought all the right things to help him learn and get ahead. Shortly after they were married, he had decided to study Spanish, and Lali had recently donated the stack of books to the local library. She told herself that this was just another flashing interest, a variant of the typical middle-age crisis. He would get bored and they could go back to their hikes and early dinners, followed by a movie.

Instead, Jonathan found a Reform temple and started

going to services every Saturday, because his Fridays were too unpredictable.

He asked her to accompany him, and she went because she wanted to be supportive. Initially, she had been enchanted by the warm welcome. The people were so different from the members of the church she had attended in India.

Church was serious religious business in Kerala, but Sundays were also social, an opportunity to swap information and show off new clothes. The girls of marriageable age wore their best, and nine-year-old Lali had been riveted by Sara, who was studying in a college in Bombay and came in a low-cut blouse and transparent chiffon saree that the older women gossiped made her look like a prostitute. When Lali was small, the older women grilled her about school; when she was older, they asked when she was going to get married. "I'll send you an invitation to my wedding, Aunty," she told one particularly annoying woman, who promptly asked, "That is very good and all, but when will the invitation be coming, when, when?"

The Jewish congregation didn't ask why she and Jonathan were suddenly attending services; they simply embraced them. She didn't even mind that she could not understand Hebrew. The priest back home liked to intersperse his Malayalam services with Syriac, which no one understood.

But the more she went, the more awkward she felt. She didn't know how to explain her change of feelings to Jonathan. It wasn't that she was a Bible-thumping Jacobite Syrian Christian, and it wasn't that she thought less of Judaism. She just didn't belong, the same way she had felt like an outsider those times she had gone to Hindu temples. Both the church and the temple had incense, yet they had different scents; both the priest and the rabbi used the Bible, but the stories sounded different.

It didn't help that the yarmulke on Jonathan's sandy hair

made him look, for the first time in their lives, foreign, like a figure in a photograph. One morning she had a headache and stayed home. The next Saturday she had a hair appointment, and soon it became normal for him to kiss her good-bye before leaving for the synagogue.

Then Jonathan decided to take religion classes on Saturday evenings and needed more time to study. One evening he was even reluctant to join their neighbors, the Reidels, for a barbecue.

Lali explained that he had to go. She had already RSVP'd that both of them were coming, *and* that he was bringing his famous potato salad.

"I'm taking this class that's challenging," he told the Reidels when they suggested going to a movie the following week. The Reidels, themselves nonreligious Jews, were amazed and delighted that Jonathan was studying the Talmud.

"Always wanted to," James Reidel said, "but never had the time."

Jonathan had smiled and said, "Got to make the time."

She wanted him to make time for *her*, and, thinking about his love of music, bought tickets for a concert conducted by Sir Neville Marriner, an old favorite of Jonathan's. He went with her, but she saw him looking at his watch. They drove straight home after the concert and he disappeared into his study.

Lali sat on the bed, alone, desolate, frightened, wondering what she was going to do about the growing distance between them. They had become the sort of couple who lived in the same house, ate at the same table, and read at the same time—except that they were on very different pages.

He tried, and every time he did, she was hopeful.

One day he saw her reading *People* magazine online and said, "Honey, why don't I get you a subscription?"

"No, please don't do that," she responded immediately,

embarrassed that he had caught her reading such trash. "I don't like supporting paparazzi publications."

"Reading it off the screen isn't supporting it?"

"It's not the same thing. The parts I read are free on the web. A subscription is over a hundred dollars a year, *and* uses paper."

"If you say so," Jonathan agreed, and she knew, once again, that he did not understand her.

Their lives were filled with such instances of disconnect. Was it all due to Judaism, she wondered? Should she go back to the synagogue? But she was already so far behind him.

Did he now see her as a *shiksa*, and resent the fact that, because of her, their son would have to convert to become a Jew?

She had always thought she was very lucky to have married Jonathan. Even her parents, who had disapproved initially, had been assuaged by the fact that he was a Harvard-educated cardiologist ("No one in Kerala can say anything negative about *that*," Amma had noted with satisfaction), and they were relieved that he was family-oriented. Appa had read that so many American men were more interested in their hobbies than having children. When Lali took Jonathan to India, he had not made a fuss about the food, and he had been interested in everything from how rubber is tapped to the little children fishing with makeshift rods in the flooded paddy fields. She had felt that she had married a man who was the best representation of the West precisely because he was open to the ways of the East.

Then he had parted the curtains to his own religion, and she found herself offstage.

"I know he's not having an affair," she confessed to Mary one day in the office, "but it feels as if he is."

"First of all, be happy he's not seeing another woman. It's just religion. He'll stop when the studying gets tough," Mary prophesied.

She hoped Mary was right, but Jonathan kept at it. Every now and then, he would confess that he felt he was moving backward rather than forward. Lali would be sympathetic on the outside but jubilant inside. But he never stopped reaching for his books, and she realized that he was going to stick with Judaism.

She just didn't know how she fit in. And what she was going to do about it.

"Excuse me," a voice brought Lali back to the café, "can I use this chair?"

"Sure," Lali said. There was no chance that Jonathan was going to join her. He didn't even know she was here.

He left for the temple and she took off for Starbucks. She always made sure to return home before he got back. Jonathan would wonder why she needed to take her computer to the café. He knew she used it only to write to her friends and to read *People* magazine, neither of which was urgent.

Lali was just about to go to the *People* magazine site when a small box appeared in the lower right-hand corner of the computer screen.

Her heart did a somersault.

Aakash was online.

"Are you there?"

"Just looking out at another beautiful day," she responded, blood surging through her entire body as if she had just come off a gravity-defying roller coaster.

"If I were there, you would not have to look outside to find your sky," he wrote, alluding to his name, which meant *sky* in Hindi. She laughed. She did not recall his being this playful when they had met at UCLA. She had known him for a brief, intense time back when she was getting her master's degree. She had not thought about him for years and years.

Then, six months ago on a Friday, Jonathan called to say that a new friend from Berkeley had just invited them to Shabbat, and he had accepted.

Lali was furious. "You told me you were free, so I bought movie tickets. I thought we could get a quick bite before seeing it."

"Honey, I'm sorry. It's just that we never seem to do anything, so I accepted the invitation. I think you'll enjoy the evening. His wife works in advertising."

"I really don't want to drive across the bridge," Lali said, hoping that would make him change his mind, her own churning with the unfair "we never seem to do anything."

"I'm sure they'll understand," he said.

She was just about to say she *would* make the drive, when he suggested, "Why don't you go see the movie yourself?"

She wanted to strangle him. What was the use of having a husband if she had to go to the movies alone? Besides, he thought he was being magnanimous, but he was just doing what he wanted to do—and didn't want her to stop him.

She had stayed home, sulking on the couch, trying to find something good to watch on TV, when she decided to turn on the computer.

"It's my new best friend," she had joked with Mary.

"I thought I was your best friend," Mary responded.

"That's true during the week. But on the weekends you become a wife, with a husband who wants to do things with you."

"Yeah, he drags me all over the city to look at houses we can't afford to buy. It's making me crazy."

"Mine stares at books all day. You know, I always thought people loved their jobs because they enjoyed the work. I don't really like providing the same student with the same information for the nth time, or giving yet another prospective parent the college website address. I just like being around people who pay attention to me. I'm pathetic, aren't I?"

"Nah," Mary said, "you've just been married longer than I have. Give me a few years. I'm sure Larry and I will start doing different things. I keep telling him I want to train for a marathon. Larry will never give up his beer and couch to go running. So who knows? One day I might be running the Boston Marathon and he might be watching the Celtics on TV."

Lali looked at the blue screen of her "best friend," at the words Aakash was writing.

She blamed the computer for getting her into this situation.

That Friday night when she had turned on the computer to go to the *People* magazine site, she had seen ads for *Class of 1985* and *Are you looking for someone*? She had read about people who had connected with each other after ten, twenty, thirty years. She had no desire to find classmates from her all-girls college in India. She had not maintained any friendships after she left Bangalore, and even if she suffered a sudden bout of nostalgia, she would not know how to find them, because they were married, with their husbands' surnames.

She was still in touch with Jay and Frances from UCLA, and she exchanged Christmas cards with a few others from her department.

Then she remembered him.

Aakash Khan wasn't a very common name. All she had to do was type in the words.

They had met each other at the Student Store at UCLA. He was wearing a khadi kurta with jeans, very comfortable in the mix of Indian and American clothes.

He suggested they go out for a chai, and ten minutes later they were sitting in a small café in Westwood.

He was studying engineering, and informed her that he was dating an American woman named Claire who was spending the semester at Cornell.

"What makes you think that you have to tell me this?" she had inquired, immediately dismissing him as one of those Indians with a severe case of "white fever," desperate to marry a white girl.

"I just think honesty is the best policy, and I didn't want you to get the wrong idea."

She was taken aback by his answer. She had presumed of course that he liked her. Had he only suggested tea because she was Indian, and there weren't that many Indians then at UCLA?

Their encounters continued and became lunches, matinees, even the occasional late-night teas that reminded them both of India. He made her a tape of Madonna songs, and she proofread one of his papers.

When her former roommate Sharon invited her to a party, she told Lali to bring along her boyfriend. "He's not my boyfriend," Lali said—but she had taken Aakash.

It was the first time in her life that she had gone to a party with a man. Until she arrived in America, she had only sat beside a strange man in a bus, never in a classroom. The males she knew were the ones her parents knew. And those males knew better than to ask her out.

Her mother had cautioned her to remain true to herself, to keep away from boys. But Amma had always couched her warnings: "Those Americans are not like us, so please be careful. They like to go out with girls, but they don't believe in marriage."

Aakash wasn't an American, and she felt no guilt as she waited for his phone calls, then rushed out to meet him.

She had, however, felt uncomfortable the time they ran into Frances and Jay. Frances was always open about being Jay's girlfriend. Goans made love marriages, and Frances had said that if she didn't find a man on her own, her parents weren't going to come up with one. But Lali was a Malayalee, and her parents were even now looking for a suitable husband. She had purposely not told Frances anything about Aakash because she did not want to answer questions. When they saw each other outside Royce Hall, she pretended not to hear Frances's whispered "good-looking bloke you have."

"We should get together," Jay had suggested before they drifted away to study in the library.

"Get together?" Aakash had asked after they had gone, then repeated, "Get together? What sort of friends do you have, anyway? They are so smug and happy with themselves. And what's with the kissing you on the cheek? Does he think that makes him European? Fraud!"

"They're not that bad once you get to know them," Lali said, though she too was a little tired of the way Jay and Frances acted as if everything they did was the best. But she was feeling more charitable, because Frances had recently told her she wasn't sure whether Jay was ever going to marry her.

Frances was alarmed because she had just heard that Loretta, her good friend back in Goa, had been dumped by her boyfriend. The boyfriend had gone to study in Wisconsin, and right after Loretta had spent a fortune sending him flowers on his birthday, he wrote her a good-bye letter. Frances was worried that the same thing was going to happen to her.

Lali had reminded her that she wasn't stuck in India, Jay and she were in the same school, and besides, she was absolutely positive Jay wasn't a "use them and leave them" guy.

"Well, *you* might put up with them," Aakash said, "but I'm sure that swashbuckling Jay isn't going to be putting up with Frances's puppy eyes much longer. I bet you anything he'll ditch Frances and go home and marry the girl his parents have chosen for him. I'm his complete opposite. I've already told my parents that I'm going to propose to Claire when she comes back."

"She might say no."

"I doubt it."

"You're very sure of yourself, aren't you?"

"More sure than of you," he'd thrown back at her. "When I saw you looking at the windbreakers in the Student Store, I thought you were a surfer! How was I to know you were a *bevakuuf* and didn't know the difference between a windbreaker and a jacket!"

They were getting to know each other's stories and habits. Lali automatically sprinkled his coffee with cocoa, and he knew that she drank her tea black.

Then, one day, Aakash told her it was over with Claire. He didn't seem sad, just matter-of-fact, the information divulged between sips of tea.

Lali already liked him, and his sudden availability made him very desirable.

All week long she pondered how to let him know that she liked him—not as a friend but as a man. And that she liked him enough not to care that her parents would go berserk because he was a Muslim.

She invited him to dinner. Bought a bottle of wine. Made brownies because they were his favorite dessert. After all the plotting and sweating about how she would let him know her change of feelings, it had seemed natural to place her hand on his. She looked into his eyes. Didn't say a word. He, too, didn't speak. When she finally spoke, they were on the bed, clothes on the floor, and she whispered, "Yes, it's okay, keep going."

"Why me?" he asked, when it was all over.

"Because."

"I'm flattered."

She thought those two words meant everything, until he didn't call the next day. Or the day after. When she finally broke through her pride and phoned him, he said that he was very sorry. Claire had flown back unexpectedly. Told him she had made a mistake to break up with him. He had proposed, and she had accepted.

"I told you about her from the beginning," he reminded Lali.

She was too devastated to remind him that he had also told her it was over between them. He hadn't given her any details of the breakup, and she had stupidly assumed that he had been the one to pull away—because of her.

She felt foolish, betrayed, terrified.

She had slept with him. She knew that even Frances hadn't gone all the way with Jay, though they had been dating for almost two years.

She was a fool. But it had seemed so—natural. Ever since she had come to America, she had seen couples behaving in ways not possible in tradition-constrained India. Men and women kissing, holding hands, leaving a party together. It had made her feel, for the first time in her life, that she was missing something. Did she really want her parents to provide a husband for her? Couldn't she be like the other girls in her class and find her own man?

Many American men asked her out, but she was not comfortable enough to say, "Yes."

She definitely wasn't attracted to the ones who liked her because she was exotic. They were easy to spot because of the way they looked at her when she wore Indian clothes. They weren't interested in getting to know her; instead, they made her feel as if she had just posed for *National Geographic*, wanting to know about the *bindi* on her forehead and the rings on her toes. She got so tired of their questions that she started making up stories. She told one man that she had come to America to escape her evil mother-in-law who kept demanding that she ask her parents for more money, that the dowry she had brought with her just wasn't enough. From there, it had been easy to embroider more, and Lali had said she was married at fifteen, had three children by the time she was seventeen, and had left them all behind. Part of her was intrigued that the man still wanted to go on a date, but a greater part thought that anyone who believed such a story was an idiot not worth her time.

The men she liked presented an entirely different problem. Since she had never dated before, she had no idea how to gauge a suggestion for tea versus dinner, how to react when they leaned forward to kiss her. She envied her American friends, who had sorted through all that when they were teenagers and knew how to behave on dates.

Aakash had been the perfect blend of East and West. She had worried that an American man might mock her for being a virgin in her twenties. Aakash would expect it, and would know exactly what it meant that she had given up her virginity to him.

His betrayal was—brutal.

Not only had he rejected her, he was already engaged to another woman. Lali had never seen a picture of Claire. Her very name was the epitome of a blonde-haired, blue-eyed Clairol woman. The semester at Cornell meant she was smart. The fact that Aakash would so readily go back to Claire right after they had slept together for the first and only time proved the other woman was incredibly alluring.

Lali was heartbroken with disbelief as she put down the phone after their brief conversation. She kept hearing his flat "I'm sorry," as she slumped on the edge of her bed and got under the covers. She stayed there. She was never going to leave her studio apartment. She didn't want to risk running into them.

She didn't care about missing classes, or the paper that was due. She ignored the phone and didn't eat. The pan of brownies grew mold, and she threw them away. Then she threw up in the sink. The brownies were just like her, stupid and unwanted.

She could not stop going back to that night. Why had she

invited him over? Why had she put her hand on his? Why hadn't he just removed it, eaten the food, and gone away? She had even kissed him at the door when he finally left in the early hours of the morning.

She no longer remembered whether he had kissed her back or just fled.

She couldn't sleep. The dark circles under her eyes grew blacker.

She was too ashamed to tell Frances, and though her American friends were nonjudgmental, they hadn't shared intimate details—"I'm so sad," or "I don't know what to do about this"—of their lives. They also seemed to consider breakups normal. When Angela's boyfriend told her he was seeing another girl, she cut her hair as a way of moving on. The next week she was dating someone new, and shortly thereafter, she went on a double date with her old boyfriend and his partner.

All Lali knew for sure was that she never again wanted to see Aakash.

On the third day, she realized that she needed to rid herself of him—completely. She erased his name from her phone book. Threw away the teddy bear he had given her, "for no reason other than that you are also a Bruin," he had said as he handed her the package. She changed the sheets. They smelled of him and of what they had done. She had just balled them into the laundry basket when she heard a knock on the door.

Her hope jump-started. Was it Aakash, coming to see her with a change of heart?

She rushed to the door. She was just about to open it when she raised her eye to the peephole. Black hair. Her chest felt as if it were going to explode. He had come back for her!!!

"Lali Manali! Are you there?" Only Jay called her that silly name.

She slumped against the wall. Was she really wrong? She looked again and then heard Frances. "You knock," Frances was saying. "Maybe she can't hear me because I'm not as strong as you."

Lali crept away from the door. She didn't want them to know what had happened. Perhaps they hadn't heard her.

The knocking continued. It was shaking the walls and the constant *rat-a-tat* was driving her crazy. Finally, she went back to the door and whispered, "I'm sick."

"Open up," Frances insisted. "We can take you to the hospital."

Lali knew there was no getting away from them.

"Just you," she whispered. "Tell Jay I'm not fit to be seen." Tears leaked down her cheeks as she thought of the last man who had stood outside her door.

Frances made her a cup of tea. Checked her temperature. Then she asked Lali what had really happened.

Lali had never felt so vulnerable in her life. She could not think of a lie, so she told Frances part of the truth, that she and Aakash had been going out for a while but he had gone back to his American girlfriend.

"That *harami*," Frances said. "If we were in India, I'd get some *gundas* to break his legs."

It was comforting to hear Frances's outrage. But she wanted Frances to leave, wanted to get back to her bed, wanted to go to sleep and wake up a virgin.

She didn't tell Frances that she had slept with Aakash and Frances didn't ask. After that morning, Lali refused to talk about Aakash.

But Lali always wondered whether Frances had guessed that she had done more than "go out" with Aakash.

Frances told her that the best revenge was not to let people like Aakash dictate her life. She needed to throw him out of her mind, get back to the plans she had been making. Frances insisted that she start by taking a shower. "Change of clothes, change of attitude," Frances said firmly. She made her eat a sandwich. Then she walked Lali to the library and sat with her as she started writing the overdue paper.

"I'm better," Lali acknowledged, regretting that she had laughed when Aakash said that Frances and Jay were the sort of people who got into bed and made love to themselves, not each other. She felt bad that she had automatically assumed Frances would belittle her. It was her own insecurity, the knowledge that she hadn't behaved as a proper Indian, the fear that another who found out what she had done would find her lacking.

If Frances hadn't come to her aid, she would still be in her apartment.

"Thanks," Lali said, and repeated, "I'm better, so you can stop worrying about me."

But Frances shook her head. "Not yet, you're not. First you feel sad because things didn't work out, then you feel an even greater sadness for what you think you have lost. You have to wait until you get angry to know that you are getting better."

Lali listened, then asked, "How do you know so much?"

Frances shrugged and responded, "*Cosmopolitan* magazine? It's better than that *People* magazine you always flip through in the checkout line when we go grocery shopping."

Lali never reached that last stage, but she did return to her routine, took tests, wrote papers, applied for and got a job in San Francisco, and counted the days to graduation, grateful that it was just two months away.

The day before Lali left LA, a newly engaged Frances came over to help with the packing. "I don't know if I should tell you this, but I ran into that *harami* Aakash last week. He was alone. I tried to get some information from him, but he was very cagey.

He's going back to India, but he didn't mention anything about getting married. He said to say 'Hi' to you."

Lali didn't respond, just kept on stacking books into a carton.

"You okay?" Frances asked.

"Yes, yes, of course," Lali lied.

Frances's news stayed with her all day. She tried to think of other things, even went to see a movie alone, but she finally rushed back to her room and picked up the phone.

She dialed his number, her fingers remembering the digits that were no longer in her phone book.

She had no idea why she was doing this, what she was going to do about the cardboard boxes and the job waiting for her in San Francisco.

The sound of the connection buzzed in her ear, as various possibilities jumbled together in her head.

"Hello?" It was his voice, and her body lit up, arms attentive with gooseflesh.

She was just about to respond when she heard a voice in the background. A soft, female voice. She broke off the connection and promised herself that she would never again be such a fool.

A year later, she had met Jonathan in a grocery store in San Francisco. He had followed her to the vegetable aisle, he confessed a few months after they started dating, and came up with a question about how to choose eggplants.

"Lame, totally lame," he told her, "but I couldn't think of how else to talk to you."

His question had caught her at a time in her life when she no longer believed the reasons that had kept her from refusing dates with graduate students at UCLA.

She had decided to live in America, and she knew that her only chance to become a wife was to choose her own husband. She informed her parents that she did not want to have an arranged marriage. They would go about it assuming that she was a virgin. She could not risk telling a man the truth *before* they got engaged, or having him find out *on* their wedding night.

Her parents were upset, but she was too far away for any pressure to be effective. When she called home, her mother whined about being the laughing stock of the Malayalee community in their town. "I'm the *only* mother whose daughter is still not married," she kept saying. It always took Lali a few days to recover from the great guilt she felt during those conversations.

But she had no one to blame but herself. She had removed the option of an arranged marriage when she gave herself to Aakash. He, too, would have known that, which was why his refusal to go all the way to marriage had been so painful.

So she kept herself open to dating, but felt that her fiasco with Aakash had left her cursed, because she only met married or gay men in San Francisco. Jonathan had, from that initial encounter, been a wonderful surprise.

But now, just when she thought they could return to the early days of season tickets and weekends away, he had become a man she no longer recognized.

Six months ago, while he was spending Shabbat with a new friend, she had Googled the name of an old one. She had not expected to get any information about Aakash. But when his name popped up, she suddenly could not resist doing more.

Enough years had gone by, with enough successes, for her to be able to contact him without dissolving into shame. She was the wife of a cardiologist, the mother of a Harvard undergraduate. Her husband was white. She had no need to fear that Aakash's life was superior to hers.

Before she could change her mind, she wrote, *"Are you Aakash from UCLA?"*

Aakash had responded immediately. She had been flattered. And had deliberately waited a whole week before writing back. Jonathan was home, but studying, when she answered his questions.

She provided abbreviated bits of her life—I'm married and childed—and initially, she wrote more about Jay and Frances and their three children. He was amused that she was still in contact with them, surprised that Jay had actually married Frances. He did not remember meeting any Vikram or Vic, but he had heard of VikRAM Computers.

"So you have friends in high places. I'm glad I make the cut."

He was still honest, still not given to providing details.

"I'm living proof that one out of two marriages fail. Clare and I went kaput some time ago."

She had thought he was engaged to *Claire*, not *Clare*. Had assumed his marriage would last forever.

"I'm sorry," she wrote the right words, though she wasn't. She was happy that he, too, had suffered. His failure allowed her to continue writing.

He had, in the years since they knew each other, become flirtatious.

"Maybe I should have listened to my parents. They always said Indian girls are the best. Are you still the best?"

She began writing every Saturday, when Jonathan went to the synagogue. She spent the entire week thinking about what to write Aakash.

It had been ages since she had felt so excited, so wanted. And it took her right back to her small studio near UCLA, where she would look at the phone, willing it to ring, hoping it was his deep voice on the other end. She used to change her clothes five times before going out to meet him, and after she returned, would dissect her conversation, looking for things she never should have said. She felt the same way now. Every newspaper article she read, any interesting tidbit she heard, was filtered through the "should I write this to Aakash" lens? Would he think she was smart? Would he compliment her?

Then one Saturday Aakash wrote as she was online, and it seemed perfectly natural to fall into instant chat. But the give-and-take made her uncomfortable; what if Jonathan returned early?

Starbucks provided a better alternative, so she started going there.

She convinced herself that she wasn't doing anything wrong. She was simply e-mailing an old friend. He was living in San Diego, and they hadn't even spoken on the phone, much less made plans to meet each other. She was enjoying the Hindi words that crept into their e-mails, and was amused that he even threw in a few Yiddish ones. *"Learned them from my boss. I find they perform the same function as our Hindi words."*

He probably knew more Yiddish than Jonathan did.

Now, in the aromatic café, she moved her tea out of the way and debated how to answer his very flirtatious, "I am your sky" declaration.

"I prefer a blue sky," she wrote, then added, *"We don't get too many such skies in San Francisco."*

"Aren't you a Marin memsahib*?"*

She wondered how he knew that. She had only told him Jonathan's first name. Then she realized he knew her surname from their e-mails, and he had attached that to Jonathan. Personal information was easy to get these days.

They bantered on, recommending books, agreeing that it was nice, albeit strange, that Bollywood movies were now going mainstream.

"We can thank Slumdog Millionaire *for that,"* Lali typed, *"though I thought it wasn't the genuine article."*

"Definitely for the phoren moviegoers," Aakash agreed. *"No way a street chap could end up on TV!"*

Lali loved, again, that he both understood and agreed with her. If she said the same thing to Jonathan, he would believe her but would never really get what she was saying.

"Freida Pinto a sex bomb?" Aakash queried. *"These Hollywood types should go to Goa. They'll find much prettier girls, and ones who can actually act, not pose."*

"So you must have thought Frances was pretty, since she's from Goa."

"God no. Forget Frances and Freida. I thought the children in Slumdog *were excellent. Too bad they didn't get more money."*

That took them to a debate about Western power, and how amazing it was that so many people were interested in India today.

"No one had heard of Bangalore when I first came. Now everyone seems to know about it," Lali wrote.

"I get frustrated by the ones who think they know more than me. Should I blame the History Channel or the newspaper articles?"

When she finally noticed the time on the computer, she realized that Jonathan was going to be home very soon.

"Gotta run. Have to pay the maid."

Aakash didn't need to know that she left the house to keep in touch with him. And she wasn't lying. She, not Jonathan, paid the maid.

"Good-bye, memsahib. *Till next Saturday. You know that I only get through the week because of Saturdays."*

Lali rushed up the stairs to the house and apologized to Rosa for making her wait a few minutes.

"Ees okay," Rosa said, "I jus' finish."

Lali stood by the bay window, watching Rosa walk down the street. She was glad that Jonathan, too, was a little late today.

A blue-clad figure appeared on the horizon. The postman

was trudging toward their house, pushing a cart that she guessed was probably filled with more junk mail than letters. Gone were the days when she used to rifle through the mail, looking for a letter from her mother, an unexpected note from a friend. Now she Skyped with Amma, and everyone used e-mail.

She had just started making a sandwich when Jonathan opened the door.

"Honey, there's something Indian-looking for you."

Her hands froze. Had Aakash sent her something?

How was she going to explain it to Jonathan? He trusted her.

Then she calmed down. Aakash was too American to send anything too Indian. She was just suffering from her normal dose of Saturday guilt.

Jonathan held out a large envelope, and the last remnant of fear disappeared. It was probably from one of the Indian doctors at the hospital. Jonathan had been so excited to make the introductions, but she hadn't connected with any of them. The men were typically too pompous, and the women were often so caught up in their various Indian cliques of "who did what, when, where" that she had nothing to say to them. But because she was Indian, she and Jonathan invariably were invited to weddings and big parties.

She checked the return label. She had been wrong on both counts.

"It's from Vic," she said.

"Do I know him?"

"No. I knew him when I was at UCLA; he was always better friends with Jay."

It seemed odd that Vic would invite only her. She looked at the envelope. It was addressed to Dr. and Mrs. Feinstein.

"It isn't just for me," she corrected him. "It's addressed to both of us. He's celebrating his son's graduation from MIT."

"Isn't that a little odd? Most people celebrate high school graduations."

She heard the surprise in his voice and, as so often in their marriage, felt the chasm between them. He would never understand what it meant to be Indian. She, at least, lived among Americans and knew them well enough never to have to ask such a question.

"Vic's very Indian. Any opportunity to throw a party. He must be very proud that his son is an MIT graduate." Aaron had gotten into MIT but had chosen Harvard because Jonathan had gone there. "Here, take a look." She showed him the invitation.

"Colorful," Jonathan said. "What sort of party will it be?" he asked.

Lali laughed. "It will be like the invitation, excessive. Vic will probably invite a hundred people at least. Lots of food. Loud Indian music. This must be a large event, because he's inviting people from out of the area." She imagined samosas and curries and people talking in accents caught between America and India, so they emphasized the *r* in *party* but still said *tomahtoh*.

"We would have had a big party if Aaron had had a bar mitzvah."

Lali didn't respond. She never knew what to say when Jonathan went Jewish nostalgic. He hadn't had a bar mitzvah. Aaron didn't want one, so she didn't understand why Jonathan brought it up every now and then.

"I think I'll go," she decided. The invitation was just another example of India reaching out to her these days.

"When is it?" Jonathan asked.

"June eleventh."

Jonathan checked his Blackberry. "I have a conference in Santa Barbara that weekend. My paper is in the morning, so I would be able to join you."

His offer was as unexpected as her response to it. She felt warm all over, happy.

"That will be great," Lali said enthusiastically. Perhaps this could be the start of other weekends away.

She saw the added benefit of Jonathan accompanying her. He would be living proof of how well she, the odd one of the group, had done since leaving UCLA. Frances and Jay had each other, and Vic had his dreams. She had had no one and had gone limping up to a crummy job in San Francisco.

Now she could fly down, not worry about paying for a hotel, and be able to look everyone in the eye and let them know that, "Yes, life has been good to me." Jonathan would not be the phantom husband she had to talk about. If Aaron was home from Boston, he, too, could go. It would be nice to show her son his Indian side. It would be nicer to show her old friends her Harvard-returned son.

"The eleventh is a Saturday," Jonathan said. "Why don't we go down to San Diego on Sunday?"

Lali almost laughed.

"We'll see," she said, staving off making a decision. How could she tell him why she didn't want to go there? What if they ran into Aakash?

"Let's do it," he urged. "We've been wanting to go for a while, and this is the perfect opportunity. You will have seen your friends the day before, so they won't be expecting to spend more time with you."

She couldn't come up with a good excuse.

Then she realized that Jonathan was right. They had been talking about a San Diego trip ever since Aaron was in fourth grade. Aaron had wanted to see the aquarium and the zoo, but something—work, another commitment—had always stopped them.

If they hadn't gone in all this time, she reasoned, there was hope that once again, something would intervene.

"Dad!" Nikhil's voice resounded in Vic's ear, "are you out of your mind?"

"I am quite fine. I went to the doctor only last week. He announced that I was hale and hearty, in body and mind."

"I told you I didn't want you throwing another party for me. The one when I turned eighteen was enough."

"That was not for your age," Vic corrected his son. "It was because you had graduated as valedictorian from your high school and were going to MIT. Now you have graduated again, so naturally we are having another party."

"You better not have mailed out the invitations."

"We posted everyone's invitation three days ago. Yours took a little longer to reach you because you are on the other side of America."

"Dad, don't you ever listen to me? I told you when I came home for winter break that no way was I going to have anything to do with a party."

"What? A father cannot be proud of his son's achievement?"

"Don't make this about me, Dad. It's always been about what you wanted. Look, I went to MIT because you wanted me to go there. But I told you that after I graduate, I'm a free agent."

"Here, speak to your mother." Vic handed the phone to Priya, who, as usual, was hovering, waiting to talk to Nikhil.

"*Beta*, did the package of spices I sent you arrive?" he heard her ask as he left the room.

Priya invariably had the right words and touch to calm Nikhil.

He knew his son did not want the party, just as he knew that Priya would make sure Nikhil attended it. He hadn't lied when he told his son he was proud of him. He had hoped, from the moment he saw Priya holding the tiny baby in the hospital, that, unlike him, his son would have easy access to the numerous opportunities America presented.

He had worked hard to come to this country, beginning in the mud-walled school that went from kindergarten to tenth standard. Vikram, as he was known in the village, learned on the first day that the teachers hit bad students. Teacherji took out the ruler for those who spoke during class, forgot to bring their slate to school, and could not recite the alphabet. He never wanted to feel the whack of the wooden ruler, so he studied hard, even though his father kept saying that history and English would not help him grow better crops. But as Vikram learned about other places in geography class, he learned that there were other ways to live besides farming. He read stories about tall buildings that reached the clouds, and long bridges that spanned great rivers so that a man could live on one side and work on the other.

No one in the village had ever gone beyond the tenth year of school. That included some of the teachers, many of whom had tormented his own father. They were given the job because there was no one else able to do it, and they took it because teachers were afforded more respect than farmers.

Vikram knew that his only opportunity to get away from the village was to do well in the final, the ICSE exam taken by every high school student in India. Surely, he reasoned, it would be ranked, just like the report cards the teachers handed out after every exam. He routinely came in first in his class, and, in his final year, studied extra hard to achieve the same rank for the big exam.

He took the exams, two a day, in January. The results would

come months later. All the other children soon forgot about the results, but Vikram kept track of the days and weeks and months. The festival of Holi came, and everyone in the village celebrated the onset of spring by throwing colored powder and water on each other. It was the only time in the year when old and young, rich and poor were equals. Along with his classmates, Vikram hid behind a tree and, as their former teachers came into view, pelted each one until they were dripping wet, shirts a crazy kaleidoscope of colors. The teachers could not scold them, and the boys took advantage of their one day of freedom, rubbing powder into their faces and hair.

Now that Vikram did not need to attend classes, he tried to encourage his younger brother Vijay to study. But Vijay hated school, and kept quoting Pitaji. "Why do I need to know about Yumrica or Inglaand?" he asked Vikram. "I am never leaving our village."

So Vikram went about his chores, all the while wondering if he had done well enough on the exam to achieve a rank. He helped his father ready the land for the next crop. As the sun blazed overhead, every field was tended to by bent bodies, the men plowing the land, the children and wives planting seeds.

When the plants were a foot high, Vikram went out with his father to check for bugs and to water the crops.

"Vikram! Vikram!" he heard, and he looked up to see Mr. Pandey, the main class teacher for the tenth standard—the only one who had not come out during Holi—running toward them.

"Your name is in the paper," Mr. Pandey said excitedly, waving the newspaper.

"What has he done?" his father asked in a frightened voice. Vikram could almost hear Pitaji thinking there was no money to bribe the corrupt police, and how would he manage the lands while his son was in prison?

"He has achieved a rank in the ICSE exam," Mr. Pandey beamed. "That is why his name is in the paper. See here, Vikram Jha. I knew he would do it, which is why I was always searching for the results every day."

Vikram remembered the weight of his class teacher's hand as the cane smashed the soft skin behind his knees. He had challenged Mr. Pandey one day, and even though he had proved that his way of solving the math problem was easier and faster, the old man had picked up the thin cane he always kept near him. Mr. Pandey had a reputation for being the only teacher who truly enjoyed hurting students. The other teachers would halfheartedly whack outstretched palms and deliver a few strikes on the backs of legs, because corporal punishment was expected. But Mr. Pandey loved to hit where it hurt the most. He had drawn blood that day, and Vikram had no power to stop him. The only power he had was not to cry.

Vikram looked at his name, then at the date of the newspaper. "The results came out two days ago," he pointed out.

"Ah, yes, yes. But you see, it is not easy to get the paper in a timely fashion in our village."

Vikram savored his first victory. He had now gone beyond every single person in the village. He had even surpassed the head landlord, the man who owned the village, to whom the villagers bowed down and called *seth*. The seth had not achieved a rank. The seth's three sons studied in some big, fancy school up in the mountains and never played with any of the village children. The maid who cleaned their huge house told the villagers that the seth hired tutors to teach his sons during the summer holidays. One son had recently returned home, and though the seth said it was to learn the family business, the maid told everyone that he had been kicked out of the school because he had failed his final exam two years running.

Vikram folded the newspaper and tucked it under his arm without asking Mr. Pandey if he could have it. For the first time in their relationship, Mr. Pandey didn't say a word. He raised his hand to pat Vikram's shoulder, but Vikram stepped away. He was done with the cruel old man ever touching him again.

Pitaji thanked Mr. Pandey profusely and pointed out that they were busy. The crops needed a good soaking, and it had to be done now or the day would get too warm, causing the water to evaporate before seeping down to the roots.

Pitaji carried buckets of water from the well to the fields. As usual, he did not speak, his mind focused on the work that needed to be finished.

Mr. Pandey had already told Mataji, so when Vikram and his father went home for lunch, they sat down to a special meal, the parathas shiny with ghee.

"Our son has done the best of all the students, past and present," Mataji beamed.

"Now he can concentrate on the crop," Pitaji responded.

Vikram kept quiet. He hadn't expected his father to be pleased. All these years of coming first hadn't impressed Pitaji. His father delighted in Vijay, who did not mind skipping class to help during harvest season.

But later, when Vikram said he was going to IIT, in a place called Kharagpur, Pitaji had plenty to say.

"I need you to help me with the land," he said. "We are in so much debt to the *seth* that if even one crop fails, we are done for."

"You have Vijay, and I will help when I come for holidays," Vikram promised. But once he got to IIT, he started working for the professors in any way he could. His visits home were sporadic, and short. His family could not understand what he was studying at IIT. They had never heard of it, and when Vikram explained that thousands apply but very few get admitted, his mother said they should thank the gods for such luck. Pitaji grunted. Then he said it must be very crowded, how could Vikram live in a place filled with people?

He always brought back small gifts for his family, but no matter what he said or did, Pitaji behaved as if Vikram was deliberately hurting him. Mataji was sad that she didn't see him often. She worried that he was getting thin, was studying too much. His father just grumbled that all his thick books and papers would not help create better plants or crops, unlike Vijay, who was already so fast at digging.

At IIT, Vikram was on his own, unlike other students, whose parents had helped them get into the school by arranging for them to take special cramming classes. Those parents sent large food packages to augment the so-so food in the dining hall and used their contacts to set up internships and job interviews.

When he announced he was going to America, Mataji wept. She had heard about that country, she cried. It was across the ocean. The gods would be so angry he was crossing the ocean they might not let him live. If he did survive, he would be polluted by their meat-eating ways.

He told her not to worry, told her that Gandhi, too, had gone over the oceans.

"To the same place?" she wanted to know.

Vikram couldn't tell a direct lie to his mother. He knew about Gandhi's trips to South Africa and England. Then he remembered Nehru. Along with Gandhi, it was a name Mataji knew and respected.

"Nehru went to the same place in America," he fudged. He had read an account of the great man visiting the University of California at Berkeley shortly after Independence, and how pleased he was when the band played India's brand-new national anthem.

His mother's fears had briefly resurfaced when he almost

missed his flight in Amsterdam. He had taken advantage of the two-hour layover to hunt down the escalator Homi had told him about. Homi was a Parsi from Bombay, and his parents worked for the United Nations in The Hague, which meant he went abroad every year and returned with stories about underground trains and automatic doors. Vikram had been eager to see the engineering feat Homi said took people from one floor to another without their having to expend any energy. Vikram had only read about such marvels, and when he finally saw the smooth undulation that connected two floors, he didn't care that a number of people stopped and asked if everything was okay. As he stepped on it, he realized that Homi had lied to him.

"You had better be careful if you ever have to go on one," he had warned Vikram. "The first time I put my foot down, the step came up and threw me backward." He should have known that Homi was having fun at his expense.

It was because of people like Homi that he had never told anyone at IIT about his background. He was "one of the boys" in the brains department because everyone at IIT had to be smart to get in, but he knew that the others would make fun of his poor family. So he listened to them talk about vacations in Kashmir, parties where both men and women drank, and he never joined in. If he told them that his parents lived in a mud-walled house without running water, and could not understand him when he spoke English, they would only laugh. Then they would bring it up later for more laughs. He learned to protect himself, just as he had learned to believe in himself from a young age.

The only person who knew his trajectory was the president of UCLA. He liked and trusted the man, who was the first one to start calling him Vic.

"What an incredible story. You're just like Horatio Alger," the president had said, and that was when Vic knew that people in America, too, though much kinder, would never really understand him. He was not like anyone else. Horatio Alger was one in a long line of individuals who had risen from nothing. The difference was that Alger knew of other such men. Vic had not had any blueprint to follow, any hero to imitate. He had done this on his own, in spite of all the barriers—and jokes—along the way.

So of course when Nikhil was born, he didn't want his son to grow a watchful eye. He wanted Nikhil to know that he would never need to learn things on his own.

Yet Nikhil had started out doing just that. Priya insisted on speaking Hindi to Nikhil, who answered in the same language. Vic had not been worried. Everyone in India spoke a number of languages; there was no reason to fear that his son would lag behind just because he said "*paani*," instead of "water," at home. He anticipated that once Priya started meeting other mothers, Nikhil would pick up enough playground English so he would not feel lost in kindergarten. But he was completely amazed when Nikhil learned to read from watching *Sesame Street.*

One day Priya had taken him shopping, and he pointed out the cereal she was looking for. Priya assumed he had remembered the color of the box—until she realized it was a new cereal she wanted to try out.

"Nikhil can read," she told Vic when he came home that night.

Vic thought of all the things he had done, and simply picked up his son, put him on his lap, and asked him to read from the newspaper.

Nikhil skipped kindergarten and started school in first grade. He was the youngest in his class, but he always got A's. By the time Nikhil finished fifth grade, Vic determined that a public school—even the good ones in Newport Beach—was not the right place for his son. He put him in the best private school in the area and made sure Nikhil took every AP and Honors class that was offered, which brought his GPA even higher.

The only trouble Vic remembered with his son was in regard to sports. Nikhil preferred cooking to hitting a ball, and Vic had been very concerned that his son was growing up to be a sissy. He himself had laughed at the boys who could not throw a curve ball, and he hated the thought of his son being a joke on the field.

"Every man has a sport," he told Nikhil.

"What do you play?" Nikhil had challenged him.

"Cricket," Vic answered readily. "It's too bad they don't play it here, otherwise you would see what a top-notch player I am."

After much discussion, Nikhil decided on swimming. He liked the water. Vic also knew that the individual sport suited his son because he was uncomfortable about physical contact and the attendant risk of injury.

As soon as Nikhil signed up for lessons, Vic contacted a designer and built a pool with a lap lane. Nikhil had practiced every day and won quite a few prizes before he stopped swimming in his last year of high school. By then he had gained early admission into MIT, and Vic had let it go.

But Vic wasn't going to cancel the party. He was proud, of course, but he also wanted to make an occasion of giving Nikhil a position in his company. He had long planned that once Nikhil got his computer-science degree, he would start tutoring him to ultimately take over VikRAM Computers, his software company. He did not want Nikhil to begin at the bottom, the way so many Americans determined was the best path. There was no need for Nikhil to know every aspect of the company. He could start in middle management and then eventually take over, by which time Nikhil's brother, Nandan, would be old enough to start working. Vic had worried that Nandan had come along seven long years after Nikhil, but now he realized it might end up being beneficial. His oldest son would be able to guide the younger one, just as when they were small. When both boys were working at VikRAM Computers, Vic could become a consultant, stop going to the office every day.

Vic checked his watch. It was time to go and meet his biking buddies. He had just pocketed the keys to his motorbike when Priya called out to him.

"Where are you going?"

"I am meeting the group."

"Are you going to drink with them?" Priya started, then saw his face and switched subjects. "Nikhil is very angry."

"I'm sure you were able to make him see sense."

"He wants me to make *you* see sense."

"We're having the party, and that's final. The invitations have already been posted."

"Actually, the invitations are still in the house."

"Why didn't you post them when I told you to?"

"I thought Nikhil should see it first."

"Post the invitations today itself." Vic was furious. Who was she to go against his wishes?

"It's Saturday. The post office is closed by now," Priya reminded him.

"I know what day it is. The invitations are stamped, are they not? You can put them in the mailbox outside the post office. Give them to me. I'll do it."

"You will be late for your motorbike ride. I'll do it."

Suddenly he did not trust her. "You already posted them, didn't you?" he demanded.

Her silence confirmed his suspicion. "What were you going to do? Call all those people and tell them the party is off because Nikhil does not want to celebrate his graduation?"

"Nikhil is very angry. He says you don't listen to him—"

"If I had listened to him, right now he would be taking classes at the community college, and cooking in some stupid restaurant on weekends."

"He did what you wanted. Starting in the fourth grade, he took swimming lessons and practiced every day."

"What did you want him to do? Stand by the stove and stir some vegetables? I made sure that his body was strong."

"So now his body is strong, and his mind also is strong. He wants to become a cook."

"I'm not sending my son to a cooking school," Vic shouted.

She was soft, just like Nikhil. She had been raised to believe that she would always be looked after—first by her parents and then by the man they arranged for her to marry. She had never struggled to fill out applications, never crammed all night, never known what it felt like to walk past the IIT canteen as if the food were bad, because in fact there was no money to buy a cup of tea, the cheapest item on the menu.

Nikhil was even luckier. He had slept in a bed from the day he was born. He had pocket money, a bike as soon as he asked for one, and a swimming pool in his backyard because he did not like contact sports. It wasn't just that he had never been hungry for one day in his life; he had never needed to desire more than he already had.

"He's my son, too," Priya stated.

"Your son, your son," Vic raged. She had started saying that when Nikhil began helping her cook. Vic would come home for dinner and Priya would announce that Nikhil had made the dal. Vic was always so tired that he only half-listened. He just wanted to eat and rest.

"He's *my* son," Vic shouted now, suddenly remembering the day Nikhil had received the acceptance letter from MIT.

Vic had been ecstatic. Some of his classmates at IIT had

applied there, but Vic had had only enough money to try for admission to one college. His professor had gone to UCLA and advised him to apply there, saying he would write a letter on his behalf. Vic looked at the MIT admission letter he had never received and wanted to call everyone and tell them the news. But, just as he had done when he got his UCLA acceptance letter, he kept quiet. His mother had raised him to fear the black eye, had always told him never to share good news in case someone's jealousy would cause it to go away. The seth had only known that Vic was at IIT in his second year. They had been able to keep it from the seth that long, by which time his own son was in a college in Delhi, so he hadn't minded that one of his workers' children was also studying.

Nikhil hadn't said much about the acceptance letter. He put it in his room, and, later that day, Vic heard him talking to his best friend Jeff. Instead of bragging, Nikhil had told Jeff he was lucky to be going to college in Long Beach. "You won't have to brave the winters," Nikhil said. "I hear Boston's cold for half the year."

Vic had never taught his son the art of deliberate modesty. Yet Nikhil was behaving just the way he had, when his roommate back at IIT had gotten a job in Bombay but not admission to the University of Wisconsin. Vic had told his roommate that he was luckier, because he knew exactly what he was getting, while he, Vic, might have to return to India if things did not work out at UCLA.

"He's my son," Vic shouted again.

Nandan came into the room.

"Are you two fighting again?" Nandan inquired.

"We are discussing things," Priya said.

"And it is not any of your business," Vic said.

"It is when you disturb me," Nandan responded.

"Then close the door," Vic instructed his son. "I bought a big house so we can all have our own rooms, and you don't have to be disturbed when I am having a discussion with your mother."

He had done all this for them, and now they were being ungrateful. Nandan was just fourteen and already cheeking him, Nikhil didn't want to have a party, and Priya was siding with their son.

That got him the angriest. He had taken her out of the small village where she had attended a one-room school, and had married her even though she hadn't finished college. Her parents had given her just two gold bangles and one necklace, and her dowry was so ridiculous it wasn't worth mentioning. But because his parents had arranged everything, he had flown home, gotten married, and returned to the States in one week.

When Priya first arrived, everything frightened her. She did not know how to use the stove, preferred washing clothes in the bathtub, and even though she desperately wanted to make friends with the neighbors, stayed inside the house the whole day.

He had been convinced that the best thing for her was to get pregnant, and he had been right. After she gave birth to Nikhil, she began going to the park, meeting nannies and mothers, and arranging play dates.

Next thing he knew, she was speaking English easily and telling him that she needed more time before having another baby.

He had been pleased by her adjustment, relieved that he no longer came home to a crying wife.

But now that adjustment had led to her sassing him. He, the man who had built a two-story house for her parents, who had provided such large dowries for her younger sisters that they were able to marry doctors, and who had sent her brother to college. Two years ago, he had even brought over her idiot cousin Rajesh.

Rajesh had a BCom from a nothing college in North India, but every time they visited, he begged Priya to use her influence with Vic to give him a job. Vic had signed the papers only after it was clear that Priya's immediate family had no intention of leaving India. Like his own younger brother, they were happy to write long lists of requests, but no one, other than Rajesh, wanted to emigrate. So Vic had a lawyer take care of things, and, when the time came, he bought airline tickets for Rajesh, his wife, and three children under the age of six.

Rajesh had assumed that America was just like India, where relatives got high-paying jobs without the right qualifications. Vic had warned Rajesh that he would need excellent computer skills if he wanted a top job at VikRAM Computers. Rajesh kept assuring Vic that he was taking such-and-such classes, but it turned out that he only signed up for them and never completed a single course.

Still, Vic had listened to Priya and given her cousin a job. Rajesh, however, soon started complaining. He wanted his own office, more money; he wanted a *good* position in the company. But on this matter, Vic remained firm. He wasn't going to inject Indian rules into his American firm.

After numerous attempts, Priya stopped asking. Perhaps it was because Priya herself was getting fed up with Rajesh's wife. She complained all the time about the lack of servants, about how she missed her family, and could not understand why she needed to drive. If America was such a great country, she asked Priya and Vic one night when she came for dinner, then why were the shops so far away from the people? It wasn't just an inconvenience for her, she reasoned, it showed how stupid this country really was. Back home, she only needed to call out to the vegetable man as he walked down the road. She never needed to leave her house in order to cook a meal.

After six months, she decided to return home. Vic bought the tickets for her and the children and encouraged Rajesh to leave as well. Rajesh refused. He had found a job selling insurance. "There is a very big Indian population here in the Los Angeles area, so I will definitely make plenty of money. Then I will bring back my wife, and this time I will make sure we have some servants. Maybe I will even bring a servant from India." He moved into an apartment, and every time he saw Vic, he had another insurance scheme to sell.

Did Priya think that just because he had given in to her nagging and bought some unnecessary insurance policies from her cousin, she was now in charge of their house?

"You are forgetting who is the boss of this family," Vic said.

"I always remember," Priya said calmly, "but you keep forgetting that in this country, parents can't be bosses forever. Nikhil is twenty-one now. He can vote, and drink, and he can also just walk away from us."

"That he will never do," Vic waved his hand. "He has never worked a day in his life. How will he support himself?"

"He knows computers and cooking. America has plenty of jobs for such people."

"Not in this economy."

"He has been talking of going to India."

"What?" Vic exploded. "I raise him here, send him to MIT, and he wants to go back to India? What have you done to him?"

"Me? I didn't do anything."

"You were the one who was always wanting to take the children to India every summer. You kept telling them stories about your village, making it seem so wonderful."

"As if you stopped me," Priya scoffed. "You liked it when we left for the summer, because you could work all the time."

"And who did I work for? You tell me that."

"For us," Priya said. "You always say it was for us."

"I did everything for this family. I didn't take holidays, I even walked to save the bus money when I first started my company.

Did I buy fancy suits and eat lunch in expensive restaurants? No, I took my lunch and shopped at Target. Now, when I want to have a simple party, you are saying that I am asking for too much."

"I am not saying it."

"You just make sure that Nikhil comes back," Vic said. "Now I am not going to be on time, and it is all because of you." He stomped into the garage.

It wasn't good to be late with this group. Thank God they were meeting just to discuss the next motorbike trip. The men took their rides very seriously and did not wait for latecomers. He had been left behind a few times in the beginning, until he realized that 5 p.m. meant exactly that. Back home, being on time was reserved for exams. He even used to be a few minutes late for classes when he first started UCLA, until he adjusted his thinking.

He ignored Priya's "Don't drink" and got on his BMW motorbike, which still gleamed with the shine of new paint and chrome. He revved down the road, picking up speed, all the while watching for the police. If he made every light, he just might be on time.

Vic had stumbled across this group of six expat French motorbikers a year ago when he had wandered into the BMW showroom. He had thought he knew about bikes until he heard them going back and forth about gears and sprockets and drive-lines with the salesman. He hung around, pretending to check out the different bikes but actually listening to the men and making mental notes.

For some reason he followed them outside and then blurted out the obvious: "You have Harley-Davidsons."

"So what is that to you?" The man who had harangued the salesman now challenged him.

"Nothing. I just thought, because you know so much, that you must have BMWs."

"We like to give those BMW types a hard time. What do you have?"

"A Jaguar." He heard one of them snort, and said quickly, "But I am going to be buying a motorbike, which is why I came here."

"A BMW?" the man asked.

"Yes." He knew that hard-core riders preferred Harleys, but he had wanted a BMW from the time he was a little boy.

His village didn't have tar roads, and there were no streetlights. People had bicycles, and the better-off ones had scooters. The fat seth, who owned most of the land that the villagers tilled, was the only one with a car.

Mahesh was the sole man who had something different: a BMW motorbike. It had belonged to Mahesh's father, who said he got it from a British soldier years earlier. The bike was old, and Mahesh didn't ride it often because it was hefty and difficult to maneuver on the uneven roads, especially after a heavy rain. But whenever he did take it out, everyone came to watch the wonder that had been born in Germany, taken to England, and finally brought to India.

Vikram begged Mahesh for a ride, but he always refused, giving the same answer the other children had heard for years: "I don't want you to get hurt. Your parents will get too angry with me if this ancient machine harms even one precious hair on your head." Vikram could only watch as the stately motorbike rolled down the road, Mahesh waving to the people as if he were the prime minister.

He promised himself that one day he would make enough money to buy it from Mahesh. Mahesh didn't have children, and Vikram guessed that when he died, his widow would be willing to sell the motorbike. Vikram was in his final year at IIT when he heard that Mahesh had been killed by a snakebite. He was conjuring up ways to get enough money to offer the widow when his mother, who remembered his love for the motorbike, wrote and said that Mahesh's cousin had taken it. So even before he could try it out, the motorbike was gone. That was when Vikram decided he would buy himself a brand-new motorbike one day. It would be as similar to the old one as possible.

Other desires—the house, private school, the Mercedes, the Porsche, the Jaguar—had intervened. He also did not think it was practical to have a motorbike when he needed to take the children to their various activities. But now only Nandan was at home, and Priya was able to manage his schedule on her own.

Finally, the time had come for him to drive that dream he'd had as a boy when he had watched the bulky, pre–World War II BMW *putt-putt* down the dirt road.

"Good luck," the Frenchman said, climbing on his bike.

"Wait a minute," Vic put up his palm. "Are you members of a group, a motorbiking club?" He came up with the right phrase. Until this moment, he had only thought of buying a motorbike. But now he considered how much more fun he would have if he rode with others. "Maybe I can join up with you?"

"We're all French."

"The French and the Indians are not so different," Vic smiled. "Maybe you know that your emperor Napoleon, and Tipu Sultan, the king we all called the Tiger of India, gave each other advice on how to fight the British?"

"For that reason we should let you join us?"

"When I was in Greece, a shopkeeper lowered his price when I informed him that the Indian king Porus was the one who stopped Alexander from conquering any more countries."

"What are you, a historian?"

"Actually, I am the CEO of VikRAM Computers."

"And now you want to ride with us?"

"Yes."

"Do you even know how to ride a bike?" the man asked, and the one to his left added, "And you will have to get a Harley."

"As you point out, I am Indian and you are French. So my bike, too, will be different. I will ride a BMW."

The next week he had the bike and took his first ride with the French group. Pierre, the one who had done most of the talking when Vic approached them outside the showroom, had been in America the longest and had started the club three years earlier as a way of meeting other French expats. He told Vic that they had agreed to break their "French only" rule because he had been so persistent, coming up with history to push his point.

Vic didn't care why they let him in. He liked riding with them and also found them unexpectedly useful. Since he was now one of them, Pierre told him which shop sold the best riding gear, and which mechanic knew the most. He showed Vic his bare chest and recommended that Vic also shave the hair to make himself more aerodynamic.

"I thought that was for swimmers." Vic wondered whether Pierre was making fun of him.

"No, no," Pierre insisted. "All serious riders do the same because the air is like the water. This makes it easier to cut through it."

He also told Vic to start building muscles on his arms if he wanted to wear the tight, sleeveless shirts that went so well with bikes. Priya had been appalled by his bare chest, and it had hurt so much that Vic never shaved again. He did, however, install exercise equipment in his house. Though he had started out pumping iron every day, now he only had time once or twice a week.

Vic had never enjoyed free time before this. Until he met the Frenchmen, he had meetings over lunch and often went to the office during the weekend. His company was well established, but he still needed to ensure that it kept up with the changing times. And ever since a newspaper had written an article about him, he had become involved in numerous Indian civic ventures.

The once-a-month ride was his only indulgence. The summer trips Priya insisted on were more for her than for him. He usually spent half the time on the phone, staying back at the hotel while the others visited a museum or toured a castle.

Today he was meeting the bikers to discuss a trip to Las Vegas. The group went every year, they said, as a sort of pilgrimage to good shows, casinos, and booze. Vic had never been to Vegas and was excited just thinking about it. Nikhil and Nandan had gone on numerous school trips, many around Newport Beach, some as far away as Washington, DC. Now he, too, could do the same. Last month he had gone up to Santa Barbara with the Frenchmen. Vic had given a talk at the university, but it had been a quick trip, up and back in a day. The men took him on narrow roads that had spectacular views, and they had eaten a take-out dinner on the beach.

Vic turned into the parking lot of the bar. The Harleys were already there. He set his bike alongside the others and entered the bar. He knew exactly where to find them. They were in the back, playing darts.

"Twenty dollars says you can't put this in the center," Pierre handed a dart to Vic.

Vic aimed, and threw.

"How do you do that," Pierre shook his head, "every time?"

"Good aim," Vic shrugged, accepting the money.

He had bought a dartboard after he realized they always played while drinking beer. He had practiced for weeks before finally, reluctantly, agreeing to a game. Now he was able to beat their challenges and pocket their money.

"Sure your wife will let you get away for a three-day weekend?" Pierre poked him in the ribs.

"Just because you are not married does not mean your girlfriends don't mind," Vic reminded him.

"But we change our girlfriends every time they make a fuss," Pierre laughed. "Wives are more difficult."

"Not Indian wives," Vic said smugly. "My wife always does what I ask her."

"So what we hear about Indian women is correct, then?" Pierre ascertained. "They are the opposite of that Indira Gandhi."

"Some are like her, but I did not marry one like that."

"Okay, then, good. You will come with us to Las Vegas, and we will show you a good time. Wine, women, the tables, bring it on," Pierre rubbed his hands together, "especially the women."

Vic enjoyed his liquor, but he had never understood the lure of the gaming tables. He only gambled when the odds were in his favor, as with the darts. He had never had the time, or interest, to study cards, and never considered risking his money on a game of chance. He also didn't understand the need to see naked women dance, or take them back to the hotel room.

The Frenchmen weren't the only people he knew who enjoyed the company of loose women. He had met a few Indians in recent years who talked of prostitutes, and one man was very open about his American mistress. Vic knew that those Indians viewed such behavior as a mark of their success, and the man with the mistress felt superior to his countrymen because he was sleeping with a white woman. Vic had done all that while at UCLA, but once he married Priya, he committed to being a faithful husband. The only French he knew was the term *ménage à trois*, which had led him to believe that they were a people who did anything and everything sex-related. This opinion had been confirmed by the Frenchmen, who claimed that relationships were like musical chairs, and they got up or sat down depending on the girl passing by. "When is the trip happening?" Vic took out his Blackberry.

"June tenth."

"That is not a good weekend for me."

"Why? The wife wants to do something?" Pierre jeered.

"No, nothing like that." Vic had purposely not told them much about himself. It was the same tactic he had employed at IIT. Back then, he had feared ridicule because of his socioeconomic conditions; in America, he knew that some people thought Indian customs were strange. So he kept his house to himself and only let others know what was absolutely necessary.

"Come on, you can tell us."

"Why don't we just look for another time that is suitable for all of us?" Vic prevaricated.

"Now you are making us very suspicious. What is so important on June tenth that you can't even tell us?"

Vic almost made up a story about his company. Then, at the last minute, he decided it was okay for them to know about Nikhil's very American success.

"I am having a party for my son."

"Change the date. You don't have to give the party on the real birthday."

"It's not for his birthday. He has graduated from MIT and is returning home to join my company."

"MIT. Wow. Congratulations. Your son must be very smart."

Vic shrugged. He didn't want to brag. Most of the men were construction workers. They had come to visit America and then stayed on. Pierre was the only one who worked at a desk.

"I really thought your wife didn't want you to go to sinful Vegas," Pierre said.

Vic hadn't even told them her name. From the moment they knew he was married, they enjoyed poking fun at him. If he didn't want another beer, they'd sneer, "He's married." When he didn't turn to look at a girl with a tight-fitting dress, they would mock him, saying, "Has your wife put a detective on you?"

About six months ago, he got fed up, and said, "Look, I can get unmarried anytime. But none of you can get married just like that," he clicked his fingers, making a sharp sound. For a while they stopped the "he's married" joshing, but it had recently crept back.

The irony was that Priya had actually been very happy when he first told her about his new hobby. "It's good you are making men friends," she stated, and he had harrumphed, wondering which talk show or movie she had learned *that* from.

Even when he started meeting them for drinks, she had not said anything. But she blew up when he got a DUI ticket three months ago.

The men had warned him that the police did not like bikers and took any opportunity to give them tickets. Pierre said that one time he slowed down at a crosswalk, saw that the woman was talking on her phone, and so accelerated. Next thing he knew, a pig of a policeman had given him a ticket. When he tried to argue that the woman had given no indication that she wanted to cross the street, the pig told him to take it to court. "But you won't win," he said. "I'll make sure I'm there."

Vic knew about the police. Back in the 1990s, they used to pull him over all the time. They assumed that a brown man could not possibly own a Mercedes. But these days brown men were driving all sorts of cars, including Jaguars, and Vic had long ago stopped watching out for cops.

So when the men told him their stories, he didn't think it applied to him.

He had been the first to leave that evening, and a cop had been waiting to bust whoever came out of the bar. The DUI turned out to be an unexpected seal of acceptance from the group. They each had one, or two, or three. "You are finally one of us," Pierre had bought him a drink to celebrate.

Priya, on the other hand, had been hysterical. She had cried and carried on. She worried that he would get into an accident and die. She couldn't comprehend that he wasn't a drunk, that he had only had a few beers, that the cop was probably trying to make his quota for the day. She fretted that this would get out in the Indian community, and it would tarnish their name.

He had been more concerned about getting his license reinstated. He had only had two beers; he knew how to control himself. Priya did not need to worry that he would ever get caught again.

But the DUI had changed Priya's attitude about his biker friends. She claimed that she was never easy when he went with the group. She did not like him wearing tight T-shirts that showed off his muscles. She didn't object to his exercising, she said, because that was good for his health, but the thin T-shirts made him look like a low-class *gunda*.

"In actuality," Vic now told Pierre, "my wife would be more than happy to cancel the party."

"Then make her happy and make yourself happy," Pierre recommended. "Vegas is something you should not miss, especially the Vegas we can show you."

"I can't go that weekend," Vic said firmly. "Sorry. You all go and have a good time. I'll let you make your plans. Good-bye." He left before they could say another word.

Not wanting to go home, he headed for the beach. He had never seen the ocean before coming to UCLA—his family had never, ever gone on vacation.

As Pitaji used to say, "The land does not allow us to rest."

"Unless you are the seth," Vikram had reminded his father, while his mother told him to keep quiet in case someone was listening and reported back to the fat man who owned their land and controlled their destinies.

People in America were surprised that though he had grown up quite close to the Taj Mahal, he had only seen it once. He never told them that he had gone there *after* living in America.

Vic sat on the soft, yellow sand and gazed at the water. If he returned tomorrow, it would be the same view, except that it wouldn't be the same water. The constant change used to fascinate him.

But he was too distraught right now to do anything but think about all the things that had gone wrong today.

He had hoped that planning for the Vegas trip would improve his mood. Instead, the men had annoyed him. Why did they make fun of his wife? He used to enjoy their company, but these days he only went for the rides.

Priya, too, made him angry. She was the one who had made Nikhil into a sissy who loved cooking more than sports. She had never liked canned and frozen foods, so from the very beginning, had cooked as if they lived in India. Her only allowance that this was America was to use the blender to make the masalas, instead of grinding the spices by hand.

When Nikhil took rice and dal and vegetables for his lunch, his classmates used to make fun of his food. Priya had wanted to give him sandwiches, but Vic had stopped her. "He will always be different," he told his wife. "Let him learn early how to make it work for him."

Now, of course, America had gone mad for "real cooking," and it was fashionable to be vegetarian and eat ethnic. Their neighbors were always asking Priya for recipes, and she had even demonstrated how to cook a few dishes in Nandan's school. Every now and then, Nandan returned home hungry, because some classmate had begged him for his lunch. Indian food was popular, and though not as chic as Japanese sushi, it was garnering a lot of attention.

But Nikhil needed to realize that Americans were fickle where food was concerned. Their interest in Indian cuisine would go away, they would go back to eating meat—but computers were here to stay.

Now he worried that Nikhil wanted to go to India. Was this a recent plan or did it go back to when he wanted to give up MIT and take cooking classes in various parts of the world, including India?

Vic would have to stub out this new, stupid idea. His son did not know the real India. He was being seduced by the news, which was coming from the mouths of foreigners who would never understand India—and politicians, who never told the truth. Vic discounted every statistic that claimed India was on the cusp of becoming great. The country was too corrupt—from the government on down—to ever move ahead. Didn't Nikhil realize that he himself would return to India if it truly was a better place? Here he could run VikRAM Computers the way he wanted to, hire the best people, and not worry as long as he kept to the law and paid his taxes. In India, he would have to bribe all sorts of officials and everyone, from relatives to the friends of friends of friends, would demand a job. Perhaps he should tell Nikhil exactly why Rajesh wasn't working for him anymore.

He couldn't allow Nikhil to go to India. His son was raised in America. He would have no idea which hand to oil, how to grease the system.

Vic heard some shouting. A group of people were running into the water. They were Nikhil's age, maybe younger. They laughed and pushed each other, as if nothing were wrong with their lives. When, he wondered, was the last time he had been so free? Had he ever really been unfettered, allowing the future to come to him, not wanting to control it by doing, planning, thinking ahead?

His first taste of any freedom had come when he was at UCLA. His classes had been easy, and he only needed to study a little in order to ace his exams. He got a job as a teaching assistant and did tutoring on the side. His combined income allowed him to rent a tiny studio apartment that was close enough so he could walk to campus. He also had a phone, a small black-and-white TV, and a well-stocked fridge. He even had money left over to send home every month. His parents still weren't happy that he was so far away, but his dollars had paid off the onerous loans Pitaji had taken from the seth when the harvest failed. Yet Vic hadn't felt burdened, and every now and then he enjoyed a restaurant meal.

He had loved those early years in America. He had tasted meat for the first time but had quickly gone back to being a vegetarian. These days, he no longer had to explain his food choices to people, and he had recently hired a man who was vegan.

He had even slept with white girls at UCLA. He had been so surprised the first time it happened. He was tutoring a very pretty girl, and she suggested they meet in her apartment rather than at the library. He didn't care where they met, as long as she paid him his fee. She had opened the door dressed in her nightgown. There had been no studying done that day, or the next time, or the time after. But he made sure that every girl knew that he was not available for marriage. They found his concern very "gentlemanly," one girl said, but each assured him that marriage was not in their near future. They simply wanted to have fun, experience new things. He was in the novel position of being wanted just for himself, and he luxuriated in the many girls who chased after him. But he never fell in love, never had the desire to keep up any relationship. And, unlike so many Indians he met these days, he didn't get a case of "white fever."

It was while he was at UCLA that he took the initial steps toward forming his own company. Even that had been easy. Many people approached him, and the system was set up in such a way that he could get help with his business plan as well as find out who might give him seed money.

It had all worked out, right down to having two sons who would carry on his name and his work.

"James!" a girl shouted as she ran right in front of Vic, kicking sand onto his legs. He suddenly thought of Jay. He had first seen Jay at the UCLA orientation party, watching from afar as he smiled and spoke and charmed everyone. And of course a man wearing blue jeans and a silk shirt *would* go up to one of the few Indian girls present and start a conversation. Vic had been talking the entire time to another computer nerd from Japan. Kevin Ozaki had come to UCLA with the same ambition of starting a company, except that he planned to do it in his hometown of Kyoto.

Then the president of UCLA came over and insisted Vic meet the other Indians at the party. Vic had tagged Jay, from the very first "Hello," as the son of a rich man. It was there in the way he assumed everyone was listening when he spoke, in his casual shrug when he told the story of losing the textbooks he had just bought. They gradually began meeting each other more often, and Vic had been very amused when a few Americans thought they were cousins, friends, brothers. How could the Americans know that Jay would never have befriended Vic if they had met in India? Jay would have been the one in the first-class train compartment; Vic would have been in third class, just another body amid the hoi polloi.

Yet Jay's rich beginnings hampered him in the United States. Jay expected things to work out; he didn't work, really work, because he had never had to do so. His life had been decided from the moment he entered kindergarten in his fancy school, which fed into a top-notch college in India, which in turn gave him the right education to do well enough on the GMAT to gain admission into UCLA.

But all that did not help him in America when it came time to get a job. Vic had watched as Jay started to flounder without the societal support he had always enjoyed. When Vic had tried to help, Jay dismissed him. Jay thought he knew more, knew better.

"Why don't you come with me to check the job listings?" Vic had suggested. He wanted to keep all his options open, so, even as he set about creating his own company, he looked for a full-time position.

"I have an 'in' with this company my adviser used to consult for," Jay shrugged. He was so sure that influence would get him a job. Jay did land a job, but Vic always thought that he would have done better if he had sent his resume to more, rather than fewer, companies.

Jay had let his guard down only once, when he spoke about his relationship with Frances. But Jay had drunk a lot that night, and Vic thought it was the liquor, rather than their friendship, that had caused Jay to blurt out his worries.

Vic hadn't attended their civil wedding, but he had asked one of the girls he tutored what type of present to give. She had suggested towels, and he had bought them a matching set.

Their lives, as he had always known, had diverged after UCLA, but those few years had created a bond that gained in importance as he grew older. He had met hundreds of people since then, had made scores of friends. But only one took him back to his early days in America.

There had been such comfort in coming from the same country, comfort in knowing that none of the other students' parents could eat with their fingers. There was so much he knew about Jay from just one glance, from hearing just one word. The Frenchmen? He would never be able to place them in their society, even though he had been in France.

Vic pulled out his phone. Jay hadn't moved in years, and one of the benefits about being a computer expert was his facility with numbers. He pressed the phone against his ear as he heard the ringing. He'd ask Jay if he had received the invitation, tell him that this time he wasn't going to accept any excuses. The thought of seeing his old friend melted his dissatisfaction with the Frenchman and his family.

The call connected, and he was all set to shout, "Hello, remember me, Vic the stick?" when the answering machine kicked on.

Jay's voice was saying, "You know who we are, but we don't know who you are. So tell us. And we'll call you back. If we want to."

He hung up without leaving a message. Maybe he'd call again tomorrow. Maybe by tomorrow Nikhil would have come to his senses. But even if Nikhil was still resistant, they had to start planning the party.

Preparing for the Party

Frances looked up the new listings and then scrolled back to the old ones. She loved seeing the jubilant sold banner across the photograph of the Miller house. The Millers had, after a long evening of going back and forth and asking for more money, accepted an offer that was $10,000 below their asking price. Frances had been unsure it would go through, because the first-time buyer had a Federal Housing Administration loan and was only putting down 3½ percent. But, as each day slipped into the next, nothing impeded the sale, and Frances told Jay, "I think the market is finally turning around, you know." It had given her renewed faith in real estate, in her life in general, and she had recently signed up for a weekly class entitled "How to Increase Your Potential."

She shut the laptop, satisfied that everything was in order. There was never much work on Saturday mornings, which meant that she could have a leisurely breakfast with the family.

Frances had just filled the kettle and turned on the stove when Jay joined her in the kitchen. "Well, Vic's long-awaited day has finally arrived." Jay said what had been on his mind from the moment he woke up.

He hadn't thought much about the party until a few days ago when Harvey Goldman, his office mate, invited him to a talk at UCLA's Anderson School of Management.

"I know you're an alum, and my wife would rather go to a baby shower than listen to a panel of businessmen predict what's in store for us. Don't let this $350 ticket go to waste." Harvey had waved the rectangular paper in Jay's face.

Harvey was the office go-getter, and Jay was pleased to be the chosen one this time. "Let me make sure I'm available," he said, checking his Blackberry. "Darn it, I have to go to a graduation party for a kid I haven't seen in years." Jay shook his head sadly.

"You don't know the kid, don't go," Harvey recommended, so Jay ended up telling him about Vic, their UCLA days, and Nikhil.

"Why didn't you tell me you know Vic Jha, the CEO of VikRAM Computers?" Harvey demanded. "You could have gotten my son an internship for the summer. Instead, poor Bobby is going to teach swimming at the local YWCA."

After that, Harvey kept asking Vic-related questions. "Did he tell you he was going to start his company when you were at UCLA?"

Vic had mentioned it a few times, but never in concrete terms. Jay had wondered whether it was more a fantasy than something Vic was really pursuing. Even when they had gone clothes shopping at Macy's, Vic had said that if he couldn't get an investor, he'd make use of the new suit for job interviews. It had given Jay the impression that Vic wasn't committed to any particular path, as long as he made money.

"Why didn't you join in on the ground floor? Imagine where you'd be today, huh?"

How could he tell Harvey that even though Vic was intelligent, he hadn't thought his friend had the Western smarts to start and sustain a company. After all, the first time they ate in the cafeteria, Vic had been nonplussed by the plastic tray, the menu, the choice of toppings for a baked potato. As Jay had told Frances, referring to Vic's favorite footwear, "This bloke is flip-flopping his way through school, good in the classroom but not anywhere else." He had always assumed that his own upbringing, the fork-and-knife skills he had learned back home, would land him a great job that would take him straight up the ladder of success. He would not have been surprised if Vic had told him he was returning to India.

"College friendships are tight, so I bet this Vic will be able to help your kids if they decide to become computer people."

Jay was sure that Vic would be willing to help out. It wasn't just the ties they had formed in college; it was also the "we're from India" connection. But Jay knew that he would never ask Vic, because he could not return the favor.

The sudden interest in Vic had left Jay uncomfortable. If even Harvey wondered at the disparity between them, Jay knew that the Indians at the party would find him severely lacking. They always judged a family by the man, and it was clear that he hadn't provided for his wife and children the way Vic had.

He wished that they didn't have to go.

He recalled Frances's hysterical reaction to the invitation the day it had arrived, how she had yelled at Mandy. She hadn't brought it up recently, and given that she got nervous before going to the annual Christmas party at her firm, he was surprised she wasn't going on and on about the evening.

"We got the invitation, what, two months ago?" he asked Frances.

"At least that long," Frances agreed, a little distracted as she searched for her favorite cup. "I bought the graduation card yesterday and remembered to get a clean hundred-dollar bill from the bank."

"Don't forget to add one dollar," Jay reminded her, wishing they were able to give more money.

"Oh, right. I always forget about that odd custom. Goans don't do it, you know."

"Old Hindu tradition of not liking even numbers." Jay peered out the window. "Looks like rain, though I guess Newport Beach has a different weather pattern."

"I'm sure Vic's accounted for that," Frances said, just as Lily and Sam raced into the kitchen.

"We want pancakes," Lily demanded.

"With syrup *and* jam," Sam seconded.

"And just who do you think I am?" Jay, arms akimbo, inquired, glad to be taken away from thinking how his own life sagged when stacked up against Vic's.

"You are Sir Jay, also known as our sir-vant," Lily giggled.

"And you are to sir-ve us our breakfast," Sam doubled up with laughter.

Frances loved the giddy exuberance, the sureness with which they ordered pancakes. It had been a long time since she had felt so—at ease. The Miller sale had done more than bring in much-needed money. It had restored her confidence, and she had, after much agony—thinking yes, then no—come up with a plan for Mandy. The fact that they were going to do something for Mandy had further settled her.

"Out of the kitchen, you two," she said, shooing the children toward the family room. "We'll call you when the pancakes are ready."

Frances cracked an egg into the bowl. Jay watched the yolk hold its own, only dissolving into the albumen after Frances started to whip it with a fork.

He suddenly remembered telling five-year-old Mandy that an egg is like life: There is no knowing which way it will crack open.

"What did your egg do, Dad?" she asked him, but before he could answer, Frances had laughed and said that men don't have eggs.

"I know, Mom," Mandy had said, "men have sprite, I mean sperm."

How they had laughed, eyes acknowledging that their daughter was, as her kindergarten teacher had said, precocious.

Everyone who met Mandy commented on the way her dark, shiny eyes snapped in the world around her. Now those eyes had stopped being engaged, and it depressed him that he, the father who had marveled at her from first sight, did not have the right answer for her problems. There was a time when Mandy actually thought he was like God and knew everything. But those days were in the dreamy past, and he had been feeling inadequate for months.

He and Frances had spent long nights arguing how best to recover the child they were used to, the little girl whose insatiable desire to know the most had made her such a gifted student.

Frances had thought up the solution that she and Mandy return to India for the year.

"My mother hasn't been well, and I haven't seen her in years, you know," Frances said. "My sisters have been taking care of Mama, and this way I can give them a break. And Mandy can finish her last year in India."

He knew the guilt that came from living far away, had experienced it firsthand when Papa had had bypass surgery two years ago. Frances had encouraged him to go, had assured him that this was not the time to worry about expensive last-minute tickets. He would never stop her from going home, especially since her last visit had been when Sam was a baby.

But he thought her plan was too drastic, so he suggested she go for the entire summer, alone.

"I don't want to split up the family for a whole year," he said firmly. "Lily and Sam will miss you too much."

"Oh, Jay, don't you think I'll miss them too?" Frances had asked, tears in her eyes and voice. "This isn't an easy decision for any of us. I had hoped that we could all go for the summer, so that we'd only be apart for the school year, but we don't have the money."

He knew that they could not afford five tickets, gifts, and the generous spending that people back home presumed from dollar-earners. Their families believed they were enjoying the perks of being rich immigrants, and it was easy to keep up the lie from this great distance. Papa didn't know they had the smallest house on the block, or that they routinely bought secondhand cars. They even had ironclad reasons for the long years between visits home. Summer was a busy time for real estate, and the children's winter break was too short to make the trip.

"What makes it bearable is that Lily and Sam constantly beg to stay after school. They think it's a great treat, and this way they can have it for one year, you know," Frances said. "Besides, tell me, what's the alternative? Mandy hasn't changed. We tried the therapist, and that didn't work. You said give her time, but it's near the end of the school year and she's still getting C's and D's. What else can we do?"

"What makes you think she'll do better in India?"

"I don't know. But we have to try *something*. It's breaking my heart to stand by and watch her flail."

Once Frances made up her mind, she spent a lot of time figuring out the details. She researched schools and found an American-style one in Bangalore.

"It's the exact same curriculum but with tougher teachers. If Mandy starts getting A's, she will have a chance of getting into a good university. As you say all the time, America is a forgiving country. She can even write her college-application essay on why she had such a bad year in eleventh grade."

Jay remembered his schoolteachers, each one a bulldog, never allowing him to fail. If Mandy really was like him, if she needed to be prodded, then India was the place for that. Perhaps she would rediscover her old curiosity, get back that wonderful euphoria that came from getting all A's. Jay had hoped that Griffin would help, but though he came around more often, Mandy's grades had not improved.

Frances even managed to come up with a good explanation in case people asked about the trip. "Remember that French girl in Mandy's fourth-grade class who returned to Paris for one year because her mother wanted to give her a strong base for the language? Well, we're doing the same thing, except not for the language, but for the feel of India. These days everyone knows about India, yet our children have been there only a few times."

A few weeks later, she read an article in the *Los Angeles Times* about Indians returning to the homeland and said, "See? We're not the only ones doing it."

Jay didn't want to tell her that those Indians were taking advantage of the fabulous jobs American companies were offering in Delhi, Bangalore, and Mumbai. They were returning as CEOs to live in American-style houses that were cleaned by an army of servants.

The decision had given her fortitude, a calm that Jay hadn't seen in a while, and she was able to sleep through the night again.

Frances kept saying, as if to assuage her guilt, "If this fails, at least we tried, you know."

Mandy had been hysterical when Frances told her that the tickets were booked for the end of June. "I'll come back as soon as I turn eighteen," she threatened them.

When that didn't work, she cried and cried. "Please, Mom,

Dad," Mandy begged, tears wetting her cheeks, "don't make me go."

Jay had looked at Mandy's quivering lips and felt, again, that this might not be the right decision. But as Frances said, what was the alternative? He didn't have one, outside of hoping that Mandy would improve on her own.

But that night, after Mandy went weeping to her room, even Frances's resolve had softened.

"Are we doing the wrong thing?" she asked Jay. "Remember when I forced Mandy to play with Cindy?"

That infamous play date was family lore, brought out every now and then as something that should never happen again.

Mandy had been invited to play with Cindy, who lived next door, but she hadn't wanted to go. Frances had phone calls to make, so she told Mandy to stop being silly, that Cindy had new toys, and didn't she remember having fun with her friend?

Less than ten minutes later, Mandy ran home with blood streaming down her face. Cindy had suggested a game of pirates, and though she refused to let Mandy have a sword, she wielded one herself and had cut Mandy next to her right eye. A few centimeters more and Mandy might have lost her eye.

Frances had cried all the way to the hospital. She sobbed even harder when Mandy told her not to feel sad, it wasn't hurting that much.

"What if things get worse in India?" Frances worried as they talked about the logistics. Which sister should Frances stay with in Bangalore? Should she take a computer class in case she needed to change jobs when she returned? "As you keep reminding me, this isn't something that can be corrected easily."

Their office mates thought they were crazy. They insisted that every study showed that children should not move around, especially during their last year of high school. And one of them pointed out, "What good will one year do?"

"Maybe I should go to India for the summer, see Mama, and return by September," Frances vacillated.

Then, in May, Mandy brought home a report card with two F's.

"Please, Mom, Dad, give me another chance. This time I promise I won't disappoint you."

As Frances said later, those two words, *this time*, straightened her resolve, which Jay said kept leaning like the Tower of Pisa and driving him crazy because he never knew what he was coming home to. She had heard them repeatedly this past year. *This time I'll study for the test. This time I'll be waiting when you come to get me. This time I'll turn in my homework.*

"You have exhausted your *this times*," she told Mandy. "You told us the same thing back in January. This time I'll study more, you promised us, I'll bring up my grades. Now it's going to be *our* version of 'this time.' This time you are going to a school where there are no excuses. I'm taking you to India, and that's that."

Jay finally concurred that the year away, while hard on everyone, might turn things around for their daughter. The more they talked about it, the more Frances was committed to going.

"I'll be helping out with Mama, but the other benefit is that I'll be home every afternoon when Mandy returns. I can be there for her in a way that I can't here, you know," Frances had said.

Jay wasn't convinced that Mandy would do better just because Frances was around more, but anything was worth trying. The e-tickets had been confirmed, and Frances was going to stop in Delhi, see his parents, who lived a few hours away, then head down to Bangalore.

Nikhil's party was the last hurdle before they took off for India.

As if she could read his mind, Frances said, "I've told Lily and Sam not to blurt out anything about the India trip this evening."

The children were used to the firm family policy about keeping things private. When Mandy started doing badly in school, Frances explained that her grades were not to be mentioned to anyone outside the house.

"Like a lady's age?" Sam had asked.

"Exactly like that," Frances had agreed. "It's only for our family to know."

"But you told Mrs. Greenberg that I got a perfect score in my last CAT math test," Sam offered.

"That's because she asked me, you know," Frances said. "She wants to put her daughter in your school, and your grades let her know that you attend a good school."

"But what if someone wants to go to Mandy's school?" Sam asked logically.

"I'll tell them it's a good school," Frances said. "It's just like yours, and you know how much you love your school." Frances tried to steer her son away from the question.

"Hypocrite," Mandy said softly, and Frances shot her a "keep quiet" look.

"What's a hypocrite?" Lily, who loved new words, asked.

"It's from the Greek and means an actor," Mandy responded before Frances could speak.

"How do you know that?" Frances asked her daughter.

Mandy shrugged.

"Mandy's clever," Lily said, "but she's wrong this time. You're not an actor, Mom. You make people happy by helping them buy a nice house."

Frances spooned batter into the skillet as she continued talking to Jay, "I also told them it's Nikhil's big day, and we don't want to take anything away from his celebration. But we'll have to say *something*, you know, because people will ask us about the children."

"The less said the better," Jay maintained. "We'll tell them that your mother is sick, and you and Mandy are going to India to help her."

"It's the truth," said Frances, flipping the pancakes.

"At least we won't have to worry that Mandy will say anything."

"I'm actually grateful that she won't say a word. She'll probably sulk in some corner—" Frances was interrupted by her cell phone.

"It's the Millers." Frances was surprised to read the caller ID.

She hadn't heard from them since their house sold. Were they calling because something, somehow, had gone wrong? Frances took a deep breath and answered, even as she ladled another batch of pancakes.

Jay set the table and stayed in the dining room. He knew from experience not to disturb Frances while she was on a business call.

"Jay," Frances called him back to the kitchen. "You won't believe what just happened. The Millers called to say they had recommended me to their friends who want to sell their house in Toluca Lake. That's going to be a huge sale."

"But you can't take it," Jay reminded her. "You're leaving for India in a few weeks."

"I'll get a partner. Susan Hayman has been asking me to partner with her for ages. If I get this listing—and the Millers seem to think it's a done deal—I'll have Susan take over if the house hasn't sold by the time I leave for India."

"You sure you can do this?"

"Of course I am. Why? Did you want me to look this gift

house in the window and say, 'Hmm, there's a problem with the dates. No thank you, go elsewhere?'"

She almost sounded like him, turning gift *horse* into a gift *house*. "It's nice to see you in such a good mood."

"I really feel like things are finally getting better, touch wood."

"Here, you can touch my head," Jay offered. "Solid teak, unlike the pressed stuff they sell here."

"The pancakes are done," Frances knocked against his head and picked up the platter.

"Come on, everyone. Breakfast!" Jay called.

Lily and Sam came running. Mandy always had to be pried out of her room.

"I'll go get Greta Garbo," Jay said, but as he was walking toward her room, Mandy came out.

"Just in time for breakfast," Jay said, "and just in time to celebrate your mom's new listing."

"Yay! Pizza tonight!" Sam said.

"Sam, let me look at your head." Jay bent down and examined the black-curled skull.

"What do you see, Dad?" Sam's voice was a little frightened.

"I was looking to see if you had Alzheimer's."

"Is that bad?" Sam's voice was even more worried.

Lily, who knew what her father was up to, giggled into her napkin.

"It's bad if you're little. It's something that happens to old people."

"But you don't see it in my head, right?" Sam ascertained. "Right?"

"Still looking, Sam," Jay answered.

"Why do you think I have it?"

Jay started laughing. "Because, Sam, we've been telling you

for days and days that we're going to a big party tonight, and instead you want to have pizza."

"Dad!" Sam finally realized he had been had.

By now Frances and Lily were laughing loudly, though Mandy wasn't participating. She was pouring syrup on her pancake.

"And speaking of tonight," Jay rubbed his hands together, "are you ready to par-tay?"

"I am," Sam spoke through a mouthful of pancake. "Will there be Coke and 7UP and Sprite?"

"There should be," Jay answered. "You can bet that there will be good Indian food. Yummy in your tummy." He tousled Sam's hair.

"Do they have good Indian drinks?" Sam asked.

"Of course they do. Lassi and lemonade and even limeade," Jay counted off. "I'm sure Uncle Vic will have those, as well as a whole bunch of American sodas."

"I'm wearing my red shoes," Lily said with satisfaction.

"Mandy, are you all set to have sodas and watch your sister dancing in her red shoes?" Jay wanted to include her. She was eating her breakfast with a faraway look. As always when he saw it, he worried.

"I don't like dancing," Mandy stated.

"Aren't you looking forward to wearing your new dress?" Frances asked gently. Ever since she had booked their tickets, she hadn't been getting angry with Mandy. It was easier to put up with her, knowing that soon they would be in another country, where things were going to be different. Mandy was the real American here, and there were many times when Frances let her daughter lead the way. But in India, she would be in charge of everything.

So when Mandy kept complaining about not wanting to go

to the party, Frances hadn't reacted. Instead, one evening she took her shopping.

Frances used to long to go shopping with Mama when she was a girl. But because she was the youngest, she inherited most of her clothes. It hadn't mattered when she was very small. She used to look forward to wearing what Mama said were "hand-me-overs." But when she grew older, she wanted new outfits. Mama would explain that since the clothes were in good condition, there was no need to buy anything new for her. But the clothes looked old, and she was always hearing that she looked just like the sister whose dress she now wore, and then like the other sister whose skirt now fit her.

Frances would cry in the bathroom, because she felt that her sisters had gotten everything first. Her oldest sister Gloria was the family beauty; Ivy was the smartest; Hazel had beautiful hazel eyes; and Alba had the best figure. It was almost as if even God, who had forgotten to make her a boy, had neglected to give her something special that made her stand apart from the others. She never wanted her daughter to feel that way, and decided that though it would make the party more expensive, she would buy Mandy a new dress.

Frances assumed that the other Indian girls at the party would wear colorful, mirror-decorated *ghagra cholis* that they had either bought in India or ordered online. Mama had never allowed any of her daughters to wear Indian-style clothes. Tight churidars with calf-length kurtas were popular when she was young, but these days the infusion of Bollywood films had started a trend for the fully gathered ghagra skirts that came down to the ankle, along with a midriff-baring choli. She could not imagine Mandy in something so—ethnic—and decided to stick with what she knew, which was Western clothes.

She had found an off-the-shoulder, floor-length black dress. Mandy tried it on, and even though she didn't say much, Frances could tell that her daughter liked it.

"You'll look beautiful in your dress," Frances now said.

"It's okay, I guess," Mandy mumbled.

The phone rang. It must be the Miller connection.

"I have to get this," Frances said quickly. She was en route to the kitchen when she realized it wasn't her cell phone.

Jay glanced at the ringing phone. They had a rule about not picking up any phones during meals, but Frances had just broken it. Lily was at the age when she loved answering the phone.

Feeling a little like the God he used to be in Mandy's eyes, Jay told Lily, "Go ahead, you can answer it."

"Hello, Bakshi residence. How may I direct your call?" Lily's voice was high with happiness at the unexpected treat, her lips bowed in a smile that seemed to go all the way to her ears.

"Mandy, it's for you." Lily covered the phone and said, "It's your boyfriend, I mean *manfriend*."

Sam chanted, "Mandy's got a manfriend, Mandy's got a manfriend."

"Sam, not so loud," Jay admonished his son. "We don't want Griffin to hear."

"You're so lame," Mandy told all of them before taking the phone from Lily.

Jay was surprised that she didn't go to another room. He had not invited Griffin over for a barbecue, but shortly after he had seen the boy outside their house, Mandy had started working with him. Apparently things were going well, because Griffin came by at least once a week. Mandy didn't ask to go on dates, or use the car, but Jay figured she was doing things her way.

Mandy walked over to the sofa and was talking softly, so Jay could not make out any of her words. Lily and Sam were still acting silly, and he told them to clear the table.

"I thought we had that rule about taking calls during meals?" Jay asked Frances. She had come up with it.

"I know, I know," Frances agreed. "It's just that I didn't want to miss the O'Sullivans."

"O'Sullivans," Jay said. "That's a name I haven't heard since India."

Frances stared at him. Did he know? How could he know? She had never told him about Rich O'Sullivan. It had happened so long ago that this morning, when the Millers told her their friends' name, she hadn't made the connection.

"What do you mean?" she forced herself to ask.

"Enid Blyton," Jay said, looking a little sheepish. "I know that boys didn't read the St. Clare boarding-school series, but I was bored one day and read the first few. Didn't you read them?"

Frances let out the breath she had been holding in. He didn't know. He was talking about the O'Sullivan twins who go away to boarding school and have all sorts of adventures.

"I read the St. Clare series too," she said. Then, wanting to move away from the subject, she added, "I'll go make a fresh pot of tea."

Mandy came back to finish her pancake and Jay asked, trying to keep his voice friendly, not nosy, "What was that about?"

"Nothing."

"Ah, Shakespeare might have written that 'Nothing begets nothing,' but in my experience nothing always comes up with *something*."

"Oh, Dad, I've heard you say that a thousand times," Mandy grimaced.

"Can you imagine how many times I've heard it?" Frances placed the teapot on the table and took her seat.

"I think Dad's funny," Lily, ever loyal, took up for her father.

"Now, Lily, I hope you meant funny as in ha, ha, not funny as in peculiar," Jay said.

"Both," Lily said, thinking she was being agreeable, then she smirked when her parents started laughing.

"When you grow up, you can be both," Jay said grandiosely. "I'll stick with making people laugh."

"I want to be just like you, Dad," said Sam, who didn't like it when he wasn't the center of conversation. "I'll tell people what to do, and they will have to listen to me."

Jay felt the rush of love from his son and remembered how once he, too, had wanted to be like his father. He hadn't come close. Vic's son, however, must be following his father's lead. His degree was in computer science. Vic had a company to give his son. Jay shifted in his chair, uncomfortable. He didn't want Sam to be like him.

"This is America," he told Sam. "You can be anything you want."

"But you told me I couldn't be a stunt man," Sam reminded his father. He had seen his first James Bond movie and had been riveted by the action, then amazed to learn that most of the stunts had been performed by a double.

"That's because we don't want you to get hurt," Frances interjected. "Do you remember what you wanted to be at that age?" she asked her oldest daughter.

Mandy didn't answer.

"I remember," Jay said. "Mandy told everyone that she was going to be just like Mom."

Frances recalled the days when people, even strangers, said that Mandy looked like her. She knew that Mandy had Jay's features, and she often told him, "It's so unfair. I carried her for nine months and she turns out to be a mini you." Yet when Americans saw the mother-daughter duo they didn't look beyond the brown skin, brown eyes, and dark hair, and said they were copies of each other. Frances always loved hearing it.

Mandy used to try on her mother's shoes, spray on her perfume, and one time Frances walked in as she was imitating her sales speech, "This is the living room, and it has a very nice fireplace."

"Mandy wanted to become a real estate agent." Frances smiled at the memory of her daughter selling an imaginary house to imaginary clients. She wished she could have taped it, but Mandy had stopped talking as soon as she saw her mother. These days, Mandy rolled her eyes when Frances said that she had saved every tooth that fell out as well as all the notes Mandy had written to Santa.

"I only said that because I thought it would be cool to see my name all over town," Mandy shrugged. "I'd rather be a stunt woman than a real estate agent."

Frances knew that Mandy was being deliberately mean, knew that she was doing this because she was being forced to go to the party, and after that to India. She felt her happiness plummet, but then she steadied herself. She wasn't going to let Mandy affect her mood today. She had prepared everything, from Mandy's dress to the pretty one Lily would wear, and had even found a jacket for Sam in a secondhand store. She was going to recycle the dress she had worn to last year's Christmas party. It was made of thin wool, a little warm for June, but Vic's house was close to the ocean and the evenings could get chilly.

All that remained was to dye her hair.

For years she had worn her hair in the same short style, the ends curved into the nape of her neck. She sometimes wished she had longer hair, because the gray would not be so exposed, but she loved the sleek, chic cut too much to change.

She used to have her hair colored at a salon, but now it was just too expensive.

"I can do it myself," she told Jay. "It's so easy, I don't know why women bother having it done for them."

It just required time, and she had given herself plenty of that today.

"Okay, you four," she stood up from the table. "I'm going to beautify my hair, so please don't use my bathroom."

"You mean you're doing that stinky stuff?" Sam asked.

"Yes I am, Sam I am," Frances wrinkled her nose. "If you need anything, ask your dad."

She squeezed on the dye, starting with her temples and neck, which were the most offending areas for gray hair. She used a toothbrush to spread the dye evenly, then put on a shower cap and waited twice the recommended time suggested on the bottle. She had been very nervous the first time she had kept on the dye for that long. A distraught client had called and Frances had kept talking, conscious that the dye was still in her hair but unable to get off the phone. She had worried that her hair would fall out or turn brittle. Instead, the dye job had lasted longer than usual, so after that she did it routinely. It had given a new meaning to Jay's adage that there are no mistakes in life.

It was only after she washed and dried her hair that she realized she had used the wrong bottle of dye. She had meant to return the black one, but had forgotten, and now, in her anxiety to get going, hadn't checked the bottle. The color was too dark, and, as so often happens with black, her hair looked obviously dyed.

She stared at herself in the mirror. How could she have been so stupid? Why hadn't she just gone to a salon for once?

A salon! She glanced at her watch. It was only 2 p.m. There was time to get it corrected.

Frantic, she called the nearest Supercuts. She passed by the shop every day, knew that it was only a five-minute car ride away. After six rings, an accented voice told her the next available stylist would take her at 4 p.m. Frances tried another salon. Same story.

"Saturdays are one of our busiest days, madam," a woman at the third place reminded Frances.

This was it. She was stuck with the wrong color. Then she remembered the highlight kit. It would be the perfect solution to her problem.

There was no need to beat up on herself for making a mistake. No need to taste, again, the acridity of a last-minute failure. This time she could fix the problem.

She picked up the highlight kit and read it carefully. She wasn't going to risk making a mistake.

Lali watched the bright green lines on the digital clock rearrange themselves from one to two to three. She had not spent such a wakeful night since Aaron left for Harvard the previous year. Aaron was in Boston, packing. Lali suspected that he was keeping away as long as he could. He probably didn't want to face her while she was still so furious about his announcement to not return to Harvard for his second year.

"How can you make such a decision without consulting us?" she had demanded when he called with his "news" two weeks earlier that he would take a year's leave from Harvard and use the time to figure out if he wanted to go back or stay on the West Coast.

"Because it's *my* decision, Mom," Aaron had responded. "You told me that your parents didn't want you coming to the United States, but you came anyway."

"I had a scholarship," Lali reminded her son. "And my parents were not opposed to my coming here. They just wanted me to come as a married woman."

"But you didn't, did you?"

"They were very proud that I had gotten into UCLA," Lali said, and then added, "If I tell them that you are not going back to Harvard, they won't understand."

She had gone over and over that conversation, tried to figure out what she could have said to make him change his mind and continue on at Harvard. But Aaron was as stubborn as Jonathan.

She looked at her sleeping husband. Last night they had fought over Aaron—again. Except that this time it wasn't about forcing Aaron to go back. Lali had begged him not to tell Frances and the others that their son wasn't returning to Harvard.

Jonathan had refused. "*I'm* not going to lie," he said.

She had turned her back to him, infuriated by his sanctimonious response. He could afford to be honest. He was used to students switching majors, dropping out, even giving up a degree with only one class left to finish. She had explained that in India, children need to know their career path when they start college. "It's a big shame to change majors, and an even bigger one to give up a good school," she had said.

"Aaron's not giving up," Jonathan stated. "He's simply taking a year off, and if people don't understand that, it's their problem."

Jonathan had gone straight to sleep, his arms flung over his head, undisturbed by her constant movements.

Their argument, the upcoming weekend they were to spend in Southern California, kept her awake, and at four thirty she slipped out of bed and went to the bathroom. The shuttle was going to pick them up in an hour for their midmorning flight to Santa Barbara. It was dark outside, too early for the birds to chirp, too late for the nocturnal animals to make any noise.

Lali turned on the mirror lights and leaned in to get a closer view of her face. No matter what else was troubling her, she needed to look good this weekend. The dark circles she had inherited from her mother—the telltale sign of being an Indian, she explained to her friend Mary—were worse from the sleepless night. Her eyes looked tired and sunken. Now, on top of everything else, she was going to look ugly.

She knew she was obsessed about her appearance, but she didn't want to go to Southern California looking middle-aged and saggy.

"I didn't even worry this much when I was getting married!" she told Mary.

"You were younger then," Mary reminded her. "And cellulite was something that happened to *other* people. But you're meeting college friends you haven't seen in more than twenty years. Let me tell you, if we had the money, I would have had plastic surgery before going to my thirtieth high school reunion!"

Right after Lali mailed off the RSVP in the bright red envelope, she had rushed to the calendar to calculate the number of days she had left to redo herself. She switched to a salad plate and took smaller portions. She signed up for Pilates classes and walked for half an hour on the days she didn't have a class. Despite all this, she didn't lose a single pound.

"You do know that Pilates is about toning, not weight loss, right?" Mary confirmed.

"You mean I spent all those hours on the mat and the exercise ball for nothing?"

"Don't you feel better?"

"I don't care about *feel*. I only care about how I *look*."

Now she scrutinized her neck in the mirror. Along with hands, it was one of the first places to show signs of age. She had bought a black dress with a low, round neck for the party. The beautiful turquoise necklace Jonathan had given her for their fifteenth anniversary would cover her neck, but also draw attention to it. Her neck was still wrinkle-free, thank God.

She drew herself up tall, and was checking to see how she looked with her stomach sucked in, when Jonathan walked into the bathroom.

"What are you doing?"

She had been so focused on the image in the mirror that she hadn't heard him open the door.

"I'm getting ready." She immediately rearranged her pose and reached for her toothbrush.

"I'm going to make some coffee," Jonathan said. "Tea for you?" It was a peace offering after last night's unresolved argument.

Amma had always said it wasn't healthy to go to bed angry. She would say the same about starting a journey together.

"Okay," Lali said, trying to take the grudge out of her voice. "I'll be there as soon as I get ready."

The part of her that wasn't furious with him wished they weren't fighting. For one thing, it was so tiring. If only they could go back to being the happy couple who mingled at parties but always returned to the other, in what Lali told Mary was "the magnet effect." She had always counted on the comfort of holding his hand, of giving him a look when someone made an outré comment. That was the image she wanted to present at the party.

But right now their lives were like the separate bags they had packed.

It was as if their entire past was a piece of luggage they had misplaced or lost. It didn't matter that she knew he had packed two days ago, that all he needed to do was wash up and change into his travel clothes. When they first got married, every new detail she learned about him had thrilled her.

In the past few months, she had been discovering their many differences.

Was it a factor of age, as Mary claimed? That people, when they reach their forties, settle into being who they are meant to be? It typically meant that they returned to the ways of their youth. But that didn't make sense with Jonathan, because his parents hadn't raised him to be Jewish.

She knew that bits and pieces of her were, unexpectedly, definitely, turning Indian.

Like just now, when she was spending so much time getting ready. She used to make sure she looked nice before taking the train to her college in Bangalore. But after marrying Jonathan, she began to appreciate his theory that since they weren't going to be seeing the other passengers again, why bother getting dolled up?

Today, of course, was special. It wasn't who she was going to see on the plane.

It was who she was going to meet after she landed.

It was with that in mind that she put on her makeup. Concealer under the eyes, powder all over, and, finally, mascara to define her eyes. She just needed to brush her hair and put on the clothes she had set out the night before.

She was pulling up her pants when she heard something fall on the floor.

"Shit!" she muttered. The button had come off. She bent low to the floor, searching, and was about to kneel down to look under the chest of drawers when she felt a crunch under her foot. The button was in two pieces. She didn't have time to find another one, size it, and sew it on.

"Dammit," she said, throwing the pants on the bed. This

was her best pair. Now she would have to make do with the only other "good" pair of black pants she had. The pants were a few years old, a bit faded from repeated dry cleaning, and they didn't fit as well.

This was not a propitious beginning.

"Five minutes," Jonathan picked up their luggage and took it to the front door. "Just enough time for another quick cup of coffee. You having that tea?"

She didn't want the tea anymore, but this wasn't the right moment to discard his peace offering. There still might be time to talk, to get him to agree to her wishes. She definitely didn't want to arrive so—separate—at the party this evening.

She took a sip of tea and burned her tongue. "Ouch!"

"Honey, you okay?" Jonathan asked. "I thought you knew it was hot."

This was his fault. It was because of his conference that they had to leave so early. Now she was stuck in the wrong pants with a furry tongue.

Before she could respond, the doorbell rang. The shuttle had arrived.

The airport was busy even at this early hour, and they moved silently from check-in to security.

She took off her shoes and placed them in the basket with her purse. She stepped through the security arch and heard the loud *ding!*

"Check your pockets," Jonathan recommended, as he retrieved their bags.

"I don't have any pockets," Lali said. Then she saw the small brass studs decorating her blouse. She had been thinking only of how nice she would look when she bought it last week. She hadn't been concerned about setting off alarms.

"Must be these," she told the official.

"Step aside, and stand here," he indicated a spot that did not interfere with the other passengers.

"Can't you see it's those little buttons?" Jonathan asked the man while looking at Lali.

She stared into his deep blue irises, so familiar and reassuring. Their joint annoyance united them.

The man's voice broke their connection.

"Move away, sir," he said sternly. "Which one is your bag?" he asked Lali, and Jonathan brought it over.

"This is ridiculous." Jonathan banged it onto the counter just past the conveyor belt.

"Keep back, sir," the man said threateningly, and Jonathan did as he was told.

When the man got on his walkie-talkie, Lali felt as if the entire airport could hear him. She avoided the eyes of the other passengers and didn't talk to Jonathan, in case it drew attention to the fact that she was waiting to be allowed to join him.

After one of the longest ten minutes of her life, a tall, thin, official-looking woman approached her, wand in hand. Lali spread out her arms and legs, like Da Vinci's Vitruvian Man, as humiliation and anger pounded through her.

As she had expected, the wand beeped at the studs.

"Satisfied?" Jonathan asked the man, who shrugged his shoulders.

"You may go," he told Lali.

"It's the aftereffects of 9/11, honey," Jonathan said as she joined him. "Remember the old days when we needed to check in ten minutes before our flight and you could pretty much carry anything on board?"

Jonathan would never be able to truly understand what she had just gone through. The attacks on the World Trade Center and the Pentagon had made travel more inconvenient for him. He was an American, and his blond hair and blue eyes would always protect him in this country. She, too, had an American passport. But her face fit the profile of a female bomber, and her blouse could send the security staff into high alert. She was sure that the same blouse worn by a white American would not have produced such a response.

She was still feeling estranged when they took their seats in the waiting area.

She had just opened her book when Erik Muller came loping toward them.

"Jonathan, Lali," he said, "Fancy running into you here. Where are you going?"

Erik was the pediatric dentist who still took care of Aaron's teeth. "I'm off to see a friend get Mauied," he joked, pointing to the coconut palms on his shirt. "Now that destination weddings are the rage, I'm sure Maui is going to become an even more popular locale."

"Have fun. Nothing that exotic for us. I'm going to the Santa Barbara conference," Jonathan said.

"And what will you do while Jonathan is conferencing?" Erik asked Lali.

Lali felt the first finger of discomfort constrict her throat. She had tried to avoid thinking about those hours when Jonathan would be busy with his colleagues.

She was collecting her thoughts when Jonathan answered, "Oh, Lali's been to Santa Barbara before. She's tagging along because this evening we are driving down to LA for a party with her Indian friends."

"A Bollywood party in Hollywood?" Erik asked, shaking his hips slightly.

"We'll find out, I guess," Lali said, still assessing Jonathan's "her Indian friends" comment.

"Just get me a picture of Jonathan dancing," Erik said.

"That won't happen," Jonathan shook his head. "I don't dance. Why do you think I kept telling Lali we should have a small civil wedding? I was afraid that she would change her mind when she found out I have two left feet!"

"As long as the hands do the job, eh?" Erik waved his fingers. "You might not have a choice, Jonathan. I've heard that Indian parties go on for hours. Someone will pull you onto the floor."

Frances was just about to tell Erik that no one would ever presume to drag Jonathan, or anyone else they had just met, onto the dance floor, when the loudspeaker blared.

"That's my flight they just announced. Bye!" Erik rushed off.

"You'll tell them I really can't dance, right?" Jonathan looked worried. He was acting like Erik, as if an Indian party was utterly different from an American one.

She knew he was phobic about dancing, a result of his mother's insistence that he attend Cotillion during middle school, plus something that had gone terribly wrong at a dance. He had never told Lali the whole story, and she hadn't asked. She had been relieved, because she didn't know Western dances, and it was one more American thing she didn't need to learn.

She weighed her irritation against his anger at the security man. "If you stop every passenger wearing buttons on their clothes, the planes will never take off on time," he'd told the man when Lali joined him.

"No one is going to make you dance," she said, and suddenly she wished they could laugh about the party together. If this had happened when they first married, she would have told him not to worry, that she, too, would feel like an outsider if Vic brought in

Bollywood elements. But that happy past had become hazy from their conflicts in the present.

"Erik had me worried for a second," Jonathan said. "I've never met your friends, and I don't want to embarrass you if everyone dances while I'm sitting."

In this context, his "your Indian friends" comment no longer angered her. His concern surprised—and shamed—her.

"You won't embarrass me," she said honestly. She was proud that she had married a nice-looking man who was a cardiologist. Frances and Jay would no doubt dwell on the fact that he was short, but they would be impressed by the Harvard pedigree. Lali knew it was silly to give in to the Indian pressure of education and status and looks, but all those qualifications she had stuffed down for so long had come out because she would be seeing her friends at the party.

"You sure about that?"

She knew he wasn't being literal.

"I'm sure." She paused. "I just wish we weren't fighting."

"I'm not fighting," Jonathan started, then saw her face. "Okay, then, I'll say it again, I still don't know why your friends would care either way whether Aaron goes back to Harvard or not."

"It's because you aren't Indian," she said, stating what was obvious to her. "It's difficult to explain, but we all grew up assuming that people never tell the whole truth. Maybe it's because there is so much competition in India, but people are very protective of what they have. It could be about something really silly like the shop where they bought their saree, or it could be withholding an important ingredient from a recipe. People are so used to hearing a partial story that they try to figure out the missing part, and then they often think the worst. I remember when Amma told people I was engaged to you, someone asked if you had been married before.

When Amma said, "No," they asked to see your picture. They wanted to see if there was something physically wrong with you. So now, if we tell Jay and Frances that Aaron's not going back to Harvard next year, they will think that I'm hiding something, that he actually failed and can never return. None of them will believe that he is voluntarily taking a year off from such a great school."

"I got that bit," Jonathan said. "You certainly feel that way."

"Think of it from my perspective. Harvard is the one school everyone knows about back in India." Lali shook her head. "I can just see their brains clicking if we were to tell them that Aaron is abandoning Harvard."

"I wish your brain had clicked into understanding why he needs a year off," Jonathan said. "You just flew into a rage."

Aaron's announcement had immediately divided them. Lali had shouted, then cajoled, then threatened, until Jonathan took the phone from her and hung up. After that, Aaron refused to speak to her. Jonathan kept telling her it was Aaron's life, and that they should support, not upset him.

"Let him take some time off," Jonathan had said at the time. "He was so concentrated on getting into Harvard that he never had a chance to think if it was the right school for him."

"Harvard will not wait around for him to make up his mind," Lali had said as she left the room.

Even Mary told her it was a shame that Aaron was giving up such a good school. It was when Lali heard Mary's words that she switched from just being upset at Aaron's stupidity to feeling the stress of answering questions from Jay and Frances and the other Indians at the party. She wished she could cancel their plans, but it was too late to back out.

Then the perfect solution came to her. Aaron was still in Boston. She would tell everyone that was the reason he could not attend the party. She would simply omit telling them that he wasn't going back next year. Jonathan was sure that Aaron would return, that the year away would give him a better appreciation for Harvard. So her lie wouldn't be a *total* lie. But they had fought over it—again—the previous night. This moment at the airport was her last chance to get Jonathan to agree with her.

"Look," Lali said, "you will never understand the way Indians think. Take this party, for example. Yes, it's to celebrate Nikhil doing so well, but the people attending the party will also be celebrating themselves. They will be checking out clothes, finding out who drives the better car, even discussing whose lawn is greener—literally greener. I remember going to a party in Silicon Valley before we met and listening to an engineer go on and on about the superior grass he had used for his lawn. He was very serious."

"Then why are we going?"

"I wasn't thinking about that aspect of the party when we got the invitation. I just thought that I hadn't seen my friends in a long time. But now things are different, and . . ."

"We don't have to go," Jonathan suggested. "It's not too late to join the other doctors for dinner tonight."

"Oh, we can't cancel *today*," Lali said, stressing the last word. "Vic is expecting us, and I also told Jay and Frances we'd see them there."

"But from what you just said, they aren't that nice," Jonathan pointed out.

"They're nice," Lali insisted. "They're just Indian. They'll be thrilled to see us. I just don't want them to think Aaron's a failure." Lali suddenly had an idea. "When the Jews first came to America, they also wanted to become successful, right? I'm sure they tried to outdo each other."

"I suppose so."

"Is it so bad that I want to show off my doctor husband and

Harvard son? I mean, it's not a lie, because technically Aaron is still at Harvard."

Aaron had called them with his decision on the very morning that Lali had slipped a picture of him wearing a Harvard sweatshirt into her wallet. She had imagined Jay and Frances and Vic asking about him. Vic's son was already a success, and if Frances's occasional e-mails were anything to go by, her children were doing extremely well. So when they inquired after her son, Lali had thought she would show them the picture, let the Harvard colors flaunt themselves.

Jonathan paused, then sighed. "Okay, if you're sure you want to go. I won't say a word," he promised. "If they ask about Aaron, I'll just say he's doing fine."

"And if I say he's at Harvard, don't correct me," Lali added quickly.

"I'll pretend I didn't hear you."

"Thank you. I'll try not to say it in your presence."

Lali sighed deeply and rested her head against the back of the chair in the airport waiting area. She felt she had checked one problem off her list.

The other issue was something she didn't want to think about, but could not stop her mind from running in that direction.

It was what she had been considering when she parsed her body in the mirror this morning, when she tried to make those black circles disappear.

Aakash.

"I'll be busy until later this afternoon," Jonathan reminded her as he adjusted his tie in the mirror. "You're sure you will be okay, honey?"

"Yes," Lali said impatiently. He needed to leave their hotel room. She could not make up her mind in his presence.

"I'm just asking," Jonathan put up his hands as if in self-defense. Then he said, "I've been meaning to tell you that you look lovely."

She immediately felt guilty, and rushed to explain, "I wasn't sure I'd have time to change, and I wanted to look nice in case we met any of your colleagues."

She wondered if he could hear the lie that lurked beneath her words.

He hardly ever commented on her appearance because, as he told her right after they were married, he thought she always looked pretty. So she knew, she knew, that the compliment came along with the tea he had made her earlier. But she could not quell her unease, and now she wanted him more than ever to leave for his conference. She needed to be alone to figure out the next step.

"See you later, hon," he kissed her lips. "One more time," he kissed her again.

Lali had started the three-kiss custom the very first time he had gone to a conference after they were married. "It's the magic number," she had joked, and Jonathan had simply accepted it. Now he was waiting for her to complete the ritual.

She didn't say anything, just kissed him on the cheek. He looked at her, then shrugged. "Okay, I'm off. See you later."

Lali glanced at her watch, then at the clock on the small table between the beds. Almost eleven o'clock.

She had told Aakash she would meet him at 11:20.

"Typical of you to pick an even number that's an odd time," he'd written. *"I'll be there. In case you don't remember what I look like, I'll be the one with the big smile and a dozen roses."*

Lali sat on the edge of the bed, watching time move forward.

It was just like last night. Then she could not sleep. Now she did not know what she should do.

It had started so innocently.

"Vic is celebrating his son's MIT graduation in true Vic style," she had written.

"Don't tell me, he's going to have bhangra *dancers and fly in a long line of good* desi *girls so his son can choose a bride without needing to make that long trip to India."*

"I'll let you know."

"You're actually going?"

"I haven't seen Frances and Jay and Vic in ages. Might as well laugh and eat good khaana *at the same time."*

"You haven't seen me in ages either."

"Too bad you weren't invited!"

"Maybe I'll just invite myself."

She knew their banter was high-schoolish and would have died of embarrassment had anyone read it. Yet while she was going back and forth with Aakash, she felt like an overeater, unable to stop reaching for the next cookie.

"You're coming down just for the party?"

"I'll be driving down from Santa Barbara. My husband is giving a talk the same day." She hardly ever mentioned Jonathan, but every now and then she slipped in some information. She wanted Aakash to know that though *he* had not wanted her, she had found someone who had given her a good life. Santa Barbara was a beautiful place, and while she had been there enough times to wish they were going somewhere else, many people thought of it as a resort.

Aakash was slow in responding. Immediately she regretted typing "my husband." In their computer chats, they typically avoided personal information, just as they had back at UCLA. She knew he didn't have children, he knew she had one son, but other than that, they acted as if they were sitting across from each other in a Westwood café. She had spoiled their rhythm. Was he angry?

"There indeed is a medical conference in Santa Barbara that weekend. What will you be doing while your husband is busy?"

He had been Googling Santa Barbara events while she worried that he didn't want to hear about her home life. Instead of feeling hunted, she was—flattered.

"I'll hang out at my favorite bookstore and then have lunch at a wonderful Thai restaurant." Her sentence had such a cosmopolitan ring to it. Neither of them had ever heard of Santa Barbara when they were in India, but now she was intimate with the place.

"Maybe I'll meet you at your favorite bookstore. Unless your husband will object."

And so, what began as a good laugh at Vic's expense ended up with her agreeing to meet Aakash.

Yet as the days curled into nights, and Saturday was no longer a faraway day on the calendar, she remained undecided. When they were writing each other, she acted as if she were going to meet him for lunch.

That was all he wanted, he said. *"I'll leave San Diego early in the morning and drive straight on up, which means I'll be starving by the time I get there. Thai food sounds almost as good as Indian* khaana.*"*

She had dressed this morning as if she were going to rush out of the hotel room as soon as Jonathan left, grab a cab, and tell the driver, "Chaucer's Bookstore, please." She had bought the brass-studded blouse at Nordstrom in order to look good for Aakash.

The entire morning had been an obstacle course in her race to the bookstore. The button, the burnt tongue, the *ding!* at the airport. Was she deliberately ignoring the signs that she should not go?

Yet, after feeling so conspicuous at security, everything had gone well. Jonathan had agreed to keep quiet about Aaron, they had arrived in Santa Barbara on time, and Jonathan had taken off shortly before eleven for his conference. She had already told the other wives that she would be busy this morning. She had already planned to say, "What are the odds of running into an old friend?" if anyone saw her with Aakash.

11:13.

She tried to switch her mind to the evening party. She had been so excited about seeing her old friends—until Aakash decided to meet her for lunch and filled her imagination with various possibilities: What he looked like now. How he would greet her. If he would flirt with her in person. Now she forced herself to think of Frances and Jay. Had they put on weight? Were they still full of themselves? How would they react to seeing her married and living a successful life? Both she and Frances had given up their original careers. Frances was probably doing well despite the weak market. Would they think her job at the college was dinky? Jay and Vic had kept to their professions.

But she just could not bring herself to care about the party.

She looked at the clock: 11:14. Only one minute had passed.

If she really didn't want to see Aakash, then why was she feeling bad?

It was just lunch. Not dinner, no candles or wine. And of course Aakash was joking about the roses. They were friends meeting after years. It was no different from what she would be doing later in the evening at Vic's house. There was no reason not to go. She stood up.

There was a knock on the door.

Jonathan had returned.

That was it, she thought. Her decision had been made. She could not go to meet Aakash while Jonathan was in the vicinity.

"Coming," she called out, even as she scanned the room for the key he must have forgotten.

"I so sorry," the woman from Housekeeping apologized. "I did not know you was inside."

"We just checked in," Lali said, as her heart continued to beat rapidly. "There's no need to clean it." She glanced at the clock.

11:20 exactly.

She raced to the elevator, and, as if she was meant to go, the doors opened. A taxi pulled up just as she approached the revolving doors of the hotel.

They made every light. But as the taxi wove its way toward the bookstore, Lali wavered.

"Stop," she instructed the driver when they were one block away.

"But it's farther down." He continued driving.

"This is fine," Lali insisted, as she paid him.

She imagined Mary telling her not to go. She hadn't told Mary she was corresponding with Aakash. She didn't want her friend to think less of her.

She thought of Jonathan's compliment, his concern that she be happily occupied while he was giving his paper. Their recent rapprochement had filled her with thankful love, had almost made her forget that he spent all his free time studying and going to the temple. Would she even be on this street if he hadn't turned so Jewish on her? For months she had worried that he regretted not marrying a good Jewish woman whose children would automatically be Jewish. When he had mentioned that it was too bad Aaron hadn't had a bar mitzvah, he had also said, "Of course he will need to convert."

"*Unless your husband will object,*" Aakash had taunted.

She hadn't objected to the days and evenings Jonathan spent away from her. She never asked if he was meeting a woman or a man. Why should he object to her having lunch?

She started walking toward the bookstore, staying on the opposite side of the street, eyes fixed on the glass door.

"I'll be standing just inside," Aakash had written.

She had prescription dark glasses, but, as she told her optician, her vision was blurry at a certain distance. She strained her eyes but could not detect a brown figure.

"I'll be wearing a Madras check shirt in honor of your South Indian heritage."

She glanced at her watch. It was 11:40. Had he come and gone? Her disappointment was so fierce she needed to stand still for a moment. Why hadn't she come on time? How could she have missed this opportunity?

But wouldn't he have waited? What was twenty minutes after all these years?

She remembered the time they had planned to see a movie. Her adviser had kept talking to her, and she had run all the way to the theater, even though she was sure he had gone inside by then. But he was standing near the box office, neither angry nor upset. He had laughed away her apology and told her that of course he knew she would not ditch him. She had been so relieved when he suggested they go in and stay behind for the next showing. "We can see the beginning after the ending," he had said.

He would not have come up all the way from San Diego and left because she was late. He knew about airplanes and hotels—and spouses who could cause delays.

Perhaps he hadn't come, had never planned on coming. He would write next Saturday and joke that he would not be caught dead wearing a check shirt because that's what cab drivers wear in

India. And of course, she of all people knew that he would never be able to stand inside a bookstore. He would be reading books, making a pile of the ones he planned to buy. He had never invited her to his apartment near UCLA because he claimed it was too full of books.

She stopped, abashed, then realized that she had nothing else to do. She might as well go to the bookstore. She hadn't lied when she said it was her favorite one.

She was waiting for a group to go ahead of her on the crosswalk when she saw a man in a khadi kurta rushing toward the bookstore.

Aakash?

Lali had never known that her heart could speed up so suddenly. She had read somewhere that racing cars and hearts have the same ability to go from zero to 150, but until now she had never experienced that surge.

The man was on the bookstore side of the street. She focused in on him. It was definitely Aakash. The kurta, the jeans, the cloth book bag slung across his chest, coffee cup in hand. If she erased the coffee, he could have been the person she had met in the UCLA Student Store all those years ago.

She hadn't allowed herself to think how *he* would look, too concerned with her own appearance. But deep down, she had imagined a more elegant version of the man who had always attracted attention because he carried himself so well in both Western and Indian clothes. When he suggested they meet for lunch, she had, without realizing it, pictured him in a nice pair of slacks with a polo shirt, or a striped shirt accentuating his height. He would look like a man who had stepped out of a fancy car with leather seats. The shirt he told her he would be wearing counted as fashionable.

Instead, he had the grungy appearance of a lingering graduate student still working on his dissertation. He could be the barman who told a good story about the PhD he had never finished. He didn't give off the rich whiff of a man with a corner office, or one who even worked in an office, for that matter.

She looked down at the $150 blouse, the old pants, the ten pounds she had tried so hard to lose as she attempted to gain back the lithe, elastic body of her youth.

He had simply found some old clothes and thrown them on. He hadn't even had a haircut, or shaved.

He was at the door of the bookstore, about to open it. He was late, yet he obviously was so sure she was inside, waiting for him, that he didn't even look around.

Then she saw it. A rose. A single, long-stemmed rose that was drooping.

"I'll be the one with the dozen roses," he had written.

She didn't want the roses, considering them a ridiculously Western gesture for two Indians. But she felt the insult of just the one. Wasn't she worth the money?

Years earlier, she hadn't been worth the courtesy of an "I'm sorry but Clare's back, and we're engaged" call.

She had been taken in by him once, had misinterpreted the gift of a stuffed animal, had thought their meetings over tea and food signified a growing relationship.

This time it was clear that he was expecting something—with one lousy red rose in his hand.

"Will your husband mind if I keep you all afternoon?" he had asked.

She turned and fled the way she had come. The taxi was still idling at the corner.

This, she knew, was a sign.

"You forgot something?" the driver asked.

"My dignity," she wanted to say. Instead she looked out the window and responded, "I changed my mind."

When the taxi deposited her at the hotel, she ran in. As she kept pressing the UP button of the elevator, she heard her name.

"Lali! Lali!"

All she wanted to do was go to the room and lock the door. She turned around, reluctant, nervous.

"Hi, Lisa." Lisa Frost was a cardiologist whose husband had left her for another man. She had lost weight, and Lali could feel her bones as they hugged.

"Are you going to hear Jonathan's paper?"

"Oh, no," Lali brought out her stock response. "I wouldn't understand it."

"Don't sell yourself short. Jonathan's always saying how smart you are."

"He's the smart one," Lali protested. At another time she would have used her other standard line, "After all, he chose me." Now she wanted to hurry upstairs and call Reception, tell them to hold any calls for her. She didn't want to take the chance that Aakash might phone the hotel.

"Well, it's back to work for me," Lisa wrinkled her nose. "I'm sorry I'll miss you tonight."

The elevator came, and Lali was glad it was empty. She watched, impatient, as the numbers changed from four to five to six, relieved that it rose, uninterrupted, all the way to the eleventh floor.

Jonathan had told Lisa she was smart. He had told her she looked pretty.

Thank God it had been Lisa, not Jonathan, downstairs. Jonathan would have realized something was wrong, would have wanted to talk about it. He had always been like that, asking questions, telling her that problems should be resolved, not allowed to marinate for days.

What would he say if she told him about Aakash?

And, as if the trick pattern she had been looking at suddenly revealed itself, Lali saw her actions from Jonathan's perspective.

He had told her about his previous girlfriends, had assured her, "They were as wrong for me as you are right." Then, after seeing that her album contained snapshots only of family and friends, he had thrown away all the pictures of his ex-girlfriends. "This way we're equal," he said.

She had never told him about Aakash. She wasn't worried that Jonathan would run away because she wasn't a virgin. She was terrified that he might think less of her, as a woman, when he heard that Aakash had discarded her after sleeping with her for one night. She had never wanted to give him any reason to lose his high esteem of her.

Today, too, she had hidden Aakash from him. And for what reason? To meet a man who had walked out of her apartment after accepting her virginity? Who had married another woman six months later, not caring how that night had scarred her?

She held her head in her hands. Even she could not understand her actions.

She had blamed her Aakash adventure on Jonathan and had whined to Mary and others in the office that her husband preferred Judaism to a real-life wife.

Yet he had never stood in her way—for anything. When they were first married, and he was still paying back his loans, he had not made a fuss about going to India. He had even agreed to baptize Aaron as a Jacobite Syrian Christian, then he commiserated with her when the priest refused, because he was a Jew.

What if she had decided to return to the church? How would she feel if Jonathan corresponded with another woman while she was attending services? Would she understand, forgive, that it was just e-mails and a lunch?

She took off the wretched blouse, the pants, the shoes she had polished the night before, and took a long, hot shower.

She suddenly remembered that other shower, the one she had stood under after Aakash left in the early hours of the morning. "I'm a real woman," she had thought as she scrubbed her arms, legs, all the places he had touched.

She had thought, then, that she was taking a shower because that was what she did every night just before going to sleep.

But she hadn't washed away Jonathan's scent after she first went to bed with him. She had slept in his arms, awakened in them.

The glass door of the shower fogged up and Lali closed her eyes. All these years she had been so upset about giving up her virginity, had been so humiliated by Aakash's cavalier disappearance that she had never considered why she had taken that shower.

These past six months, she had enjoyed stepping back in time, yes, but she had also wanted affirmation that she was worthwhile, that he should never have left her apartment forever.

Today she had lied to her husband, had given up shopping and chatting with the other wives, for a man who thought so highly of her that he had been late.

Aakash had been sauntering down the sidewalk and at one point had slipped, glancing down at his feet. Was it possible that he had even resurrected his old *kolhapuri chappals*?

"We're both wearing *kolhapuris*," he'd said that day in the UCLA Student Store, pointing to the very distinctive slippers that have two straps separating both the big toe and the little toe. "This means either we both have good taste or we're from the North."

"Well, I know I have good taste," she had responded. "In fact, I have such good taste that I hail from South India."

He had laughed and laughed, and she was feeling very

pleased that he appreciated her joke when he stopped and said, "I haven't heard *hail* used that way in ages. Thank you, thank you, for taking me back to India without needing to pay for a ticket."

She had thrown away her *kolhapuris* a few months after moving to San Francisco. It was too cold to wear them, and the soles had become slippery with age.

He, on the other hand, seemed to have kept too much.

She was done with him, her nostalgia for what had never been.

Thank God I didn't tell anyone, not even Mary, she thought. She could simply bury this episode in a spot where she would never venture again.

Vic had been awake half the night, tracking the weather on the computer. He had become a little nervous when Nandan announced at dinner that there was a 50 percent chance of rain the next day.

Vic had immediately dismissed the possibility. "It was nice and sunny today," Vic said. "It will be exactly the same tomorrow also."

But all night long he clicked onto the weather page, and his mood changed depending on what he read. The weather people were so fickle. At midnight they reported it was going to be sunny all day; at one, that changed to morning showers. Then at three, there was the possibility of scattered showers. "Scattered?" Vic scratched his head. The idiots didn't say when during the day those scattered showers would come down.

He was worried because he had deliberately not ordered a canopy, even though Priya had begged him to do so, and the owner of the store where he rented the tables and chairs suggested it as insurance. It wasn't stinginess, as Priya had accused him. It was hard science. He had checked the weather for the past three years, and the entire week around June eleventh had been sunny.

Then, his final check at 4 a.m. had put him into a hopeful mood. *Scattered* was gone from the forecast, and there was just a 20 percent chance of morning showers.

When he awoke at 6 a.m., Vic immediately looked out the window. The sky was dark, but not full and low as if pregnant with condensation. He breathed in the air. He was sighing with relief that it didn't smell like rain when Priya came into the bedroom and pronounced, "It's going to rain."

"Who are you?" he asked, "The god of rain?"

"I just heard the weather report," she said. "They are saying there is a 50 percent chance of rain, so you had better order some canopies."

"That means there is a 50 percent chance it will *not* rain. Those weather people are idiots. How many times do they announce it is going to rain and it doesn't? Look outside. It's a little dark, but that is only because the clouds are still covering the sun."

"What will we do if it rains?"

She was always asking him to fix problems, whether they existed or not, always looking on the gloomy side of things.

"I told you, it isn't going to rain," he shouted.

"You can't control the weather, Dad," Nikhil said from the doorway. "Mom's right. It is going to rain, and since we can't possibly fit all the people you invited into the house, I suggest we cancel."

"When I want your suggestions, I will ask you," Vic shot back.

"Might be too late," Nikhil warned, and disappeared before Vic could rebut him.

"You just make sure your son is dressed and ready to greet the guests this evening," Vic told Priya. "I'll manage everything else."

He wanted to remind her that she had hardly helped with the party, and this wasn't the time for her words or worries. He had made every single arrangement, from choosing the guest list to picking out the invitation to ordering a cake big enough for 150 people. Compared to all those details, today was easy. He simply had to make sure that everything fit together. As he had told Priya's cousin Rajesh, who had wanted to come in the morning to help out, it was like writing a computer program. Vic had already done the hard part. Now all that remained was the follow-through.

He had told their cleaning woman, Flora, to come at 9 a.m. and bring two friends. She usually took all day to clean the house on her own, and he wanted her to be finished by 3 p.m. Flora used to help Priya when Nandan was born, and after he started kindergarten, she began cleaning for them. She knew them, and the house, and didn't need to be told what to do.

When she arrived on the dot at nine, he simply said, "Make sure everything, everything, is very clean."

An hour later, a big truck pulled into the driveway. The chairs and tables had arrived. Vic rubbed his hands together. It was, as his classmates at UCLA would say, starting to be party time.

Within a week of arriving at UCLA, a student he had just met had invited him to his first party. It was in a house that five people shared. All night long, men and women traipsed in and out. Vic had never seen something that luxurious at IIT. There was wine, cigarettes, food, music, and someone had even bought a keg of beer. He didn't drink in those days, so he had spent the time watching the others. They were so free with their kisses, their food, their bodies touching each other as they swayed to music.

Jay had invited him to a number of parties, and Vic was

amused that Frances always made sure to tell him to bring something. Once she even told him where to buy cheap wine. He knew that some offering was expected, so he usually brought chips, nuts, anything crunchy. He never told Frances—he just let her believe that he didn't know how to behave at American parties.

He had wondered, at that first party, when he would have the chance to throw one, and whether he would be as generous with his invitations and food. These days, money wasn't a problem, and he had been able to invite everyone he wanted to and serve whatever he wished.

So far, everything was going according to his careful plans. Vic hurried to the kitchen to remind Flora that she would also be cleaning the tables and chairs that were being unloaded from the truck. Then he ran to the front to instruct the workers where to set them up.

"Hey, hey, stop," he called out to the men who were already arranging the tables and chairs. "Who told you where to put everything?"

"The lady in the house, she gave to us this paper." A burly man who seemed to be in charge handed Vic a detailed drawing showing the layout for the round tables where the guests would sit, as well as the long buffet tables.

"Why are these here?" he pointed to the buffet tables that would, by the evening, be weighed down with pakoras, samosas, biryani, two dals, four types of vegetables, pickles, papads, and, at Priya's insistence, tandoori chicken and lamb kebabs.

"We don't eat meat," he had told her, because he knew she would get angry if he mentioned cost.

But she had a ready answer that he could not dismiss: "So many people make sure we have vegetarian items when we go to their houses. We should do the same."

"Why don you ahs her?" the man pointed behind Vic. He

turned and saw Priya walking toward them, her knee-length kurta fluttering in the breeze.

"The buffet tables are in the wrong place," Vic announced, not sure whether he was annoyed that she had taken over or pleased that she was helping.

"They are all correct," Priya countered calmly. "I arranged it that way so two lines of people can serve themselves at the same time. It will go faster, and, just as you are always saying about your computer programs, faster is better."

"Ees going to rain," the man said. "You have cover for the tables?"

"It's not going to rain," Vic refuted, just as the first drops of fat, cold rain started bouncing off the tables.

"Thank God they're plastic," Priya said, as everyone rushed back to the house. "Vic, you had better arrange for canopies. I only hope we can get some at this late hour. I don't want to be sitting and worrying the entire evening about whether it's going to rain or not. As it is, people are going to have enough problems walking on the wet grass."

Vic sighed. He was sure this was a freak shower. The drops of rain were too big and far apart to turn into a downpour. He wondered how the idiot weather people made their forecasts.

"You fellows have some canopies?" Vic asked the burly man.

"I will call and check. But that will be more spensive."

"Just find out," Vic said, though, as he had suspected, it stopped raining. But now moisture lingered in the air, and Vic wasn't sure if the day was going to turn into the wrong 50 percent.

Perhaps he should have listened to Priya and arranged a catered dinner at a hotel. It wasn't tightfistedness that had prevented him from booking one of the local hotels. He had wanted his son's party to be special, didn't want it to be just another revolving event at a hotel. He had attended too many receptions, conferences, dinners that were all jumbled up in his memory because they were so similar. The ugly carpets, the impersonal rooms, the flat-tasting food. He wanted to greet his friends in his own home, not rent a large one that would be transformed for an entirely different event the next day. Years from now, he wanted to look outside his window and recall the arrangements of the chairs, the people talking in groups, the purple flowers of the jacaranda tree, the scent of the roses that Priya had planted when they bought this house.

"We can make the cover for you," the man said. An hour later, Vic looked outside and saw a large white canopy flapping between poles.

By 3 p.m., the heaters had been set out. Almost everything was in place. Nikhil had returned from exercising and Nandan was inspecting the numerous tubs of sodas that Flora had placed on the edges of the lawn.

"Don't spill any on your clothes," he cautioned his younger son.

Nandan was so careless with his things. He was always leaving his jackets in school, and one time when he was very small, he had handed over a $20 bill to buy some ice cream and grandly told the vendor to keep the change. Vic had lectured him for days afterward, until Priya begged him to stop. Nandan, she said, had got the message, and he would never make such a mistake again. Vic wanted his sons to get all the benefits he had never enjoyed, but he didn't want them to behave like little rajas who don't know that earning money is hard work.

"Dad, I haven't spilled stuff in years," Nandan said as he started drinking a Sprite. Vic was about to remind his son of the number of times he had spoiled his shirts, then decided it wasn't that important.

This party was about Nikhil. Nikhil was the VIP today. Nikhil was going to be wearing the suit he had worn a few weeks ago at his graduation. Vic had been saturated with pride that day, greeting other happy parents, including many Indians. The Indian men were bragging about their children's GPAs and the jobs they had lined up. Vic had listened. He didn't say a word. Didn't tell them that his son didn't just have a job, he already had a company that he was going to inherit.

Vic inspected every room in the house. He had bought the house because it was the biggest one on the block. Priya had preferred a smaller house that was closer to the ocean, but Vic had remembered how the seth's large house in the village had inspired admiration and envy. He was aware that though many Americans were happy to welcome him to a country to which their own ancestors had immigrated, just as many considered him an alien. He would, he thought, force them to account for him. He had long practice at being an outsider, at needing to find ways to make people look at him with respect. At IIT, he had used his brains; in America, where money was just as lustrous as back in India, a huge house would make everyone know one thing: He was rich. And, just as in India, wealth gave status to a person.

The house had five bathrooms and four bedrooms. The dining room could easily accommodate twenty-five people, as could the living room, and both had fireplaces that had never been used. Priya complained that the house was too big for their small family, that she did not like the boys' bedrooms being so far from theirs. She did, however, agree that the garden was beautiful, and she especially liked the apple trees. She had eaten very few apples when she was young, because they were expensive, and considered Western fruit. Now she could eat as many as she wanted, and she had learned to make delicious, chunky chutney.

Flora had done a good job of cleaning, and the furniture gleamed. She had put new rolls of toilet paper in the bathrooms and had boiled cinnamon-laced water so the entire house had a lovely aroma. She had also helped Priya put bright tablecloths and vases of flowers on the round tables.

Vic thought the flowers were as unnecessary as gift wrapping. "People only care about drinks, food, and the company," he told Priya, but she shook her head and said that he was just being stingy.

"Stingy?" he looked at her in amazement. "Do you know how much this party is costing me?"

"You wanted to have it, so you must do it properly."

The one thing he made sure to do very properly was the drinks. The French bikers had asked if he was the sort of Indian who did not serve drinks at home. He had laughed and told them that all Indians love to drink, and his countrymen would be very disappointed if he didn't have an open bar.

"I'm having two stations with four bartenders," he told them, and they had raised their glasses to him in thanks.

"We will drink enough to make a boat float," they promised, and, for a moment, he regretted inviting them. But they had changed the date for the Vegas trip to accommodate him, and they kept asking him about the party. So he finally invited them, expecting to hear excuses.

Instead they said, "We'd love to. We promise not to tell your wife any stories about you."

The bartenders were setting up, and Vic was happy to see that they had followed his instructions and come well stocked.

The only item that required double-checking was the food. Vic had worried about the food from the moment he gave the order to Kumar, who owned a local Indian restaurant. He had warned Kumar from the outset that since he, too, was Indian, he knew all about his countrymen's penchant for late deliveries, as well as the inevitable issue of something, somehow, going wrong with the order.

"You are in America now," he reminded Kumar, "so make sure you give me exactly what I ordered. And you better be on time."

Still, to confirm that Kumar was going to do his job properly, Vic phoned him at 4 p.m. Three rings, four . . . he was just beginning to fret that Kumar had mixed up the day when he answered.

"Surely, Mr. Jha, we are coming there. We will definitely be at your house by five thirty."

He had taken the precaution of telling Kumar five o'clock, even though the party was set for six. When Vic heard this new time, uttered without any apology, any sign that it was half an hour later than planned, he felt as if his blood was going to explode.

"If you are not here by five thirty sharp, I am not going to pay you one single paisa."

"Surely, Mr. Jha, we will be there. And in America we are not using the paisa," the man heh-hehed over the phone, half laughing, half apologetic.

"And every dish had better be hot."

"But Mr. Jha, you were telling us only mild spices. You were telling us that you have invited many foreigners, and also many of our own people have been living here so long, they cannot stomach our hot dishes."

"I mean temperature hot, you—!" Vic shut his mouth before the word *idiot* slipped out. In this bad economy, Kumar needed the order, but right now Vic needed the food more.

And Kumar had better not have put his usual quota of chilies in the food. Some Americans could tolerate spicy cuisine, but he didn't want to take a chance. Then there were the Indians like Lali who had married Americans and had probably lost all ability to eat chilies. Vic had thought of both types of people when ordering the food. The Indians would like the familiarity, though a few might complain that the food lacked definition. The Americans would be surprised, because they would assume that all Indian cuisine was spicy, and therefore inedible.

"Bloody idiot!" Vic said as he hung up the phone.

"Is Kumar not bringing the food?" Priya asked, her face showing alarm.

"Of course he is. He just likes to play a little."

"As long as he brings the food on time, and it's tasty."

"I'm going to make a last-minute check of the outside before getting ready."

The sky was gray, and even though he heard thunder, it hadn't rained since those few drops in the morning. He had been correct, after all.

He walked around the lawn, which now looked smaller because of all the furniture and heaters. The tablecloths dressed up the plastic tables, and the flowers added an elegant yet homey touch. He hurried in to tell Priya that she had made the outside look better than he had imagined, but she wasn't in the bedroom getting ready. It usually took her much longer, because she had to comb her long hair and apply all types of powders and colors to her face.

He looked around for the *sherwani* he had decided to wear. She typically hung his chosen outfit on the closet door. The *mojari* shoes were still in their box.

He had invested a lot of thought not just in the party but also in his clothes. Should he be American in a suit? But he wore a suit every day to work, and he wanted this occasion, this moment when he publicly brought his son into the company he had created, to be special. His own father had worn cotton *dhotis* all his life and had borrowed a silk one for his own wedding. Vic had given his *dhotis* to his younger brother Vijay when he started studying at IIT. He wasn't about to go backward and put on something that would feel strange and make Americans think of a diaper. Gandhi hadn't cared, but he did.

Then Vic remembered Gandhi's right-hand man, Nehru, the prime minister his mother adored, the man who had popularized Indian-style jackets in the West. He would, he decided, wear a Nehru coat. But when he went online, he realized that Nehru jackets needed to be tailored. *Sherwanis*—the long, beautifully embroidered kurtas that come down to the knee and are worn with narrow pajamalike pants—did not need to fit perfectly. And they came in different styles. He chose one with a Nehru collar. On the bottom of the Internet page, he noticed that many people paired sherwanis with mojari shoes. It had been years since he had seen those pointed shoes that looked like something Aladdin might have worn. These shoes were special even in India. At one time, they were the footwear preferred by royalty. He had never owned a pair, because his village was far from Rajasthan. The website had a large selection, and he liked the idea that they were handmade. They would go perfectly with his outfit, and, because it was summer, he would not get cold. He had ordered a white pair, to match the pants, and he had selected blue for the embroidery, to match the color of his sherwani.

He had just stepped into the mojaris when Priya came in.

"Why are you not dressed?"

"I was talking to Nikhil."

"He'd better be getting ready. People will be here in half an hour to congratulate him."

"No, people are coming because you have invited them."

Vic stared at her. She didn't usually make stupid, obvious statements. After they were married, he had been happily surprised by her intelligence. He had not known what to expect, what to hope for, when he returned home to marry the girl his parents had selected for him. She had been in her second year of college, studying sociology. He had insisted that his parents find him a girl who had attended college, thinking it would give him more time as a bachelor. But then his parents wrote to him about Priya, and since she fit his basic requirements, he could not refuse their wishes.

She had not looked up during their only meeting prior to getting married. But he had already seen a picture, so he knew that her face wasn't scarred by smallpox or pimples, that she was, as his mother had said, fair, which meant pretty. She had been properly nervous but acquiescent on their wedding night, and though he hadn't made a big production of looking for blood, he had made sure to see it on the white sheet. Then he had returned to America and worked hard. He wrote her a few letters, though she sent him one every week. Her English was stilted but basically correct, the letters filled with information about what she was studying. She was starting her third year when her visa came through and Vic sent her a ticket. She was sad not to be able to finish her BA degree; she clearly wasn't like those girls who considered college a waiting period before getting married. She had actually learned something.

She was not afraid to travel by herself to the United States, and he had been relieved to save the money, as well as the time, it would take to go fetch her. She had not said much when she joined him, and he knew she was adjusting to being far from her parents, to living in a land she had only seen in Hindi films that had been shot abroad. She enjoyed the TV and spent a great deal of time looking through the supermarket produce aisle for vegetables. Then she got pregnant, and it seemed to Vic that as soon as she became a mother, she had plenty to say. In English.

She also learned to drive, and she asked other mothers all sorts of questions. She learned about preschools, something he didn't even know existed, and by the time Nikhil had his third birthday, she was able to organize a birthday party complete with goody bags. She also started shopping at the farmers' market. Once she knew that she could get fresh vegetables, she produced the most wonderful meals.

Her ability to settle so well into life in America had helped him, because he did not need to keep a constant eye on her. He had met many Indian men who grumbled that their wives simply could not get used to California's freeways, which meant they had to be both provider and driver.

Now, however, Priya was annoying him. She had grudgingly gone along with the party, but he expected and demanded that she smile and support him this evening.

"Yes, I am the one who invited all our friends. So get ready before they come."

"I told Nikhil about your plan for him. He does not want to work in your company."

He wished he could hit her, the way Pitaji would slap Mataji when she did something he disliked. But he had never liked it when his father did it, and had promised himself that his sons would never hear, or witness, such an action. Besides, in America, domestic abuse could land you in jail.

"How dare you spoil my surprise?" He was so angry his voice was shaking.

"Didn't you hear me? Nikhil does not want to work in computers."

"He is going to join VikRAM Computers, and that's final."

"No, Nikhil says that he wants to take cooking classes. If you don't let him do that, then he and I, both of us, won't come to the party."

"Nikhil!" Vic shouted.

"*Aree*, why are you shouting on the day of the party?" Rajesh appeared in the doorway, holding a big present. "Where is the happy graduate? I am also looking for him."

"Go wait downstairs," Vic ordered Rajesh, then shouted again for his son.

Nikhil poked his head out of his room.

"Aha, there you are," Rajesh said. "See what I have got for you."

"Uncle Rajesh, you didn't have to get me anything."

"That I already know, but I was wanting you to have some small-big present from me. You want to open it?"

"Open it later," Vic ordered his son. "Rajesh, we are busy now."

"But it is only five thirty, and our Indians are never punctual. I did not give it to him earlier because we were so busy. Surely there is enough of time for Nikhil to open the present his uncle has brought for him."

Nikhil tore open the wrapping and then exclaimed, "A wok! Thank you, Uncle."

"So it is to your liking? I went all the way to Chinatown to buy it. I told the man that my nephew is a very fine cook. . . ."

Vic could not hear another word. "Rajesh, outside, now. And Nikhil, come inside the room. Your mother and I want to talk to you."

"Go, go, *beta*," Rajesh told Nikhil. "I am sure your father has a lovely nice surprise for you. It will be much better than my small wok. . . ."

Vic shut the door and turned to face his wife and son. "Your mother says she has told you why I wanted this party."

"Dad, I guessed as much but wasn't sure till Mom confirmed it today. Like I've always told you, I don't want to work in computers."

"You want to be a servant and cook for others?"

"I want to be a chef. I'll be creating dishes, not just cooking."

"Creating, cooking," Vic spat out the words as if they were poison. "You will be in a kitchen, just like a woman."

"And what is wrong with being a woman?" Priya demanded. "Don't forget that you married one, that you are here because a woman gave birth to you."

Priya was talking like an idiot. Vic didn't bother responding to her. He turned to Nikhil: "If you do not join the company, then what was the use of your degree?"

"I did it to make you happy. But I always told you that I want to live *my* life, not the one you want for me."

The choice of words made Vic suspicious. "Are you going to India?"

"Maybe. I'm not sure. First I want to take some cooking classes in France and Italy."

"You have already decided all this without consulting me?"

"Dad, I always told you what I wanted to do. It's what I've wanted since I was in middle school."

"If you do this, if you go and take stupid cooking classes, I won't give you a single paisa. You will be on your own."

"I'm not worried about money," Nikhil said. "I was just hoping you would understand."

"Understand? What is there to understand? My son gets a degree from MIT and starts to cut vegetables."

"Vic, you did what you wanted," Priya said. "We must give our son the same opportunity."

"What I wanted made sense!" Vic screamed. "You are watching too many of those talk shows, talking to too many of your American friends. This is an Indian house. This is not a stupid American house where parents are shut away and the children do what they want."

"Nikhil did what you wanted," Priya reminded him, her voice steady. "He studied computers for four years and did very well, even though he did not like them. Are you going to let him do what he has wanted for so long or will you be greeting our guests alone?"

"So now Nandan, too, has joined you?"

"No one has joined anyone," Priya maintained, "and you must calm down before you have a heart attack."

"Oh, if I die, then everyone will be happy because you will get what you want."

"Vic, I am going to start getting ready," Priya said, "but I need your answer before I go downstairs."

"Same here, Dad," Nikhil said, and ducked out of the room.

Vic sat down on the edge of the bed. He stared at the slippers he had purchased with such anticipation. They were tight and hurt his big toe. All his carefully thought-out preparations were not working out.

He was furious that Priya had ganged up with Nikhil, that they had cornered him into this "yes" position.

"Everything is okay now?" Rajesh appeared at the door.

Did Rajesh know what was going on? Was that why he had given Nikhil that ridiculous present? He thought of the office key he had put into a small jewelry box for Nikhil. Indians usually gave gold at celebrations. He had given a gold necklace to his brother's wife when he got married, and just last year he had done the same for his two nieces, though he could not attend their weddings.

Nikhil would assume the box contained a thin gold chain or a ring.

The small box was in the side pocket of the sherwani. He had dreamed of the moment when he would ask everyone to be silent. Then, instead of a long, boring speech, like the ones his

Indian friends gave at their children's graduations, talking about everything from diaper days to college courses, he would simply open the box and show Nikhil the key. It was for the office next door to his. He had installed a statue of the god Ganesh on the side table, had already printed business cards for his son. The key was lying on one of those cards.

The bikers had asked him if he was going to give his son a gift. "I already did," he said, because he did not want them to know anything in case they blurted out something after having too much to drink. "I educated him. He is one of very few people who does not have any loans." In that sense, Nikhil was like him. He, too, had come out of UCLA without needing to pay back anything.

Now he had nothing to give his son.

Vic could feel the box. He was just about to take it out of his pocket when he thought of the perfect solution. He would let Priya believe that he was going along with her wishes. Except that he would take out the box and give it to Nikhil during the party as he had long planned to do. Neither of them would ever stand up to him in front of their guests. It would be too shameful, too disrespectful.

But he didn't want to lie outright to her. His mother had always told him that lies had a way of coming back and biting the person. This was not a good day for that to happen.

He chose his words very carefully. "I'll wait downstairs for you," he told her.

"Vic, does that mean you won't force Nikhil to join VikRAM Computers?"

She knew him too well. "I told you," he started, when he heard the revving of motorbikes.

"The bikers are here," he said.

"You invited them?" Priya asked. "Why?"

"Why not?" he responded. He had regretted the invitation but now didn't care if they teased him about his family for a while. They had already done him a service.

"I'd better go before Rajesh does something stupid. Come down soon," he said, then added, because he was suddenly happy, "They have been wanting to meet you for a long time. That is why I invited them. I told them you are the best wife."

"Nikhil," he called his son. "The guests have started coming."

The Party

"It is not your biker friends." Priya, who was standing near the window, looked outside. "It is one of Kumar's men. They forgot to bring the mint chutney, and I told them you would not pay them one cent unless it was on the table before the party started."

"I thought it sounded like many motorbikes," Vic said, rushing to the window to check for himself. "You were right."

"When will you learn that I am always right?" Priya asked.

"When you get ready on time," Vic grumbled. "Which means I will never think you are right."

"Oh ho, you and your stubbornness. But now that you don't have to rush downstairs to greet your beloved biker friends, can you help me with this necklace?" Priya held out the thick gold necklace she had bought for herself the last time they went to India. She liked to mark every trip home with another piece of jewelry, and when Vic complained, she reminded him that in India, the more she sparkled, the more it showed that he was a success. "And that means that *I* have brought *you* luck," she added. Vic vaguely remembered his father blaming his mother for their poverty because while he worked hard in the fields, she hadn't pulled her end by providing him with good luck.

He had never liked fiddling with her jewelry because, as he once told her in exasperation, *he* didn't require any help to get ready. This evening his irritation at her casual, habitual request was exacerbated by her decree that he *not* give Nikhil a position in VikRAM Computers.

He heard the big grandfather clock in the entranceway downstairs toll six times. "Hurry up, hurry up." Vic didn't hide his frustration.

"Why are you telling me to hurry up?" Priya asked. "You are the one who is putting on my necklace. You hurry up and do it."

"These Indian clasps are very badly designed," Vic said, peering at the S-shaped hook. He had to insert one end of the S into the tiny hole of the necklace, then clamp it together tightly, so that it would not open. She had already lost one necklace because it hadn't been closed properly. "How many times have I told you to take all your necklaces to an American jeweler?"

"I went to two jewelry shops," Priya said, "but they were going to change the clasp to 18-carat gold."

"So what if it's not 22 carat? Nobody sees the back of the necklace. There, I did it."

"Finally," Priya said, just as the doorbell rang. "That must be your biker friends, or maybe your American workers."

"How do you know that?" Vic asked, as he searched for his watch. He had taken it off because strands of her hair had gotten caught in the dial while he was struggling with the necklace. Vic was anxious because he wanted to be waiting downstairs when the first guests arrived. He didn't trust that Rajesh would greet people properly.

"Because Indians have a very flexible concept of time," Nikhil took up for his mother from the doorway. "They arrive an hour late and still think they are on time."

"Why are you not wearing your new suit?" Vic was immediately sidetracked by the sight of his son.

"I am," Nikhil pointed to his trousers, brazenly overlooking the white kurta Vic was referring to.

"You knew about this?" Vic accused Priya.

"He can wear what he wants," she said. "I think he looks very nice."

"Go and get the door," Vic told his son, angry because he knew he could not order him to change his clothes. He had suggested that Nikhil wear the expensive suit and tie he had bought for his graduation. But instead of looking sleek and well tailored, Nikhil was wearing an off-the-rack kurta, with sleeves so long they had to be folded back. He had wanted his son to look like an executive, not a patriotic Indian.

"I still have to comb my hair and stuff," Nikhil said as the bell rang again. "Ask Nandan. He's watching TV in his room."

"Nandan," Vic shouted, "go greet our guests."

"Why me?" Nandan answered from his room. "This isn't my party. Tell Nikhil."

"People are going to think we are the worst of hosts," Vic worried as he peered out the window. "Oh, it is only the bartender. Hey," he yelled, "why are you ringing the bell? Just open the door and go inside."

"It's locked."

"That bloody Rajesh must have done that. He is always thinking that people are going to come in and rob us. Idiot! Rajesh! Open the door. Where is my watch?"

"Here's your watch," Priya said, handing him the Rolex he had worn ever since they were married. She still wore her matching watch, though it was platinum, and all her jewelry was gold. She had once suggested that he buy her a gold watch, but Vic told her the old one still worked, and he wasn't going to waste his hard-earned money just so she could look coordinated.

"I'd better go down before that fool of a cousin creates more problems." Vic strapped on his watch.

"Don't say such mean things about my cousin," Priya admonished. "He has never done anything bad or wrong to you."

"Except ask for a job he wasn't qualified for."

Priya sighed. "Still saying that even though he left VikRAM Computers more than a year ago and is working for an insurance company?"

"Rajesh! Did you unlock the door?" Vic shouted again.

"I already did," Rajesh said, appearing at their bedroom door. "What else do you want for me to do?"

"Greet the guests and make them comfortable if we are not there," Priya said, and Rajesh answered, "Of course, of course," before disappearing.

"Why did you ask that *ullu ke pathay* to do that?" Vic shook his head.

"You may call him a son of an owl and think it's a big insult," Priya said calmly, "but in America, an owl is a symbol of wisdom, so only you will look like an idiot."

"You're talking rubbish," Vic said dismissively.

"Ask your children. Even they know. They learned it in elementary school. You were too busy working at your company to know what they were studying."

Vic did not like being reminded of those days when he had been obsessed with growing his company. He had spent all his time strategizing, worrying, thinking of new ways to make VikRAM Computers bigger, better than the other companies that seemed to start up on a daily basis. He used to get angry with Priya when she insisted he cancel a meeting in order to attend Nandan's winter program, or a swim meet for Nikhil. It was only recently that he realized what, and how much, he had missed.

His school in India had offered nothing except beatings and

old books. He had always thought he had done a great job just by giving his children such amazing opportunities. Nandan had attended a robotics camp two summers ago because he was interested in robots—and because Vic could pay for it. Vic didn't think he needed to see the robot his son had made.

The one exception Vic had made to his busy schedule was Nikhil's graduation from MIT. He had missed the high school one because he had had to travel at the last minute. It was while Vic was at the MIT graduation, hearing other parents reminisce about the various stages of their children's lives, that he realized he couldn't add to the conversation—not because he preferred being the silent one but because he had very few memories of Nikhil as a schoolboy. He had heard about them from Priya, nodded sleepily over the perfect report cards, said "Yes" to camps and evening classes, without really listening.

Vic had returned from Boston determined to correct the gap that had been growing ever since Nikhil had been born. It was one of the reasons he wanted Nikhil to join VikRAM Computers. He had watched the ease with which fathers had talked to their sons, treating them like valued friends. He wanted to be like those fathers. He didn't want to turn into his own father. When he returned home, conversation stopped after Vic asked Pitaji about his health, and about whether the fields had given good crops.

He didn't need Priya reminding him of how much he had lost by working so hard for this family. *She* had been the lucky one. She had stayed home and enjoyed the excesses of his success. Once Nikhil was settled into the office next door, Vic planned to suggest they have a weekly lunch date. They could even start each day by going to the office together. It would be one of the many benefits of having Nikhil aboard.

"Don't try to make me think your cousin is anything but a fool." Vic went back to Rajesh-the-irritant. "He will simply take everyone to the bar, and, while they are getting drinks, he will make sure to have another, until he gets so drunk he won't even know his own name."

"You are a big one to talk about drinking. What is that?" Priya indicated the empty glass on the dressing table.

"That's because of you and your son," Vic said, pointing his finger at her. "At the last minute, when I am preparing to go down and meet our guests, you make a stupid demand, and what, you think I will smile and be happy?"

"You *are* happy because you have your big, fat computer company, and you ride your motorbike like a young boy," Priya said. "I want *Nikhil* to be happy."

Vic opened his mouth, but Priya held up her palm and said, "Just make sure you don't drink too much tonight. I don't want another—"

"I know, I know," Vic grumbled. She was never going to let him forget the DUI. He had done so much for her, given her jewels and silk sarees, and yet she could not forget his one misstep.

The DUI had turned her into a nag. Vic had hoped she would forget about it in a few weeks, but when she continued to hover and question, he became sly and secretive. He started filling his water glass with vodka. He had always kept a few vodka bottles in the dining-room credenza, but now he made sure there were four. He hid the one he was pouring from behind the others, so they always looked full. Unless Priya really checked, she would never know that he was still drinking.

He didn't feel bad doing it because he thought she was overreacting to his DUI. As he told her, the DUI was an isolated mistake. He let her believe that by *mistake* he meant that he should give up drinking—except for the very occasional glass at home, or with businessmen who might think less of him if he refused to join them in a toast. She had been thrilled, relieved that he wasn't going to drink anymore with his biking buddies. He never told her that the mistake he was referring to was that on the day of the DUI he had deviated from his usual one glass of whiskey and ordered beer. The Frenchmen scorned American beer, but they grudgingly allowed that cold beer on a hot day wasn't too bad. It had been a very hot day, and the helmet had made his head feel like it was inside a sauna. That fateful evening he had decided to join the men in three rounds of beer. It hadn't affected him at all. The Breathalyzer had been his undoing. Afterward, he wondered whether he was being punished for not being himself.

Priya picked him up from the police station and lectured him the whole way home. She had watched her own father drink away their money, and she didn't want a husband to do the same thing. "When my parents were searching for a husband for me, I told my mother that I did not care how he looked, or what kind of job he had. I just did not want him to drink."

Vic recalled that when he brought her home from the airport, she had walked around the apartment he had been renting, touching the TV, the dishwasher, things she had only seen in films. The only question she had posed was about the bottles of liquor in the cabinet. He had told her that every home here had them, whether people drink or not.

"It is the same as the lawn," he said, pointing to the green patch outside the building. "Every house has a lawn, but I have never seen anyone sit on the grass to enjoy it. It is like that with these bottles."

They had had their first fight when she showed him that the bottle of Chivas Regal that used to be half full was now closer to empty. She refused to believe that it had always been that way.

"Don't tell me that my eyes are wrong. I dust it every week," she said. "I want to know why you are drinking."

After that, he became open about needing one glass every

night. He told her it relaxed him, that he never went beyond the single finger of whiskey. But slowly the one glass grew into two, and nowadays he needed three. She had tried, over the years, to stop him, but he laughed at her. "I'm the head of this house," he informed her, "and if I need to drink, I will."

The DUI had put new words into her mouth. She knew he didn't care about what *she* thought and wanted, but how would his workers react to the news? They might refuse to get in the car with him.

"I would never get into a car with someone who drinks," she asserted.

And the Indian community? He was on numerous boards, headed all sorts of committees. How could he represent them with a DUI on his record? She didn't want to live the rest of her life being referred to as the wife of a drunk. She insisted he throw away every single bottle in the house.

Vic had let her carry on, until she came up with the stupid idea of discarding the bottles. In the end, he promised there would not be another DUI.

"I never want to go through that experience again," he said, and he meant it.

She, however, had to allow him to keep all the bottles. Throwing them away was just like burning dollar bills. He would continue to drink when the occasion demanded. If he ever called her up from the police station again, then she could do whatever she wanted with the bottles in the house.

Shortly after that, he had started drinking vodka. He missed his Chivas Regal but had recently begun thinking that the Russians might be right. There was great merit to vodka, and not simply because it masqueraded as water. When he told that to the Frenchmen one evening, Pierre had said, "Firewater, that's what it is," and Vic had to agree that there was nothing like vodka for keeping a person warm on a cold night.

Vic looked at the empty glass in his hand. He had brought it upstairs with him when he came to change his clothes. "You don't have to worry about my drinking," Vic said as he left the room. "I need a clear head this evening because I am in charge of this party. I arranged everything for this evening, so now you don't need to start acting as if you are in charge."

LALI WAS so grateful, so full of love for Jonathan, that she didn't get annoyed when he hurried her out of the bathroom. She needed a few more minutes to get ready, but because all she could think of was how he had never belittled her, never made her feel bad about herself, she immediately said, "Coming!" and closed her makeup case.

Until this afternoon, she had simply accepted his spontaneous "I'll come with you to the party," hadn't considered that he was giving up time with his colleagues. She suddenly found herself feeling bad when his panel ran late, and he had to skip the next one he had hoped to hear. But he didn't complain, just changed his clothes and, as if the party meant a lot to him, worried that they were going to be late.

"You look lovely, again," Jonathan said, as they walked to the car. "Given the occasion, I thought you might wear a saree."

He used to enjoy seeing her in sarees, but she hadn't worn one in years. Her blouses got tight, it was too difficult to have new ones stitched, and draping the sarees proved to be problematic as well, so she had packed them away in the suitcase that had accompanied her on her first trip across the ocean to Los Angeles.

"Mrs. Feinstein decided to wear a dress." Lali smiled up at the man who had changed her name, changed her life. This evening her only connection to her heritage was the pashmina shawl, though because it wasn't embroidered, it could have come from anywhere.

"You've told me things about your friends over the years," Jonathan said. "But I don't remember much. Since I'll be meeting them shortly, how about a quick refresher course?"

"Now you know how I felt when we attended your twentieth high school reunion," she teased, before giving him the salient details of the Gang of Four. "Vic was an adjacent member," Lali said, "and because Frances and Jay were going steady, something only very bold Indians did back then, they were the stars."

"So Vic's wife and I will be the odd ones out," Jonathan said.

"Technically, you are the oddest," Lali said honestly. "You're the only American."

"Oh, come on," Jonathan exclaimed. "Your friends have lived their adult lives in the States. I'm sure they're very American."

"Not at an Indian party," Lali started, then stopped. She had already told him about the mean side of Indians at parties, and if she wanted him to have a good time, she needed to concentrate on the pleasant parts. "The good thing is, they'll like you just because you're married to me. And they will want to know *everything* about you, so be forewarned. You will have to answer a million questions."

For all Jonathan's anxiety about traffic and being late, they arrived at Vic's house at six fifteen, and, as Lali had suspected, the only people on the lawn were as white as Jonathan.

The lone exception was a man named Rajesh, who was using his family connection to sell insurance.

Lali tried to rush them past Rajesh, but because Jonathan didn't have an Indian filter, he engaged with the man. Rajesh had just started telling them about "the best of the best life insurance policy" when Vic, thank God, joined them and ordered the man to stop bothering the guests.

"My wife's cousin," Vic said, as if that explained the man's behavior. Vic was extremely appreciative that they had come, and he kept thanking them for making the long trip. Lali couldn't bring herself to tell him about the Santa Barbara conference and was relieved that Jonathan did not puncture Vic's happiness.

"Is Frances here?" Lali asked.

"Not so far," Vic said. "They did not come for Nikhil's high school party, but this time they sent a positive response, so maybe we will see them."

"It's really nice that you are doing this," Lali said. "Our first chance to get together since UCLA."

"No problem, no problem. You must be hungry after your travels. Please have something to eat," Vic said. "I told the restaurant not to make anything spicy, so you will be able to enjoy the food," he told Jonathan.

"I love your outfit," Lali told Vic. It was an unexpected reprieve from the shabby kurtas he used to wear all the time. "You even got the right shoes." His glasses were as thick as ever, but the frames suited his face much better than the ones he had worn at UCLA.

"All from the Internet," Vic said, waving away her praise. "You are also looking very fine. I used to think you were a little skinny when you were a student, but now you are nicely filled out."

Lali laughed to cover up her embarrassment. Vic was the only person she knew who could turn a compliment into an insult without being aware of it.

"You look the same, except that your hair is gray," she said.

"In India we are saying that is the result of too much gray matter in the head, but in America, it is because of all the worries."

"Vic, you promised not to talk about worries tonight," a woman said as she joined them. "I'm Priya, Vic's wife. You must be one of Vic's old friends."

"Not an old friend," Lali clarified. "A friend from the old days."

"Actually, you *are* one of my oldest friends," Vic insisted. "Of course *your* hair—"

"Vic, I think the caterer is looking for you." Priya interrupted him.

"It's really nice to meet you." Lali was curious about the woman Vic had married. Shortly after she moved to San Francisco, Frances had written her that Vic had gone home and returned with a wife. He hadn't informed them he was going to India, and they only knew he had gotten married when he invited them to meet his wife shortly after she joined him.

Lali had been envious when she heard the news. Jay and Frances were married, and then Vic had bypassed the uncertainty of dating and had wed someone, while she was stuck by herself in San Francisco.

She often wished that she, too, could have taken advantage of that useful ancient tradition. Her American office mates dismissed arranged marriages as primitive, the most egregious instance of parents taking away their children's independence. "How can a mother decide which man will make her daughter happy?" someone had challenged Lali. She had shrugged. It was no use trying to explain something to a person whose mind was already made up. In India, girls did not have to worry about attracting a boy. Their parents made the arrangements and it was rare to see a single girl. All Lali knew was that if she hadn't been so stupid with Aakash, her parents would have been able to find her a husband who was an engineer or lawyer, and she would then live a very comfortable life. Vic's parents had found him a pretty girl who looked like she could handle Vic, and America.

"So you're the woman who has been putting up with Vic all this time," Lali said, then wished she hadn't been so forthright. What if this Priya hadn't adjusted to American humor?

"I keep telling Vic I deserve a medal," Priya laughed. "He gets me lovely jewelry, so I guess I'm doing okay." She lifted her arm and jingled a dozen bracelets.

"These are beautiful," Lali said, bending to get a closer look, reassured that she hadn't insulted Priya. "I've never seen bangles like this before."

"It's a design from my village," Priya explained.

"In Kerala, where I come from, no one likes to tamper with the gold, so it's always yellow, yellow, yellow. I think the black inset with the band of gold on either side is stunning."

"Thank you. Oh, I can see Vic waving to me. I guess the caterer is doing something wrong," she said, and walked away quickly.

Lali and Jonathan didn't know any of the other guests, which added to the togetherness she was already feeling. They went to the long buffet tables, and though Jonathan recognized pakoras and samosas, he had never seen so many different chutneys. Lali explained that the green ones were mint and cilantro, the brown was tamarind, and the red was tomato. They filled their plates and accepted a drink from a waiter. By the time they had found an empty table, they were holding hands, and Lali was feeling warm from the wine as well as the closeness she felt toward her husband. She barely remembered last night's fight, or this morning's silent ride to the airport. It was as if she had never gone to see Aakash.

She popped an oily pakora into her mouth. She didn't care if she put on weight.

"You weren't kidding when you said that Vic would invite everyone he knows," Jonathan said, looking at the press of people.

"I told you," Lali said confidently. As she watched for Frances, she saw cars draw up, deposit passengers, and then take off to park elsewhere in the neighborhood. The men were stiff in suits, with gold cuff links, and many wore Rolex watches. The smell of aftershave was overpowering. She didn't know why Indian men in general were so attached to aftershave. She was just glad that Jonathan smelled like himself, not like something out of a bottle.

She had not seen this many sarees in years. The lawn was bright with yellow, orange, pink, and everywhere there was the glint of gold, either in the saree itself or in long earrings, wide bracelets, and thick necklaces. The Hindi music in the background, the warmth in the air, transported her back to India.

Lali was amused that the women invariably gave her a second look after they saw Jonathan. She herself was curious about the few other Indians who had white husbands. Were they delighted with themselves or, like her, had they married because they had fallen in love? A few, after giving them the once-over, stopped to chat.

It was always the same questions: Which part of India do you come from? How long have you been in America? Do you have any children? No one asked how they knew Vic. That, apparently, wasn't a significant part of their lives.

An older man who had introduced himself as Thomas considered her name and, perusing her face, stated, "You are from Kerala."

"I grew up in Cochin," Lali admitted.

"You are wearing a crooked gold cross on your chain, so you must be a Jacobite Syrian Christian."

"My father gave me this cross on my sixteenth birthday," Lali acknowledged. She hadn't given it much thought until she came to the United States, and people commented on the yellow color of the 22-carat gold she had taken for granted. A few asked about the cross, but Jonathan had been the one most fascinated by what he called her *X*. She had explained that it wasn't a letter in the

English alphabet but a symbol of how Jacobite Syrian Christians had kept their faith when others tried to convert them.

Her father had told her the story when he had given her the cross. Centuries ago, Portuguese Jesuits tried to convert Jacobite Syrian Christians to Catholicism. The Christians resisted, and about twenty-five thousand held onto a rope tied to an ancient Assyrian cross, pledging never to surrender to the Archbishop of Goa. This tilted the horizontal bar of the cross, and from then on, Jacobite Syrian Christians have worn the crooked cross as a mark of their faith. She never took off her gold chain, and she was surprised it hadn't been hidden by the turquoise necklace.

"And what is your premarriage surname?" Thomas asked.

"Chacko."

"You are saying that your family hails from Cochin?"

"They've been there for generations," Lali said.

The family *tharavad*, or home, was only eighty years old, but Chacko family members had been in the area for centuries. She had cousins three and four times removed, which had been great fun when she was young. But ever since she moved to America, it had also made going home very expensive. Her father always asked her to bring something small for everyone, and then, instead of spending all her time at home, she had to visit uncles, great-aunts, and the newly born babies of cousins. On one trip she had attended four weddings.

"Cochin used to be having many Jews. They are even having one of their places of worship there. The name Chacko is coming from Jacob, which is coming from Yacob. Yacob is a Jewish name. Was your family Jewish before becoming Jacobite Syrian Christian?"

"No." Lali hadn't known there was any tie between Jews and Jacobite Syrian Christians. Her father was very proud of being a Jacobite Syrian Christian and claimed that they were the top tier of all Christians in Kerala. Any Jacobite Syrian who "married out" could not have a ceremony in the church unless the partner converted. When Lali wanted to baptize Aaron out of nostalgia more than anything else, the priest she contacted told her that it wasn't possible because Jonathan wasn't a Jacobite. In that sense, Jacobites were the opposite of matrilineal Jews.

"She keeps a kosher house," Jonathan inserted.

Lali laughed and said, "Honey, I told you that most Indians separate their meat from their vegetables."

"Kosher and all I don't know. Although," Thomas ruminated, "there used to be a Jewish merchant by the name of Sam Kodar—Kodar, not Kosher—who had the biggest furniture shop in Cochin. Is your family knowing him?" he asked Lali.

"My family doesn't—I mean didn't—know a single Jew in Cochin. I think by the time I was born, most of them had emigrated to Israel. How do you know so much?"

"I am from Kottayam, but I worked in Cochin for some years before coming Stateside."

"Do you really think Lali's family might have been Jewish?" Jonathan asked.

"Jews have been in Cochin for two thousand years. It is my understanding that some converted to Christianity. My own family has only been Christian, but with a name like Chacko, who can tell?"

"Honey," Jonathan was excited, "why don't we find out if you're Jewish?" He turned to Thomas and asked, "Is there any way my wife can get that information?"

"There are always ways, but I am not sure how to find the path," Thomas said, and, as if his inability to further the conversation meant it was over, he left them to join another group.

"Don't get your hopes up," Lali warned Jonathan.

Thomas sounded knowledgeable, but she knew from past

experience that many Indians pretend to know a lot, even if they don't. One time she had gotten into a great discussion with a Gujarati doctor at Jonathan's hospital about where exactly one can see the northern lights. The man had rejected everything she said, even though he confessed that he didn't know much about that part of the world.

"Wouldn't that be a coincidence?" Jonathan beamed. "I mean, I don't mind you being a Christian, but if it turns out you're actually Jewish, I certainly wouldn't complain."

Jonathan's enthusiasm was contagious, and Lali felt the first brush of excitement. She had always assumed that a Hindu ancestor had converted to Christianity. Was it possible that Thomas was correct—that centuries ago a Jewish man had changed his name and religion? She would call and ask Amma. Her mother was at the age when such questions didn't upset her. Just last month, Amma told her, "I have lived so long, and seen so many peculiar things, that nothing really surprises me anymore." So Amma wouldn't mind checking the family history to see whether it contained a Jewish element. All her children were married, and if she worried about how that could affect her grandchildren, she could simply hide any newfound Jewish ancestor.

A Jewish connection would only help her marriage, Lali knew. Jonathan would be thrilled, Aaron would not have to convert, and she would no longer be an alien in the synagogue. They would welcome her as a member of the tribe, and she could tell them about Jew Town in Cochin, a place she had visited often to check out the antiques stores. It would be a replay of that first year at UCLA. In those days, she had been a novelty because many students had never met an Indian, and they were fascinated by her ability to speak English, her long hair, her toe rings.

• • •

SITTING IN THE car as they drove south toward Newport Beach, Frances kept touching her hair, kept sneaking looks in the side mirror.

The highlight kit that was supposed to have fixed the dye problem had proved to be a disaster. She had started out scrupulously following the instructions, carefully selecting thin strands of hair. But half an hour later, she was only a quarter of the way through, her arms were aching, and she was afraid she would never be done in time. So she decided to speed things up by spreading the paste all over the top of her hair. She imagined a halo appearance, similar to the result when she used to henna her hair back in India. But when she blow-dried her hair, she saw, immediately, that she should never have deviated from the directions on the box. Her hair looked like raw silk, the two colors competing against each other, a glaring advertisement of home dyeing gone horribly wrong.

By then it was 4 p.m., far too late to correct it. She wished she could cover the mess with a hat, but it was an evening event. She would have to go looking like that.

Jay hadn't said a word, though Sam had asked, "What's wrong with your hair, Mom?"

Loyal Lily had immediately said, "I like it. It's lighter, isn't it?"

Frances had smiled and nodded, but all the calm certainty that her life was on the upswing was replaced by the same feelings that had surged through her when she had stared at the invitation for the first time.

It was as if she had stepped away from firm land and was in a morass, where everywhere she looked, starting with the mirror, she saw her desires unfulfilled. She had desperately wanted to meet her friends with her head held high, a replay of the old days.

How she wished that her life was like it had been while she was at UCLA. She could not stop herself from going back in time, to when she had met Vic and Lali and had believed that she was going to have the best life of them all.

She had heard the curled syllables of Lali's Malayalee accent at that orientation party and had known, immediately, that even though the other girl had studied in Bangalore, she, Frances, was better equipped to succeed in America. She had the Western name, had eaten with a fork and knife all her life, and, unlike Lali—who said she felt "out of century" when she stepped off the plane and walked through the very modern buildings at LAX—Frances had thought she had finally come home. She had rejoiced at hearing the fragments of a dozen English conversations, so different from the languages bantered about at the dirty train station in Goa.

As Frances told Lali, she wasn't a typical Indian who speaks three languages. "I never bothered to learn Konkani or Marathi, you know," she explained, "and the only Hindi words I remember are cuss words. I used to say *harami* all the time, and the best part was, very few people in Goa knew that I was saying *bastard*. Most assumed I was speaking Portuguese!"

When both girls realized that Americans were uncomfortable hearing the ubiquitous *bastard* and *bloody* that most Indians blithely insert into sentences, Frances taught Lali to say *harami*. They grumbled about a *harami* professor who gave them a lower grade, a *harami* driver who didn't stop long enough for them to cross the street, the *harami* man in the photocopy shop who laughed because they did not know how to use the machines. Jay had been amused that out of the vast vocabulary offered by Hindi—including, he reminded them, *jodhpurs* and *cummer-*

bund—they only made use of a single cuss word. Vic was the only one who refused to use *harami*.

Then there was the matter of her clothes. Poor Lali had arrived in Los Angeles with a suitcase full of salwar kameezes that looked crumpled no matter how much she ironed them, and sarees that required dry cleaning. Frances had encouraged Lali to give up the long kameezes, and had helped her change her wardrobe from head to toe.

Lali had worn one of those sarees at the orientation party, and though many Americans made much of the color and material, she, Frances, in her pants and top, had been the one who had caught Jay's eye.

Lali also hadn't made good use of her time at UCLA and had left as she had arrived, a singleton. Back home, people would prefer Lali's racial purity and make fun of Frances's Portuguese heritage, but her Western upbringing of wearing frocks and talking to boys gave her the edge and was the main reason, Frances firmly believed, that *she* was born to succeed in America.

Jay's future was even more assured. He had been given every privilege of an upper-class Indian, which rendered him a colossus, able to prosper anywhere in the world, East or West.

Yet she and Jay had never had the money to throw a big party, and they were driving to this one in a Lexus that had been sideswiped while they shopped at the mall. They had long forgotten about fixing it. As Jay said, "Don't judge a car by its paint job. The mechanic says this one is going to last for years."

Now she wished that Jay hadn't kept in touch with Vic. And Vic being Vic had gone and invited Lali. Frances had been surprised by Lali's excited e-mail. She hadn't expected Lali to come to the party. She was intrigued to meet the cardiologist husband, but she was also envious that while things had kept getting better for Lali, the different threads of her own life were so limp.

Tonight her worries were as great as the number of people invited. She wouldn't just be meeting old friends who had done so well. She was also going to be surrounded by doctors, lawyers, engineers, each one playing the immigrant game of one-upmanship.

Jay called it the social version of cricket. "The conversational ball comes your way," he had joked after a party they had attended years ago, where one man had bragged about the size of his house, the leather seats in his car, and the tuition at his children's private school. "You hold out your responsive bat, and then you whack the show-off ball as hard as you can. If your house is bigger, or your car is a newer model, then you get to run between the wickets, and it's your score." Frances had laughed and laughed, secure in those days that Jay's hit would always be stronger than anyone else's.

But these days Jay had nothing to tout. His triumphs—boarding school, St. Stephen's College—were in the past. His current job wasn't at a high-profile company, and if people at the party started digging, he would have to tell them that he had started with the new company only five months ago. It was common knowledge that anyone who moved as often as Jay had done these past years just wasn't doing well.

She, too, had nothing to flaunt that would cause the others to look at her with envy. The O'Sullivan deal that had delighted her this morning would only remind people that she hadn't completed her PhD. She could talk up her real estate career in India, but in America, everyone knew it was essentially a menial job that anyone with some people skills could do.

She looked at Jay, at his full head of hair, the strong jawline she had noticed when he walked toward her with a wine glass. Thank God he was still handsome and, unlike so many Indian men, did not wear his suit like it was a costume. It literally suited him. She knew she was being superficial, but Mama had taught all her daughters that even though their family wasn't rich, just a few adjustments in outfits and hair could make them stand out in a crowd. That early training was one reason Frances was so good at her job. She always ensured that her houses made an excellent first impression. If the owners did not want her to stage their homes, she compensated by bringing in flowers, moving a few pieces of furniture, suggesting small changes that invariably made a huge difference—and usually brought about a sale. She had prevailed upon the Millers to relieve their rooms of the heavy, dark furniture, and it was right after they moved the side tables, bureaus, and cabinets into the garage that they had received the offer. Perhaps that was why they had told the O'Sullivans about her.

Today she had staged her family.

Frances turned around and looked at the three heads sitting in the back seat of the Lexus. Lily looked studio-ready in her white dress, the red satin ribbon in her hair matching her beloved shoes. Frances had shown her how to arrange the skirt so that it did not get crumpled, and had warned her not to spill anything on the dress. Lily's pride in her appearance was apparent in her careful posture, the faint smile that hadn't left her face from the moment she got ready.

Sam looked grown-up in his new jacket.

"Go show your father," Frances had suggested.

Jay had said, "Wow!" then added, "Sam, all you need is a briefcase, and you will be ready to go work in an office."

Sam, who had not wanted to wear what he called a monkey suit, started to take it off, until Frances assured him that his father had paid him a compliment, that he looked like a teenager, and teenagers work. Sam was at the age when he wanted to look older than he was, and this new information pleased him inordinately. He had kept on the jacket, and didn't grumble about wearing black shoes instead of his usual Nikes. He had even combed his hair, which exposed more face than Frances had seen in years. The hair, rather than the clothes, made him look older, but the overall effect was good.

She was sure that everyone at the party would be charmed by her younger children. If only Mandy had listened to her. But her older daughter had tuned her out, just as she was doing right now, earphones stuck in her ears. Mandy was slumped against the window, unaware that her dress was askew. She had waited until the last minute to get dressed and then had refused to wear stockings. Mandy's delaying tactics had made Frances anxious that they might end up being rudely late to the party, instead of just fashionably delayed. The defiant "No!" to the stockings had enraged Frances. She was just about to shout when she realized it didn't matter. The party was at night. No one was going to be peering down at Mandy's feet.

She was counting on the darkness to hide the mess she had made of her own hair.

Her stomach started tightening as they got nearer to Newport Beach. Jay was so different from her. They were going to the party and he was going to have a good time. He had grown up rich and the feeling of being better than everyone else was still with him, which was why their current financial situation did not bother him as much as it plagued her. Even though they lived paycheck to paycheck, he never thought twice about ordering the most expensive item on the menu and always left a big tip.

Now he was teaching Lily his version of "We Three Kings of Orient Are." He had got into his "let's have fun" mood as soon as he started the car, and Frances envied what he called his happy-no-matter-what personality, even as it irritated her.

Jay was perfectly aware that Frances didn't want to attend the party. He could feel her tension, see the rigid lines in her neck, but he also knew that there was nothing he could say to make her feel better. She was always nervous before going to parties.

Today the bad dye job had exacerbated her anxiety. He knew better than to joke about her "hair-raising problem." At the same time, he didn't want her nervousness to affect the children. They didn't go to many parties as a family. They might as well enjoy the evening. He was about to start their usual car game, "I'm going to a party and I'm taking an aardvark," and then have Lily come up with something for the letter *B*, when he saw the license plate in front of him: LV 4 BTLS.

Like all his compatriots in school, he, too, had loved the Fab Four. He had discovered them when he was ten and had determined to learn all their songs one summer. But the new records weren't available even in New Delhi or Bombay. His only hope was the radio, and even there, he was limited to just one English station. It was broadcast from what used to be Ceylon, now Sri Lanka, and the announcer spent half the time reeling off the names of people who had requested songs. *Manisha Dasgupta from Ranchi has requested "Strawberry Fields Forever" for her grandmother, grandfather, mother, father, brother Satish, sister Usha, and her best friend in the whole world, Madhuri Chatterjee.* When the songs finally came on, either the distance or the quality of the radios distorted the lyrics.

He had the worst time trying to figure out the words to "Michelle." Every time the song played, he'd crank up the volume, listening carefully. *So the most key vo tray be on some bell* didn't make any sense. When he returned to school, he asked his roommate about it, hoping that because his parents lived in DC he would know the words. But his roommate did not even like the Beatles.

"In America, we're nuts about Simon and Garfunkel," he had said.

Finally, another classmate, Vinod, who lived in Paris, told Jay that the Beatles had incorporated French lyrics in the song. He had even explained the meaning of *sont des mots qui vont très bien ensemble.*

Vinod, who had a poster of John and Yoko during their "honeymoon bed-in in Amsterdam" on the wall of his room, and was a Beatles know-it-all, had memorized the words of every song, and told Jay that Paul had written "Let It Be" for John's son after his parents got divorced. He taught Jay the bastardized version of "We Three Kings," and it became his favorite song. For a while, the corridors had resounded with the names of the Fab Four.

"Want to learn a new song?" Jay asked his children, then he started singing, somewhat surprised that he remembered the lyrics.

We four Beatles from Liverpool are,
John on a scooter and George in a car,
Paul on a bicycle eating an icicle
Following Ringo Starr.

Lily and Sam started laughing and begged him to sing it again.

Jay, who knew just the one stanza, obliged, rendering it with gusto.

Frances wished she could suck the joy out of this moment that Jay was consciously creating, but she saw Vic's mansion in her mind and felt diminished.

"Why are you singing a Christmas carol in the summer?" she asked. He had only started celebrating Christmas after they were married, and, as far as she knew, had never sung a carol until then.

"I want the children to be prepared," Jay said jovially.

"Do you know another song like that, Dad?" Lily asked. "It's so much more fun than the real words."

"I do know another one, but I think your mom might get angry. . . ."

"Oh, no," Lily said staunchly. "You won't get mad, will you, Mom?"

It was difficult to go against those pleading eyes, the voice that, so far, had never shouted, "I hate you," the lips that kissed her softly on the cheek every night.

Frances didn't respond.

Jay decided to take that as a "yes." He was glad that the children weren't silenced by Frances's mood.

"Okay, are you ready?" he asked. "Are you ready?"

"Yes, we are," Lily and Sam said in unison.

We four merchants from Trafalgar Square,
Selling plastic underwear
No elastic, it's fantastic,
Why don't you buy a pair?

All three were laughing by the end, and even Mandy had a smile on her face.

Frances's irritation graph dipped enough for her to ask, without a hint of displeasure, "How did you end up learning this stuff?"

"Oh, the chaps at school," Jay said airily. "They came from England, America, Europe. There was even one bloke whose parents were stationed in Tokyo. He brought back seaweed one time, and you would have thought it was poison, the way we carried on about the smell and crinkly texture of it. Now I'm sure those same blokes are eating it, along with sushi. My roommate's father worked for the World Bank in DC, and every time he went home on holiday, I benefited. Chocolates, Tang—which I can't believe I drank, much less adored—and my all-time favorite, candy canes."

Jay seldom talked about his school days, and Frances had assumed that the other students, like him, were the sons of rich people from all over India. But apparently Indians living in America had sent their children home for school. She would remember that if anyone at the party asked why Mandy was returning to India for her last year of high school. It would give their decision a cachet she hadn't realized till now.

"In fact," Jay continued to reminisce, "he bested Vinod, who came up with the Beatles version, by teaching us a very funny one about Nixon."

"Sing it, sing it," Lily begged.

"Do you even know who Nixon is?" Jay asked.

"He got impeached," Mandy said, surprising both her parents. She raised her hands high and made the peace sign.

"Mandy knows who Nixon was," Jay said, "so she'll get the references. *Jingle bells, Nixon smells, Watergate's a mess.*"

Frances's mouth went dry, and her heart felt as if it was going to burst out of her body. She knew this song. Rich O'Sullivan had sung it during the only Christmas he had spent at their house.

This was the second time she had thought about Rich. This morning she had been worried that Jay somehow knew about him, and she had only been able to dismiss his memory when she realized that Jay was thinking about the characters in Enid Blyton's books. But now, as she heard Jay singing the song, she could see Rich standing in the living room, teaching her family the words.

Mama had adored Richard and said that it made perfect sense for an American to be called "Rich," because all Americans were exactly that. Rich had been traveling through India after working for the Peace Corps up north, and Frances had stumbled across him, he used to say, while he was stretched out on the beach. Frances had been home on Christmas break from her final year in college and had gone for an early morning walk. It was her favorite time of day, because the air was still cool from the night and the beach wasn't filled with children playing, or families come to spend the day.

She had been looking at the froth-topped waves, not paying much attention to her path across the beach. His blond hair and white body blended in with the sand, so she only stopped when he said, "Hey, watch where you're going." He had been charming from the beginning, telling her he didn't want an apology—he wanted her to take him to the best shack for breakfast. Frances was used to boys asking her sisters out, but they always made sure to receive permission from her parents.

Rich was utterly different from the other foreigners she had seen. Their beach wasn't on the tourist map, so few Westerners found out about it. Those who did appear often left after one day. They were in holiday mode, wanting to make one-night liaisons, and they needed other whites to have that sort of fun. As one German told Frances, "Indian girls are boring. No drink, no smoke, and no sex. You don't know how to enjoy life." Some were couples who stayed a while, and Frances had once seen a family of four who were driving around India. The largest representation of tourists was from America, typically students who were running out of money, clothes, and soap—because many stank from afar. Frances would see the tattered T-shirt, the dirt-streaked hair, and act like she didn't speak English. She had learned her lesson the time she had talked to a red-haired man. After a lovely conversation about the tea estates of Kerala, which he had just visited, he asked her for money and became angry when she refused.

Rich was educated and was interested in India as a country, not as a sex-and-pot destination. He told her it had been his first choice on his Peace Corps application. He also had money, because he was staying in one of the better hotels instead of bedding down on the beach. That initial breakfast had segued into afternoon tea. "I know Indians always stop for their four o'clock cup, so don't try and squirm out of it."

He had planned to head down to Pondicherry to check out the French scene but kept postponing his departure. Mama was so excited. All her older sisters had been married or engaged by the time they were Frances's age, and Mama had worried that her youngest daughter would end up a spinster.

"Did you meet anyone?" she would ask every time Frances came home from her all-girls college in Hyderabad.

Mama expected her to use the years away to find a boyfriend. She told Frances that the best place to meet nice Catholic boys was in church. Frances was to go every Sunday, wear nice clothes, and smile often. The trouble was, the church was filled with older couples whose children were marrying each other. Everyone was nice to Frances, but no boy was interested in her. The ones back home were already taken, and even Frances was beginning to despair.

Then Rich, with his smooth American accent and thick blond hair, walked into their home, and Mama told Frances it was clear he loved her. Otherwise why stay on in Goa? Rich came from a large family, and Mama firmly believed that meant he, too, wanted to marry and have a family. She assured Frances that Rich would propose.

Frances believed Mama, who always knew such things. After all, Mama had told Alba to wear her best dress the evening her boyfriend asked her to go for a walk on the beach. "He is going to propose to you," Mama had assured Alba as she pinned on a brooch. And sure enough, Alba came rushing home to tell them the happy news. So Frances kept Rich company every day, showed him the grove of coconut palms that rose up tall and starry right next to the beach, and was monumentally relieved that he didn't mind using their outdoor toilet when he started coming home for dinner.

"It's a bit like camping," he said, showing her photographs of his brothers and sisters in Yellowstone National Park. "They keep sending me pictures so I won't be out of the loop when I return."

He had applied to various universities and hoped to study at Berkeley. Until Rich told her about the school, her only knowledge of the place had been the line "Down from Berkeley to Carmel," from the Simon and Garfunkel song "Cloudy." She was impressed that he was so sure about his future. He knew exactly where he wanted to go, while she was still waiting to meet the right man.

Christmas came, and of course they invited Rich to spend the day with them. He had already helped them decorate the tree and set up the manger. He had been particularly intrigued by the big star Dada made every year.

"It's like making a kite," Rich had noted, as he watched Dada bend the bamboo into a star and cover it with transparent red paper.

"Ah, but we don't fly it," Dada had said. "We leave a hole at the bottom and put in a lightbulb. Then at night we switch it on and it becomes the star that the Magi followed."

They invited him to attend church with them on Christmas Day, but he did not want to get up early in the morning. Mama and Dada liked him so much they didn't mind. After all, he was a Catholic, even if he didn't go to church regularly. He was waiting outside their house when they returned from morning Mass. All day long, they celebrated, starting with the special Christmas breakfast of eggs and sausage, then playing games, greeting neighbors, and singing carols while Mama played the piano.

At some point, Rich had belted out the Nixon/Watergate parody of "Jingle Bells."

Everyone wanted to learn it—not so much because it was against Nixon but because it was different, and represented a special connection to a land they had long heard about and would love to live in. As Mama said, their family was linked to Portugal, but every Goan yearned to go to America.

Later that evening, when everyone was tired, Rich went out and returned with a big bag of gifts. "I know this isn't your tradition," Rich said, "but in my family we always exchange gifts." He had asked Frances what he should get her family, and she had explained that they treated Christmas as a day to pray, eat, sing, and get together with friends. It had nothing to do with presents.

Rich reached into the sack and started handing out gifts. Dada, Mama, each of her sisters got one, and Frances was worried that he wouldn't give her a present, even as she felt bad that she hadn't gotten him anything.

"Here, this is for you." Rich gave her the smallest package, wrapped in gold paper. The others had received much bigger ones, and she fretted that this was his way of saying he didn't really care for her—until she saw the ring.

Mama screamed with joy. Dada told her to hush and pointed to Rich. He was on one knee, and, looking at Frances, asked Dada, "Mr. Dias, may I marry your daughter?"

Her sisters teased her that she was going to be just like the twins in the Enid Blyton books they had all read as children. "You will be Mrs. O'Sullivan," they said.

"Frances O'Sullivan sounds downright Irish," Rich had agreed. "Imagine everyone's surprise when they expect a redhead and see Fran."

Mama suggested that they marry immediately, but Rich wanted a proper ceremony in his hometown. He would keep his original plan and return to the States after New Year's. He would work and start saving money, not just for college but for Frances to join him in the summer. By then she would have her BA degree, and she, too, could start applying to study in a university—hopefully Berkeley, he said, crossing his fingers—but, as he told her ecstatic family, "Any place with Fran in it will be fine with me."

He had only kept one part of that plan. He had returned to the United States.

She had forgotten all about that song, and it had been—eons—since a white man had made her look again, to make sure it was, or wasn't, Rich.

"Sing more, Dad, sing more," Lily begged.

"Sorry, can't recall the rest," Jay said. "Ask your mother to sing you the real version."

It was the last thing she wanted to do.

She wished she could tell Jay to turn around, no questions asked, and then, when they got home, let everyone watch a movie while she got into bed by herself.

Instead, she said firmly, "This is not the right time of year to sing Christmas carols," even as her mind was back in Goa. She saw herself waiting by the gate for the postman, heard all their neighbors and friends ask, "When are you going to join your fiancé in America?" Mama was the one who finally told her there was no hope, that Rich was gone, really gone, and would never return for her.

A year later, Mama told her that he had sent a letter. It arrived six months after he had left, was very short, and mentioned that he was busy with school and was sorry but his parents had objected to the marriage. He hoped they would understand and forgive him. Mama never showed her the letter, saying that she had torn it up immediately. For a long time, Frances had wondered whether Rich had sent the letter or whether Mama had made it up so she would stop waiting.

Now, once again she forced herself to stop thinking of Rich. She had enough anxieties today without remembering that earlier, traumatic failure.

"We're almost there," Jay said, thumping the steering wheel with his hands. "Do you think Vic will have sprung for valet parking?" he asked Frances.

"That's like asking if ice is going to be warm," she responded, trying to get back to the familiar territory of Vic being inherently stingy.

"Can ice be warm sometimes?" Lily inquired.

"Don't be a moron," Mandy abjured her sister. "Mom just made up an oxymoron."

"Watch your language," Frances automatically warned her oldest daughter, and Jay added, "Careful, or your mother will wash that word out of your mouth with soap."

"Mom never washes my mouth with soap," Lily said virtuously.

"That's because you're the good daughter," Mandy said.

"Okay, everybody, say good-bye to the freeway," Jay said, as he took the exit. "Let me know as soon as you smell Indian food. We'll let our noses lead us to Uncle Vic's house."

Lily was giggling as Jay started driving down wide streets with huge lawns and obscenely large houses.

"Wow," Lily said, "how many families live in that house?" she pointed to a pale yellow mansion they had just passed.

"Just one," Frances said crisply. She had checked out what houses were going for in Newport Beach. Vic's house didn't face the beach, but a two-story one on his block had recently sold for six million dollars. Vic had probably paid less than half a million when he bought his place years ago. He really had done well for himself.

She and Jay were in the process of refinancing, but they weren't hopeful, because the appraiser had noted that though their house had increased in value, it was in a declining market.

"We just passed 10335," Frances said, "so his house should be three blocks away."

"I think I can smell the Indian food," Jay announced. "Are you excited?"

"I think I hear some music," Frances said, then added urgently, "Park here, park here," pointing to a space on her right.

"I can see some spaces up ahead," Jay said.

"It looks very crowded up there, and this way, it will be easier when we want to leave," Frances lied. She didn't want to park their car amid the BMWs (Brown Man's Wheels, as Jay dubbed them) and Mercedeses that were the preferred cars of the Indians who had made it. In this crowd, she could not get away with saying that she refused to buy German cars because the German companies had never made reparations for using Jewish labor during World War II. Americans would applaud her sensitivity. Indians would understand that she could not afford the luxury cars.

"Okeydokey," Jay agreed, and stopped the car in front of a high wall that hid the house behind it.

"A cat!" Lily pointed to the gray-haired bump that was sitting in the only spot of sun that lit up the dull brown wall. "Here, kitty, here," she called.

The cat didn't move, didn't turn an ear, just kept on crouching.

"Now that's a billy-ant cat," Jay laughed. "He knows how to make the most of the sun. He's just billy-ant. Get it?" he asked Frances, and she shook her head.

"Oh, come on, it's quite brilliant of me if I say so myself. *Billy* is cat in Hindi, so billy-ant? Just like when Lily couldn't say her *r*'s," he reminded her.

"I can say *brilliant*," Lily rejoined.

"I know you can," Jay responded. "I made up that whole story titled 'When Lily Found Her *R*'s.' This cat can say his *r*'s as well. He's billy-ant, I tell you."

The children laughed, and the cat, hearing the noise, rose disdainfully, turned its back to them, and jumped into the yard.

"Come back, Mr. Billyant, come back," Lily begged the cat.

"The cat doesn't speak Hindi," Sam informed his sister. "I'm thirsty, so let's go and find something to drink."

"You're always thinking about your stomach," Lily said. "I just want to see Mr. Billyant one more time."

"Cats aren't dogs, Lily," Jay said. "Even if this one speaks Hindi, he might take a message, but he certainly won't jump over and let you pet him. We'll look for him on the way back, okay?"

A few minutes later, they approached the canopied lawn. Hindi music announced that this was the party house, and the aroma that Jay had wanted to follow was right in front of their noses.

"Wow," Lily said, "it's a big house."

Frances assessed the residence with real estate eyes. Vic indeed had the biggest house on the block. It was probably one of those with an enormous living room that was perfect only when entertaining large groups. The structure had two levels, with dormer windows and a slate roof. There was no fence, though someone must have worried about privacy, because a row of jacaranda trees lined the narrow stretch of land between the street and the cement pathway. The jacarandas were in the last stages of flowering, and the large lawn was scattered with petals. The lawn itself was edged with vivid blue lobelias and white alyssum.

Vic had gone all out, with tables and chairs arranged in clusters. He had covered the tables with nice tablecloths and topped them off with vases of bright flowers that complemented the ones bordering the lawn. The white canopy made the open area cozy and inviting. The rain that Jay had wondered about in the morning wasn't spoiling anything. Vic must have worried about an ocean breeze, because Frances could see the warm, red glow of standing heaters. It was seven o'clock, and the lawn was dotted with people hovering around the heaters; others were sitting at the tables, eating and drinking.

"Your uncle Vic needs a big house because he's having a party, while all the other houses are just, well, houses," Jay joked. He didn't recall Vic's house being this huge. Had Vic moved? Or had Jay not paid attention the time he had dropped off Vic after a lunch?

"No valet," Frances said. She checked the sidewalk. BMWs, Mercedeses, Jaguars, Porsches lined the street, each car pristine and shiny. She was glad she had thought to park farther away. "There is someone greeting people," Jay murmured as they approached the walkway.

"Good evening, good evening," Rajesh shouted above the music. "Please, welcome, come in and annjoy."

"Thanks," Jay said. "Where are Vic and Priya? And Nikhil?" He raised his voice. Just then someone turned down the music and Jay said, "Oh, that's better. Now I will actually be able to hear you. Where's Vic?" he repeated.

"The family is all inside and outside, both. But I am party-of-one welcoming committee."

"You're Vic's brother?" Jay thought he recalled Vic saying he had a younger brother.

"Ha, ha, no, no, I am not sharing any blood relationship with Vic. I am only related by way of marriage. I am Priya's cousin brother from her father's side. Priya and I were raised in the same place. Now also we are living in the same place."

"You live here?" Frances asked. She hoped this meant that Vic had only invited family and friends, rather than everyone and anyone in the Indian community, as she had expected, and feared.

"No, no, I am having my own place. I am selling life insurance. Do you have any?"

Just last week, Frances had discussed it with Jay, and they had decided, once again, to put off buying any until they were doing better.

Before Jay, who every now and then did not think things through, blurted out the truth, Frances said, "Thank you, but we've covered."

"Ah, but is the cover you have the correct one? It is always good to have some more cover. I can give you the very best policy. You can trust me also. We are Indians, so there is nothing but good things between us, is it not?"

Frances looked at Jay. If she responded in the negative, this obnoxious man would simply disregard her words. He would, however, *have* to listen to another Indian male.

"Maybe later," Jay said expansively. "We should go in and see Vic, congratulate Nikhil." The children were fidgeting, and he knew that Sam was aching for a drink. He could see the tubs of soda, and a bartender farther up. It would be nice to begin the evening with a scotch—if Vic had plumped for whiskey.

"Later also is good for me. But in case we are not seeing each other, please to take my card," Rajesh said, taking out his wallet. "Where do you live?"

"Sherman Oaks." Jay hoped that meant they were out of this fellow's jurisdiction, if that was what insurance people had.

"I will be coming to that side next week. If you give me your phone and address, I will come see you at your most convenient time and also give you the best plan."

Jay was wondering how to get out of this without being blatantly rude when he heard a voice from behind Rajesh.

"Uncle Rajesh, are you trying to sell insurance again?" A tall young man now stood beside Rajesh.

"Nikhil?" Jay tested the name. He hadn't seen Nikhil since he was a pimply teenager. The man smiling down at him with perfect teeth also had perfect skin. If he was another one of Vic's relatives, he must have been raised here, because he spoke with an American accent.

"You guessed it. I'm Nick." Nikhil extended his hand. "You're Uncle Jay, right? Thanks for coming. I know it was quite a ride for you to get here."

Frances looked at the kurta and the wide maroon shawl Nikhil had draped around himself. He could be airlifted to any Indian village and would fit in immediately. Vic's son might have brains, but he wasn't Armani-clad. She relaxed a little. So far, it didn't look like a party where guests were going to parade their monetary success and other accomplishments. Even the lights weren't strong enough to expose the bad dye job.

"We couldn't come to your high school graduation party, you know, but we certainly weren't about to miss this one. Congratulations," Frances said, handing him the card.

"Thank you, Aunty Frances." Nikhil slipped the card into his pocket. "My dad loves parties, and I know he's been looking forward to seeing you. You must be Mandy, Lily, and Sam, right?" he pointed to each as if he were a conductor picking off sections of the orchestra.

"How did you know?" Lily asked.

"I met you when your face was about this high," Nikhil indicated his knee. "Now you're taller, but your face is the same."

"You're funny," Lily said.

"He's also got a good memory," Frances said. "You need that to get into MIT." She wanted to mention the MIT degree in the beginning, so it didn't needle her all evening as something her daughter would never accomplish. It was like getting a parking ticket. Jay always told her that it would cause them less grief if they paid it off immediately.

"Don't believe everything you hear about MIT," Nikhil dismissed. "They let anyone in. Legend has it that a dog graduated a few years ago."

"We never heard that one about UCLA," Jay laughed, surprised by Nikhil's modesty. The few American-born Indian children he had met were braggarts whose achievements were stoked by proud parents. He remembered one ten-year-old whose room was filled with the trophies he had won playing soccer. It was only after Mandy joined the local Parks and Recreation basketball team that Jay realized everyone received a trophy of some sort. It wasn't like India, where the winners alone were feted. America created all sorts of commendations, ranging from a Sportsmanship Award to a medal for Best Attitude. It had made him leery—and disdainful—of boasters.

"That's because even the dogs know that you can leave anytime," Nikhil quipped back.

Mandy laughed. Nikhil joined her.

"Did I miss something?" Jay inquired.

"UCLA—U Can Leave Anytime," Mandy explained.

"That's good," Jay said, raising his eyebrows in appreciation for something he hadn't thought up. "How did you know that?" he asked her.

Mandy shrugged, "I dunno."

"I can't claim to have come up with it," Nikhil said, "but it got Dad pretty upset when I was applying to colleges." Then he turned to Mandy and said, "I like teasing Dad because he went there, but it's a great school, in case you're thinking of going there."

"I won't get in," Mandy said flatly.

Frances wished she had the power to reel in her daughter's words. Nikhil was simply making conversation. Mandy did not have to take it seriously. But no, she had to put all her mistakes into her mouth, let him know she would never get in.

Jay heard Mandy's claim with a mixture of discomfort and helplessness, topped with sadness. So Mandy knew she had screwed things up.

"Nah, you'll get in," Nikhil waved his hand. "You're an Indian American, which means you've taken every AP class your school offers and have a 4.5 GPA. And when you take your SATs, you'll ace them."

"We're not supposed to talk about Mandy's grades," Lily offered up into the silence.

All along, Frances had worried that Mandy might, deliberately or not, say something she shouldn't, just to annoy her. But she had never been concerned about Lily. As Mandy often said, Lily was the good daughter, the one Frances was used to counting on. Lily listened, she sat without crushing her dress, she brushed her hair a hundred times every day because Frances had told her it would make it sparkle with health.

Now, suddenly, Lily was speaking out of turn, and out of character.

"Well," Frances said gamely, smiling in spite of the fact that she wanted to gather up her family and run away.

"You're right," Nikhil told Lily, "it's not polite to show off, is it?"

Frances breathed again.

Jay opened his mouth, but before he could produce something that wasn't as empty as Frances's "well," Sam explained, his voice very serious, "Mandy can't show off. She did very badly in school."

Frances felt that the firm ground she was trying to get to was turning into quicksand. Now Sam had joined in, and the irony was that he probably didn't think he was disobeying her. He had nodded with understanding when she explained that they should not tell Mandy's grades to anyone. But he was very literal, and had been that way from a young age.

Jay had first discovered it when playing baseball with two-year-old Sam, who was getting frustrated because he wasn't hitting the ball. Jay assured him that he would do better if he kept an eye on it. Sam had immediately picked up the ball and put it against his face.

It made for cute stories, except for moments such as now. She knew that Sam would think he was following her instructions. After all, he hadn't told Nikhil that Mandy got C's in all her subjects; he had just explained why she couldn't brag, which, in his mind, was not the same thing at all.

Frances tried frantically to come up with a topic, anything, to change the direction of the conversation. She knew that Jay must be trying to do the same thing.

She was still searching for the right words when Nikhil shrugged and told Mandy, "I guess you're going against the stereotype of the superachieving, nerdy Indian American. I tried that in ninth grade and realized it was better to beat those chaps at their own games. They called me names, but in the end I was a name, I mean, of sorts." Nikhil's voice trailed off.

Frances was immediately grateful to Nikhil. He might dress like a typical Indian, but he wasn't acting like one. Frances had expected him to feign concern about Mandy's grades, then use the pretending-to-be-nice phrase "I'm so sorry to hear about this" to ask probing questions, hoping that each answer would confirm that Mandy had, indeed, done poorly. She had witnessed such tactics all her life in India. Mama was an ace at it. If Mama found out that something bad had happened—a failed test, a broken engagement—she would rush over and offer her condolences. But the entire time she was actually trying to elicit information so she could run and tell it to other people. It was only when Frances grew older that she figured out that Mama also used the information to feel better about things in her own life. When Rich never came to get her, Mama insisted that her situation was much better than Denise's, because Denise's fiancé had dumped her to marry her best friend.

Jay heard Nick's throwaway words and felt as if each one was a bulb in one of those linked sequences that, when fully lit, become something unexpected. So *this* was why Mandy was doing badly! Nick had gone through a similar experience and understood Mandy in a way that he never would.

Jay had grown up in a very different environment. Because he came from a wealthy, upper-class family, he was automatically considered the best. Mandy and Nikhil lived in a land where white was still better. America had undergone many changes for the better since he had come to study at UCLA, but, in spite of the improvements, Mandy was the only Indian in her grade. It hadn't mattered when she was seven, eight, nine years old. She never complained, so he assumed nothing was amiss. Had things changed in high school? Had her classmates started teasing her, calling her a nerd? And had she responded by becoming a bad student? How else to understand the dramatic change in her grades? A's one semester, C's the next. It wasn't that Mandy had suddenly stopped trying, as he had feared. If what Nikhil said was correct, she was doing it deliberately to stop the bullying.

He'd have a long talk with her tomorrow, ask if this was true, and, if so, figure out what they should do about it.

Perhaps Mandy did not need to go back to India. If he could help her have the same epiphany as Nick, she could bring up her grades. As he imagined her staying back, he felt his heart lighten, replacing the heavy, hard substance that had taken up residence in his chest ever since he had agreed to Frances's plan.

"What name were you called?" Lily asked Nikhil.

"Valedictorian." Nikhil's answer was lost in a blast of Hindi words as a Bollywood song poured out of the loudspeakers, and then, as if the person who had raised the volume realized it was too loud, the music was turned down to background noise.

"Valedictorian," Nikhil repeated. "It's a long name for someone who has to give a very short speech. My speech was so short it was over before I began it."

"Is that what you are now? A vadelictorian?" Lily asked.

Jay laughed and patted his daughter's hair.

Lily ducked away, waiting for Nikhil's response.

Frances knew that Lily was at the stage where she loved to try out new words. She had no idea, however, that this particular one was wrong. Frances waited for Nikhil to laugh, but he was looking at Lily seriously, either trying to come up with an answer or attempting to figure out the word.

"Then you must like animals," Sam said, not to be left out.

"I do like animals," Nikhil said, "but I prefer the kitchen. I'm going to be a chef."

"I love watching the *Iron Chef*," Lily enthused. "Are you going to be on TV?"

"I don't think so," Nikhil laughed. "This is Newport Beach,

not Hollywood. Did you know that all cooks are mean?" he asked her.

"Really? But Mom isn't mean at all!" Lily wrinkled her forehead.

"I don't know about your mom," Nikhil said, "but I beat the eggs and whip the cream."

"Another good one," Jay laughed.

"Another old one," Nikhil corrected.

"Are you teasing us or are you really going to be a chef?" Jay asked. He had wondered what Nikhil would do with his MIT degree. A high-paying job in New York that allowed him to live in a fancy high-rise? Or was he going to settle into a nice office in Vic's company?

"I'm going to work hard to become a cook," Nikhil clarified. "I hope that means I can call myself *chef* one day."

Frances didn't realize how tense she had felt about meeting the Mighty Indian Triumph. She had dressed her family and herself in their best, just to be able to withstand hearing about his accomplishments. MIT graduates had their pick of jobs, even in a lousy economy. She was fully prepared to learn that Nikhil was going to be starting off at half a million dollars a year, something Jay and she together would never be able to earn. Instead, this tall boy was going to become a chef? Like the multisyllabled *real estate agent*, which elevated her kowtowing job, the moniker *chef* was just a fancy way of saying *cook*. Both jobs served other people.

"That's wonderful," Frances said, her enthusiasm encased with relief that not all MIT graduates ended up in fancy jobs. "If you tell us which restaurant you will be working in, we'll be sure to go there."

"I'm going to be taking classes first," Nikhil said. "I've signed up for the Cordon Bleu in Paris, and then I'm planning to go to Perugia in Italy."

"Like Julia Child," Mandy inserted, adding, "I saw the movie *Julie and Julia*."

"That was a fun movie," Nikhil agreed, smiling, "but Julia Child just wanted to master French cuisine in order to teach Americans. I want to learn French *and* Italian cuisines so I can do fusion cooking—you know, add touches of Western ingredients to Indian recipes and vice versa."

"Sounds weird," Mandy said.

"Mandy," Frances automatically corrected her daughter, but Nikhil wasn't offended.

"Yeah, I know it sounds weird, but fusion is the latest trend in the kitchen. Chefs do a lot with Japanese cuisine and I want to do the same with Indian. Start with French and Italian ingredients, maybe move on to Spanish cuisine. Don't worry, I'm not thinking of making tandoori pizza. It will be more subtle. Anyway, that's the plan."

Suddenly, Frances understood exactly why Mama loved rushing over to hear the latest sob story, and why she stayed until there was no more information to extract. She, too, wanted to know everything, wanted to know whether this was really going to happen, and how Vic felt about it. It would allow her to look Vic in the eye with that much less shame about her own life.

"So you will be going to France this summer?"

"Next week."

"Your father must be so happy that you know what you want to do." Frances heard herself sounding just like Mama and quickly added, "I remember meeting him when he was about your age. He also knew exactly what he wanted to do."

"Dad's old-fashioned," Nikhil shrugged. "He thinks cooking is silly. He's still Indian enough to believe that it's not for men."

"How funny that you would say that, you know," Frances laughed. "We were just talking the other day about the *Iron*

Chef being too sexist. All those men, and not one woman among them."

"I'm glad that Dad's in the minority," Nikhil said, "but I'm hopeful he will come around."

"We can talk to him if you like," Jay offered. "He and I go way back to our graduate days."

"Thanks, but I think I can manage. I just saw a friend of mine, so if you'll excuse me," Nikhil said, his eyes occupied, his hand raised in greeting. "You'll find Dad and Mom somewhere near the front door."

VIC SAW JAY and his family arrive but could not extricate himself from his biker buddies. He had heard the rumble of their accelerators fifteen minutes earlier and watched to see if this time he was correct. Sure enough, a nugget of white faces gleamed amid the mostly Indian guests.

He had only invited them because they had bugged him, and this evening, as the small hand on his watch moved farther and farther from six, he assumed their little show of excitement had been just that, a show, and that they were not going to come. Every other Westerner had already arrived, and by 6:45 he had begun to relax, because he really did not like mixing his guilty pleasure with his family life.

Now they were here, all six of them.

"Pierre," he called out, surprised that they weren't in their usual leather jackets but had worn suits and ties. "Thank you for coming."

"This is some place you've got," Pierre said, eyebrows arched.

"Did you rent it for the occasion?" Antoine laughed.

"Only the chairs and tables and heaters," Vic confessed, then added, "and that canopy. Even though I told my wife it would not rain."

"Wow! You did all this for your son?" Pierre inquired.

"Yes, yes. He is somewhere here, though I cannot see him. But ah, there is my youngest son, who is fourteen years of age. Nandan," Vic called out. "Come meet my friends. They are from France," he told him. Though he wished they hadn't come, he did not want them to feel unwelcome. He thought a quick introduction to his sons would do the job. The men were adults; they could manage the rest of the evening on their own without feeling they were being slighted.

"*Bonsoir et bienvenue*," Nandan said.

"*Vous parlez français?*" Pierre asked.

"*Un peu*," Nandan said, holding his thumb and forefinger an inch part. "*J'ai étudié le français quand j'étais à l'école. Mais pas très longtemps.*"

"Not bad for learning it only in school," Pierre complimented.

"Nandan is quite good in your language," Vic said. "He managed very nicely when we were in Paris. Food, taxis, everything he was doing for us."

"You never told us you have been there," Pierre said. "We could have set you up really nicely."

"As nicely as you set him up at the bar when he got pulled over by the police?" Priya inquired from behind them.

When Vic had scanned the crowd for Nikhil, he had also looked for Priya. Despite what he had told her earlier in their bedroom, he did *not* want to introduce her to them. He did not mind them meeting his sons; there was nothing they could find to tease in Nikhil or Nandan. But these men had a low opinion of women, and he did not want their words to tarnish his wife.

He had also worried that she would say something stupid

that they would bring up later. And sure enough, instead of greeting them in a normal way, she had said the words the Frenchmen claimed made every woman "a real pain to keep around."

Music swirled around them. He took shelter in it. "Nandan, the music is too loud. Go and turn it down," he said, as he tried to figure out how to avoid making the introductions. Should he tell Priya to check on the food? He had every right to, especially after the way she had sneaked up behind him and blurted out the one mistake he had made.

Nandan did not move. "What police?" His voice was heavy with interest.

Vic had forgotten that Nandan did not know about the DUI because he had been away on a school trip. Priya and he decided there was no need to tell him. As Priya said, it isn't good for a son to know his father's frailties.

"Nandan, you need to go and adjust the music so our neighbors don't call the police," Vic said, and only when the sentence was almost complete did he realize his mistake.

"What police?" Nandan repeated.

Vic had often warned his sons that drugs and other illicit things would not be tolerated in his house. He lectured them every now and then that he never wanted them to get in trouble with the police. It wasn't just that he had been an obedient son to his own parents, it was that he himself had never gotten a single parking ticket in all his years in America.

So of course Nandan wanted to know the connection between his father and the dreaded police.

All the pride Vic had felt when Nandan spoke in French fled, and he wanted to slap his son, just as his father's hand would shoot out any time he or his brother did something he did not like. Nandan was deliberately disobeying him, yet he wasn't frightened to do so. Instead, Vic was the one who was uncomfortable. It was, as usual, Priya's fault. She was standing there, her face serene, as if she hadn't uttered the information they had promised each other their children would never know.

"That DUI was pure bad luck," Pierre spoke up. "These American police are pigs. They were just waiting to get someone that night. If I had left the bar earlier, it would have been me."

"You got a DUI? How come I don't know about this?" Nandan demanded. "I knew you went riding with your biker friends, but Mom never told me you stopped off at bars."

Vic raised the glass of whiskey in his hand and drained it in one gulp. He didn't want his biker friends to think he was henpecked *and* chickpecked.

"Nandan, it is time for you to go and lower the sound volume. Who put it up so high? You know I never like the sound to be so loud that people cannot hear each other. Are you responsible for it?" Vic asked, sure of the answer.

"Oh, come on, Dad, it's not a party without music."

"When we have a party for you, you can turn up the sound. But not today. Go now and fix it."

"I know you're saying that to get rid of me, Dad, but I'll go anyway," Nandan said as he left.

"You have a great boy there," Pierre said.

As bad luck would have it, the song ended, and there was a lull before the next one blasted forth.

"Vic—" Priya looked at him and then at the bikers.

He wished he could tell her in Hindi to go away. The lie he had told her in their bedroom weighed down his tongue.

"My wife, Priya," Vic forced the words out of his mouth. "And these are the French fellows I go riding with."

"So you are all from Paris?" Priya asked.

"No, no, only I am from there," Pierre said. "The others are from the South."

"Didn't Vic tell you that you could bring your wives to the party?" she asked.

Vic sighed. Now the men would think it was even stranger that he hadn't told Priya that simple fact about them. If only he could get rid of her. If only he hadn't invited them.

"We are not married, sadly," Pierre shook his head.

"That's too bad," Priya responded.

"We are always teasing your husband that he is married, but of course he is the lucky one. This big house, your son, you. . . . He is a very lucky man."

This time, Vic didn't hear the sarcasm that always accompanied any sentence that had to do with his family. "Oh, yes, you have to go home now because your wife is cold," they ribbed one night when he had wanted to leave because the forecast called for heavy rain.

He was assessing Pierre's tone when Priya spoke: "Well, I think he is also lucky to have you as friends. I know that Vic always wanted a motorbike, but it is lonely to ride alone. I had thought that maybe I should get one to keep him company, but then he met all of you, so now I have to thank you."

"You can join us anytime," Pierre said gallantly, while Vic was still trying to comprehend what Priya had just confessed. She had wanted to go riding with him? Then he remembered that she had told him about a bike show, and had even looked up a few bikes on the Internet. But ride a bike on her own?

"Riding bikes is not for women," Vic said sternly.

"It's not for *some* women," Priya clarified. She paused and then continued, "Like me, for example. Thanks for the invitation to ride with you, but I prefer sitting in a comfortable car."

"Your husband's BMW is very comfortable," Pierre said. "It is not as nice as our Harleys, but you might like it."

"Hey, you two, stop talking as if I am not here," Vic protested.

"Vic, we could never forget that you are here," Priya said. "Don't panic, I will leave your beloved bike in your hands. Now I must make sure that the caterers are doing their job. Please, enjoy yourselves, and if you need anything, don't hesitate to ask us." Priya smiled and walked away.

"You never told us your wife was beautiful," Pierre said.

"Maybe she has a sister?" Antoine asked.

"All her sisters are married to doctors," Vic said and quickly changed the subject. "Let me show you the food and the drinks."

"Didn't you say you have another son?" Pierre asked.

"Yes, yes, the one for whom I am having this party. Ah, I see him there. Nikhil!" he called out. He watched as his son spoke quickly to Jeff, his best friend since kindergarten, and then came toward them.

"These are the people I go riding with," Vic said. "My oldest son, Nikhil, who just graduated from MIT."

"Congratulations. Your father is very proud of you. He tells us you know everything about computers."

"He's the one who is the computer whiz. I'm just a sous-chef."

"Ah, you also know French?" Pierre asked.

"I studied Italian in school, but I picked up a little French because I love your cuisine."

"Enough about food," Vic interrupted. "Let me take you to the bar."

"Dad, did you tell the bartenders to bring some good French wines?" Nikhil asked. "Napa might have won a few prizes, but I'm going to guess your friends would prefer French wines."

"I ordered everything," Vic said. "I am sure they will find something to their liking."

"Well, thank you for coming this evening. I hope you have a good time," Nikhil said.

Lali saw Frances, Jay, and their children walk toward the front door. After being surrounded by people she had never met, and would never meet again, she was thrilled to see the familiar faces of her old friends.

Almost as soon as Thomas left, another man had approached them. Since Thomas had been so well informed and useful, Lali greeted the newcomer with a big smile. It turned out to be a big mistake. The man proved to be the epitome of the droning-on detail-oriented Indian. When he heard that Jonathan had gone to Harvard, he began to tell him about the apartment he had rented when he had worked in Boston for a year. He wasn't content with the general location—he told them the street, apartment number, the bus line, and exactly how long it used to take him to go to the Indian store. He was starting to tell them about the vegetables he had grown, when Lali noticed Frances and Jay.

Unprepared for the gush of emotion that pricked her eyes, she blinked rapidly to hold back the tears. She hadn't seen them in decades, and they hadn't spoken for almost that long, yet, as their faces became clear in the dark, she was happy. She had been thinking of this encounter, had visualized Frances looking her up and down, when she selected her black dress. She wanted to look her best, wanted to dispel any image Frances might have of "poor Lali."

Now the old immigrant days, when they were young and new to America, returned. They had helped each other in so many ways. Frances had never before written a paper, because her college in Hyderabad only gave exams. She had come to Lali in tears, saying she was too embarrassed to ask her professor for help. Lali had explained the footnotes and bibliography and had shown her how to create a title page. Lali, meanwhile, had been plagued with foot pain, because the slippers she had brought for daily use had thin soles, not suited for concrete sidewalks and pathways. If this were India, she would have had a cobbler add some rubber to the soles. She had asked a few of her classmates whether there were cobblers around, but they said that only the extremely rich in America had the luxury of wearing made-to-order shoes. The general population went to shops that sold ready-made shoes, and no, they told her, she would never find a cobbler on a street corner.

Lali had exposed her aching, bruised feet to Frances, who had been wonderful. She immediately lent her a pair of shoes; then she took her shopping for a new pair. It was so much easier to answer the salesman's questions, to size her feet, with a friend. The shoes were the first purchase she had made in America. She was still equating dollars to rupees, so she thought that forty dollars for sturdy walking shoes was cheap. How they laughed the following year when they walked past the same store, because by then they were savvy shoppers, looking for sales and discounted, out-of-season merchandise, and would never spend that much money on shoes.

Frances had urged her to throw away her slippers, and Lali had put all but the *kolhapuris* into the trash. Even in India, *kolhapuris* were special, and she liked wearing them on occasion.

They had often made meals together, and since neither of them had been taught to cook by their mothers ("our only similarity," Frances used to claim), they would put teaspoons of curry powder into every dish and declare the outcome authentic.

Jay and Vic were the only ones who knew that Frances and Lali were terrible cooks. But they all longed for Indian cuisine, and because they could not afford to eat out often, the men (who couldn't cook at all) were forced to put up with their cooking. Jay was the worst complainer. He used to say that while American food lacked taste, their food only had one taste: curry powder. One time Frances, who preferred sandwiches to anything Indian but nonetheless cooked curries for Jay, decided to play a trick on him.

He often wondered how she could have lived in India all her life and not be able to tolerate chilies—except in pork vindaloo, a Goan specialty. "When it comes to eating spicy food, Frances has a white tongue," Jay used to laugh.

Frances told Lali what she planned to do, and together they made Jay a special meat dish—with ten chilies. Jay took a big mouthful of rice and meat, only to open and close his mouth like a fish, gasping in pain. That was when Frances taught Lali yet another trick. She gave Jay some sugar to blanket the hot taste of the chili, instead of the water that Lali had ready.

All those memories burst through her mind like fireworks, and she couldn't pay attention to the long list of vegetables the garrulous man had grown in his tiny patch of garden. Frances and Jay were here, along with their children, who until now had been only names on a page.

The party was truly beginning.

"I just saw my friends," she told the still-talking man, grabbed Jonathan's hand, and rushed away.

"Frances! Jay! You finally made it!" Lali ran across the grass, careful to lift up her heels with every step.

"Lali Manali," Jay said as he kissed her cheek. "*You* finally made it to Southern California."

"I had to come because you never bothered to drive up north," Lali shot right back. "Frances, it's been ages," Lali said, hugging her.

Frances was still chafing from Mandy's brazen confession and hadn't prepared herself to see her old friend. She had tried to spot Lali from the moment they arrived but had been looking for someone in a saree. Though she had encouraged her friend to switch from salwar kameezes to jeans when they were students, Lali had worn sarees to every special occasion. She had even worn a blue one to graduation, and so many people came up and complimented her that she told Frances she wished she had worn the interview suit she had bought.

Lali was wearing a beautifully cut black dress, with strappy, fashionable heels. Frances realized she had actually seen Lali in the crowd but had assumed the woman was another Western-dressing Indian.

Nothing was turning out as she had expected.

Taken aback by the totally fashionable person hugging her, Frances responded with a banal, "You look exactly the same," though it was blatantly false. Lali might be dressed well, but her dark circles had grown darker. She also had an unfortunate haircut. Lali had once told Frances that her face was too Indian to carry off a Western cut. She should have followed her instinct. Lali had looked much lovelier with the long braid that used to hang down her back as far as her hips.

"I know I don't, but thank you for the kind words," Lali said, patting her midriff. She had been the chunkier one, had always struggled to lose pounds. "You actually do look the same. Did you even gain a single pound when you were pregnant?"

"She gained the pounds all right," Jay laughed, "but I kept them." He patted the soft bulge around his belt. "All part of the 'no food left behind' diet."

Lali laughed and gave the pat answer she had heard when she was young: "Which means Frances has more of you to love." She had been ecstatic—filled with memories of the old days—when she saw them, but now she didn't know how to get past the stilted, trite conversation that made them almost strangers.

"I wish Frances would see it that way," Jay complained. "Why is it that charity never begins at home?"

"I thought charity *always* begins at home," Jonathan said, as he joined the conversation.

"Honey, once you get to know Jay, you will realize that he always likes to turn things upside down," Lali told her husband. As soon as she said the words, she was swaddled in the comfortable familiarity of the old days.

"And now what I want to know is, how come we never met *you*?" Jay asked Jonathan. "One minute Lali was in Los Angeles, the next she was getting married up in the San Francisco area. She didn't even invite us to the wedding," he mock-grumbled.

"Well, we didn't invite anyone except ourselves," Jonathan replied.

Lali could tell that Jay was a little taken aback by Jonathan's response. Jonathan didn't realize he was supposed to laugh at Jay's comment, not take it seriously. At the same time, it was nice to have someone speak for her. When she used to hang around with Frances and Jay, she had always been the *kebab mein haddi*, the bone in the kebab, though they were too polite to make her feel she was intruding. Now she, too, had someone. They were finally equals. She moved closer to her husband.

There was a brief pause, then insouciant Jay recovered enough to say, "Ah, but we are not just *anyone*. Lali was there to see us get hooked and cooked. I, for one, really wanted to see Lali get hooked, cooked, and curried, but alas, no invitation."

So this, Frances scrutinized the man standing in front of her, was Lali's cardiologist husband. He was smiling, holding Lali's hand, their shoulders almost touching. She had, for some reason, pictured a tall American. Jonathan was short, with short hair and a clean-cut face that looked young. He was good looking, but, because of his height, would not command the same attention Lali's previous boyfriend used to get every time he walked down Westwood Boulevard.

Frances wanted to know more about him, but instead of taking this chance to find out things, Jay was harping on about not being invited to the wedding. She, too, had felt slighted, but Lali had explained that it was a small, two-person affair.

"Oh, Jay, that was so long ago," Frances said. "Let it go. We're just happy to finally meet you," she told Jonathan.

"Ditto here. It's funny, though, that you're a woman. When Lali would talk about her friends Frances and Jay, I thought you were American, and, well, gay."

"Really?" Frances shot a look at her children.

Lali saw her unease and quickly said, "Jay may go on and on about not coming to our wedding, but I've never met any of your children. And you went and had three! Aren't you lucky!"

"We started after you," Frances reminded Lali. "I was sure we'd be playing catch-up."

Lali felt as if every word was slowly erasing the smile on her face. She had, quite unexpectedly, given that she had married later, beaten Frances in the motherhood race. But after that easy pregnancy, she had suffered four miscarriages. The final one had been the worst. She had awakened Jonathan in the middle of the night and was so weak from losing blood that she fainted. They didn't need the gynecologist to suggest they stop trying. They would be content with one child. At least she had ensured the Feinstein name.

"Frances is a Catholic and wanted to have a dozen kids," Jay explained. "I reminded her that Jesus never had any children, so he would understand if we stopped at three, which of course is a mystical number in Hinduism, though, in deference to Frances, I like to think of it as the Father, the Son, and the Holy Ghost."

Frances sighed. "See what I've been coping with all these years?"

"Aren't you going to introduce us to your trio?" Lali tightened her grip on Jonathan's hand, and he squeezed hers in response. When they were first married, they had talked of creating their own basketball team.

"This is Amanda, our first attempt, though we call her Mandy. Lily is our second child, our little flower, and this fellow here, Sam, is the one who gets to carry on the family name." Jay stood behind each child as he introduced them.

Lali looked at Mandy's bored face, at the big smile on Lily's face, at Sam's darting eyes. She didn't want to ask them the obvious "How old are you?" "What grade are you in?" questions, the adult versions of which she had just suffered through.

"Mandy, did you want to come here today or did your parents drag you?" she asked, and Mandy, who seemed to be fascinated by something at her feet, immediately looked up at her.

"Still trying to make *gul-mul*, huh, Lali Manali?" Jay shook his head. "This time you won't be able to stir up any trouble. Mandy was looking forward to coming this evening."

"I wanted to come," Lily said. "I wanted to wear my red shoes."

"And I wanted to drink sodas and Indian drinks," Sam announced.

"And I want to know where your son is," Jay said, "or am I not *invited* to meet him?"

"Aaron is still in Boston," Lali said, freeing her hand from Jonathan's grip. She didn't look at her husband as she searched in her purse for the picture. She now wished she hadn't picked the photograph of Aaron wearing his Harvard T-shirt.

"Oh, yes, I forgot that, like Vic, you are experiencing the empty-wallet syndrome," Jay laughed.

"Here's the person who has emptied our nest, and our wallets." Lali handed the photograph to Frances.

"Just one picture?" Jay remonstrated.

Frances turned the photograph this way and that, trying to view it in the best light. The crimson sweatshirt was just like the red flag that matadors use to incite bulls. The large HARVARD letters emblazoned on his chest stirred her jealousy, and she had difficulty breathing, as if envy constricted her airway. *Her* children were supposed to be the ones doing brilliantly. Instead, they were rushing Mandy to India, going backward, to try to get her on the path that Lali's son was on.

Frances said the first thing that came into her mind: "He looks like you."

"Poor fellow," Jay commiserated. "Imagine looking like Lali for the rest of his life. Let me see," he peeped at the photograph, then exclaimed, "You need to check your eyes, Frances. He looks nothing like Lali, thank God. He's as handsome as his father."

Frances looked, for the first time, at the face above the sweatshirt. Jay was correct. Aaron was as white as Jonathan, and though she could not see his eyes, the blond hair indicated they were blue. Once she had dreamed that her children would look like this. From the time she was young, she had known that it was better to look, act, be Western. Goans were very proud of their Portuguese heritage and felt superior to Indians because their forefathers had blue, green, hazel eyes. Frances used to be jealous of her older sister's brown eyes, the reason her parents had named her Hazel.

When her sisters had teased her about becoming Mrs.

O'Sullivan, they had also told her that her children might be white-skinned and blue-eyed.

It was surprising that Lali, who had the sort of skin Mama used to say was so dark it was no use hiding out from the sun, had a fair, American-looking son. He would never be called a "sand nigger," never have to worry about being shunned because he was different. In post-9/11 America, all brown-skinned people were suspects. She had seen a number of clients relax visibly when she assured them that she wasn't Middle Eastern and had been raised in India because her Portuguese ancestors had settled there.

"And he must take after his father in the brains department, too," Jay continued. "Didn't you do your medical studies at Harvard?" he asked Jonathan. He wanted to bring out the famous university early in the conversation. He knew what it was like to belong to an elite society. Was Jonathan a boastful type or would he act normal?

"Guilty," Jonathan said.

"So if anything goes wrong today, medically speaking, we can count on you, right?" Jay confirmed.

"I'll do my best," Jonathan responded.

The short answers assuaged Jay. He didn't need to worry that Jonathan would look down at his MBA from U Can Leave Anytime. Harvard, of course, was too high and mighty a school to have its name parodied.

"Let's get something to eat and drink," Frances suggested. She hadn't had anything since lunch and was hungry and thirsty.

"That's a great idea," Jay said. "Let's toast to our finally getting together, shall we? Sam, Lily, get your beloved sodas and come meet us here."

"Mandy, you can get a soda too." Frances did not understand why Jay had excluded her.

"Today's special." Jay's voice was replete with indulgence. "I'm getting Mandy her first Cosmopolitan. Would you like that?" he asked, belatedly hoping she would agree. Sometimes he forgot that his children, because they were raised in America, would not consider drinks, so common here, a treat. For all he knew, Mandy had already tried wine, beer, and who knows what else. Liquor was easy to acquire in America, unlike in India, where the good stuff either wasn't available or was expensive, while the cheap *daroo* was too dangerous to drink.

"Sure," Mandy shrugged.

"You men get the drinks," Lali said. "We'll fill up some plates. That way we can beat both lines." Jonathan and she had been lucky. They had come so early that they didn't have to deal with the crowds.

"Mandy, can you go with your sister and brother and make sure they're all right?" Frances was relieved when Mandy nodded and followed her siblings.

"Have you seen Vic?" Frances asked Lali as they made their way toward the food.

"Saw him as soon as we arrived. Priya, too." And just like that, it felt as if they were back at UCLA, walking together, chatting about other people. They had always enjoyed doing a postmortem after any party or dinner. This time they were doing it beforehand.

"I met her when she first came," said Frances. "I can't believe it's been more than ten years since I last saw her. Jay and I kept meaning to have them over for dinner, you know, but every time we called, Vic was busy, and then I had Lily and Sam so close together. Jay is the one who has kept in touch. He drives down about once a year to have lunch with Vic. Tell me, what's Priya like? She had learned to speak English, but, if I recall correctly, was one of those who never wanted to leave India."

"She must have changed her mind, because she fits in very nicely," Lali said. "And her English is excellent. She sounds like us, actually. I thought Vic had married a convent-educated girl rather than some villager his parents chose."

"I thought she'd remain one of those saree-wearing types who smiles all the time because she'd rather not speak English."

"You're right about the saree," Lali said. "but it's very elegant. Not one of those gaudy ones dripping with *zaree*," she added, eyeing a red saree, its bright color in competition with the gold threads that covered every inch.

Frances laughed and said, "That saree reminds me of the invitation."

"All that gold must have been Vic's taste. I'm telling you, Priya seems very much like us. If you haven't seen her in years, then you mustn't have met Vic's children." Lali was curious about them. Were they stereotypical products of immigrant parents or were they Americanized?

"We met Nikhil when we first walked in. He rescued us from Priya's cousin." Frances put some pakoras on the plate.

"Oh my God, did he try to get you to buy life insurance too?" Lali laughed. "Jonathan was getting caught in the 'I have the best quote' line when Vic saved us. He ordered Priya's cousin not to bother people. I guess that cousin isn't a good listener."

"Jay and I were on the brink of being rude when Nikhil appeared."

"I think we have enough food," Lali said, surveying the plates they had loaded with samosas and pakoras, making sure to ladle on some chutney. "I shouldn't be eating this oily stuff, but it's too tasty to resist."

"Can your husband handle spicy food?" Frances asked.

"This stuff isn't spicy. Vic told us he ordered food that everyone can eat. But Jonathan isn't your typical white guy. He's actually better than *you*, 'Miss I can't eat hot chilies,'" Lali said. "On our first date, we went to a Vietnamese restaurant, and he didn't flinch at the chilies. I thought they were a bit spicy, but he kept eating."

"After living with Jay so long, I've gotten accustomed to spicy food. It's funny how I could always eat my pork vindaloo but never anything else that had chilies in it. Too bad Vic's a vegetarian. I'd love to have some pork vindaloo today."

"I had never eaten vindaloo until you made it for us. People in Kerala eat a lot of beef, but hardly any pork. Hey, is it true that Goans don't have indoor toilets and let the pigs eat their poop?"

"Where did you hear such nonsense?" Frances asked.

"From this Goan girl I met who was raised in New Delhi. She said she used to freak out every time she visited her relatives. She would go to the bathroom and the pigs would come running and she could hear them eating the you-know-what. Then afterward, her uncle would kill the pig and expect her to eat it. Gross."

"Not just gross. It's false," Frances lied.

She had grown up like that but would never, ever admit to it. She had even kept quiet about it in Hyderabad. Back then, it was because Hyderabad had a large Muslim population, and she didn't want to remind people that she ate pork. In America, she didn't want anyone to think that she came from a backward home. Lali's reaction confirmed her suspicion, and she was glad that she hadn't mentioned this part of her growing up. Lali would think her home was worse than Vic's village. She preferred that people imagine beaches when thinking of Goa.

"Wonder why that girl lied to me?" Lali said.

"Here come the men," Frances said, glad to get away from Lali's questions. "And here come Lily and Sam. Where's Mandy?" she asked as Lily joined them.

"Mandy's talking to Nick, Mom," Lily answered. "She said she'd come soon."

"Can I have another soda?" Sam asked.

"If you drink too much soda, the food will drown in your stomach." Jay picked up a samosa and sighed with satisfaction. "Good food, a great drink, and oh, yes, not bad company."

"Here's to you, too," Lali raised her glass of wine.

"To the Gang of Four," Frances said. "Jonathan, we're making you an honorary member because Vic isn't here."

"Thanks. I'll drink to that."

"Delicious pakoras," Lali said. "I can't seem to stop eating them."

"Hey, save some for me," Jay said as he playfully grabbed some.

"Actually, I should give you all of mine. We ate when we first got here," Lali said.

"They also met Vic and Priya," Frances said.

"I've been keeping my left eye out for Vic," Jay said, "but every time I turn around, I see his wife's cousin. There he is, probably trying to con someone else into buying life insurance."

They looked at Rajesh and watched as he swayed and then sat down very quickly.

"He doesn't look well," Jonathan said.

"Oh, he's not sick. He's probably drinking too much. I guess Lali hasn't told you that Indians love free booze. I think airlines started charging for liquor because Indians drank too much," Jay said. "See that glass in his hand? The cousin is taking full advantage of the open bar. If he's not careful, he's going to be out of commission before dinner is served."

"I hope he has a ride," Jonathan said.

"He'll probably crash in one of Vic's many bedrooms. I won't be surprised if Vic himself gets smashed. He never drank when we were students, but since then I've seen him put away three drinks by the time I've had one."

"You're driving us home, Jay," Frances reminded him, "so you'd better stop at one."

"Yes, ma'am," Jay saluted. "See what an obedient husband I am? Ah, here comes Mandy. One Cosmopolitan for the lady." Jay handed her the glass.

"Can I have a sip, can I have a sip?" Sam begged.

"When you're seventeen, you can have more than a sip," Jay said firmly. "Until then, it's water, and soda on special occasions."

"Mandy, can I have a sip?" Sam boldly flouted his father.

"No."

"Then I'll tell Griffin you were talking to Nikhil tonight," Sam threatened.

Frances wished she had left the children at home. Sam and Lily had already opened up the can of C's that was Mandy's report card. Now Sam was hitting back at his sister because she was doing the right thing by not letting him have a sip. Mandy was so volatile these days that Frances had no idea how she would react to her brother teasing her in public.

Jay ruffled Sam's hair. "Never believe what comes out of the mouths of babies."

"I'm not a baby." Sam jerked away. "I'm wearing a suit. I'm almost all grown up."

Everyone laughed, and Frances hoped that meant the potentially tense moment had passed.

Then she heard Lily. "Nikhil's not Mandy's boyfriend, silly. He's Mom and Dad's friend."

"Griffin won't like it," Sam persisted.

"You're so lame," Mandy said, rolling her eyes. "Griffin's gay."

"What's gay?" Sam asked.

"Someone who's happy," Frances said quickly. "Go get another soda." Now everyone would think Mandy was an idiot who hung out with gay classmates. Frances wasn't so Catholic that she objected to gays because of the Bible. She just didn't like giving the impression that her young daughter was spending time with a gay boy. It made Mandy seem like a social loser.

Jay initially thought Mandy was just fobbing off her siblings. But she was serious. Was Griffin really gay?

Jay felt like a fool. He had thought that Griffin liked Mandy, that they were boyfriend–girlfriend, as they used to say in India. Why was Griffin hanging out with Mandy if that wasn't on his mind? Nikhil's comment resurfaced. Classmates must have teased Mandy. They must also have teased Griffin. Both were oddballs. Was that the glue in their togetherness? They kept each other safe from the mean comments and knowing laughter?

"I remember the days when one soda could make me happy," Jonathan said, looking at Sam's retreating back.

"Oh, yes, I know that feeling," Jay said, relieved to move onto another topic. "I was pretty young when India kicked out Coca-Cola, but how I loved Thums Up. My mother would want me to drink homemade lemonade, but of course I wanted the shop-bought soda."

"I grew up drinking fresh coconut water. My father hardly ever bought us any sodas. He told us they were made with dirty water and were bad for us," Lali said. "He was lying about the water, but it turns out he was right about all that sugar and stuff not being good for us."

"I guess your dad and mom didn't buy too many snacks, either," Jonathan nudged Lali. "Remember how you'd go shopping when we were first married and I'd ask you where the snacks were and you'd give me a blank stare?"

"No, I'd give you fruits and nuts," Lali reminded him. "I still think those are the right snacks to eat. Not the chips and cookies and other packaged stuff that is filled with salt and preservatives."

"I thought salt *was* a preservative," Jay said.

"That was in Roman times, Dad," Mandy said.

"Uh, oh, am I embarrassing you with my lack of Western knowledge?" Jay asked Mandy. Then he told the others, "I can't tell you how many times I've been told I don't have an American sense of humor, or I don't know something because I was raised in India."

"Aaron tried the same thing with me," Lali laughed. "I squashed it right out of him. I was so angry that his school only taught the Greeks and Romans that I went in and told them all about Mohenjodaro and Harappa."

"Aaron and I had a good laugh when we watched *My Big Fat Greek Wedding*. Have you seen it?" Jonathan asked the others. "Remember when the father says that every word comes from Greek, and the girl asks him, 'What about *kimono*?' Well, for years Lali would say that every good thing, from the decimal point to plastic surgery, came from India. It reached a stage where before she could even give us the answer, Aaron would say, 'Yes, Mom, I know, it's from India.'"

"Hey, easy for you to laugh, but we immigrants have to stick up for where we came from," Jay said, glancing at Mandy. She was listening intently, not with the bored, faraway look she often had.

"What makes you think I'm any different?" Jonathan inquired. "Jews aren't exactly mainstream Americans."

"But you didn't have quotas keeping you out," Jay said.

"Of course we had quotas. I couldn't have gone to Harvard a hundred years ago, and there are still some country clubs in America that won't allow me to join. Not that I'd want to join them, but it's the principle."

"I didn't know that," Jay was shocked to learn. He had assumed that Jews were as American as apple pie but with the added topping of being good academically. Lucy and the other neighbors had never let on that they did not fully belong.

"I THOUGHT JAY knew everything," Priya smiled as she joined them. "Jay, Frances, thank you for coming tonight. And for bringing the children."

"Good to see you, finally," Jay said. "And, for your information, I *do* know everything."

"Or so he likes to think." Frances made a face. "Priya, thanks for inviting us. It's a beautiful party."

"It was all Vic's idea." Priya raised her palms as if she had nothing to do with it. "I thought we should go on a family cruise, but Vic won."

"Is he still working nonstop and not taking vacation days?" Jay laughed.

"No, no. I force him to take three weeks every summer. Then I look at the map, pick a country, and off we go."

"Good for you." Frances was still getting used to Priya's poise and perfect English. Lali was correct. This Priya did not look or act as if she had been born in a small village.

She also wasn't bragging about her life. Frances had met numerous well-to-do Indians who liked to share their love of travel by listing the countries they had visited, including museums and palaces. It was one of the reasons she and Jay no longer sought out other Indians. Priya was simply being factual, not prideful. Her entire demeanor was sweet, and she seemed genuinely pleased to see them.

Frances sighed softly. So far, both Lali and Priya had proved her wrong. In spite of the behavior of her children, this might be a party she actually enjoyed.

"It's good for Vic," Priya said, "I don't work, so I don't really need a vacation. I do it for him."

"You do what for me?" Vic's voice boomed from behind Priya. But instead of waiting for her answer, he greeted Jay and Frances.

"Ah, here you are. I was wondering if today also you would not show up. But you are here. And you already have some drinks. Good, good. Please, eat and drink. Just like old times," Vic said contentedly.

All evening long, people had been congratulating him not just because of Nikhil but also because the food, the tables, the drinks, everything, they assured him, was top-notch. He told them that Priya had arranged the outdoor space, and every time he gave her the accolade, he felt his anger at her shrinking. His other main anxiety, the bikers, seemed to be doing fine, easily chatting with other groups. Slowly, he had started to enjoy himself without constantly checking to ensure that everything was going well. Now he was even happier, because his college friends had taken the trouble to come to the party.

"With a few modifications," Jay patted his belly, "and some additions," he indicated Jonathan and Priya.

"What old times, Vic?" Lali wrinkled her brow. "I don't ever remember you throwing a party at UCLA."

"Vic was too busy planning his company to plan a party," Jay said.

"I never understood those American students," Vic said, shaking his head. "Instead of studying, they were having parties. I did not want to waste one erg of my energy doing that. I would only go for a short time." He smiled at Lily and Sam. "It is good you came and that you also brought your children." The two looked as bored as Nandan did when they dragged him to parties. "Why don't you go inside the house? We just made a game room for Nandan. You can play Wii and Xbox and PS2 and also there is a TV. He will not mind if you play with his things."

"Can we go?" Lily asked her parents.

"You have legs, so of course you *can* go," Jay answered. "The question is, 'May we go?'"

"Let them go," Vic butted in. "Ah, this is your oldest girl. Hello, hello. You can also go see if there is anything to your liking in the game room."

"May we go?" Sam asked.

"Of course, but stay there until we come and get you. And don't break anything."

"Not to worry," Vic said, patting Jay's shoulders. "This is like their house. Let them also have a good time."

They watched the three hurry away, and Vic had just started to say something when he was interrupted.

"Good wine, Vic," Pierre said, raising his glass as he passed by. "Tell your son we Frenchmen approve very much."

"Your biker friends haven't left the bar since they went there," Priya informed Vic.

"So?" Vic shrugged his shoulders. "They like to drink."

"You have biker friends?" Jay inquired. "Don't tell me you've gone and joined Hell's Angels!"

"No, no, nothing like that. They are simply these French people I go motorbiking with," Vic explained.

"You're joking, right?" Jay asked.

"Oh, no." Priya answered as Vic took another sip. "One day Vic came home with a BMW motorcycle, and the next week he was riding off to San Diego with his new friends."

"They are not really my friends," Vic clarified. "I only go riding with them.

"Like those girls at UCLA?" Jay teased. Vic really liked to keep things separate. At UCLA he had ridden girls but had insisted they were not his girlfriends.

"You had girlfriends?" Priya narrowed her eyes.

"Don't believe Jay. I never had a single girlfriend."

"Is that true?" Priya asked Jay.

"So he told me," Jay joked, then relented and said, "It's true. I was the bad Indian with a girlfriend, and Lali, here, in case you're wondering, Jonathan, had the same girlfriend I had—Frances. Lali was just like Vic the Straight Stick. She didn't have a boyfriend."

"Oh, I wouldn't mind if she did have one. I'm just glad she married me," Jonathan said, as he put his arm around Lali.

Lali looked at Frances. So she hadn't told Jay about Aakash, after all. Or if she had, Jay, thank God, was pretending he didn't know. She felt a warm, thankful connection to her friends and allowed that to drown the guilt that had risen. Every now and then, she scanned the crowd in case Aakash decided to crash the party. She didn't think he would, but she wanted to be prepared if he showed up.

"And I'm just glad Vic's son graduated, because it brought the gang together," Jay said. "I'll get a refill so we can make another toast."

"Let me do it while you play catch-up," Jonathan offered.

"Whiskey for me," Vic held out his glass, "on the rocks."

"Vic," Priya said softly, "you have enough to make a toast."

"Frances, Lali, what are you going to have?" Vic disregarded his wife. This was the second time she was embarrassing him in front of his friends. He wasn't drunk. This was only his second glass of whiskey. He wanted to have a good time, and just because she never drank, it did not mean that he was going to become all pious.

"Tonight is very special. My son has become a graduate of MIT and all my friends in America are here with me. Where is Nikhil?" he asked Priya. "He must come and join us. These are the first people I met when I came to UCLA."

"I don't know where he is," Priya said tightly.

"Go find him," Vic ordered. "Tell him I want him to meet my oldest friends."

"We've met him," Frances said quickly.

"Nikhil did a great job welcoming us," Jay added. Vic had always been able to hold his liquor. Had that changed?

Jonathan returned with refills, and Vic raised his glass. "To my friends. Thank you for coming. So, tell me," he turned to Jonathan, "was the food okay for you so far?"

"Loved it all," Jonathan said.

"I think Lali loved the pakoras the best," Jay said. "Here, eat some more," he said, holding the plate toward her.

"Satan, get thee behind me," Lali protested.

"I will never understand you Christian types," Jay lamented. "You think your Jesus meant that Satan should leave Him alone. But I think He wanted Satan to get behind Him, take His side."

"You're worse than a pagan," Lali informed Jay.

"That I may be, but if I want to eat some pakoras, I better stand *in front* of you, otherwise you will gobble them up."

"Enough, enough," Lali said. Jay never seemed to recognize when his comments went from funny to hurtful.

"Please eat your fill," Vic said. "I have ordered plenty of food. Rajesh," he called out, "make sure those idiot caterers are keeping the table filled with pakoras and samosas. Go get some more," he told Lali, "or I can have Rajesh bring you some."

"I've had enough, thank you." Lali was embarrassed.

Rajesh hurried over and said, "I just now only checked, and there is plenty of everything."

"Good. Find out when they are planning to serve the dinner food," Vic told Rajesh, who scuttled away.

"He's sweating an awful lot," Jonathan said. "Is he all right?"

"You must not worry about Rajesh," Vic said. "He is Priya's cousin, and since he is the only member of our extended family present today, he is running around being important." Vic didn't want them to know that Rajesh liked his drink. He had warned Rajesh not to get drunk, and the idiot had nodded happily, all the while holding a beer in his hand.

"My cousin came a little early today because he knew we might like his help," Priya added. "He's been busy running around all afternoon."

"I'm glad you have some help," Jay said. "Looks like you invited the entire town."

"How many people *have* you invited?" Jonathan asked.

Lali knew that her husband was amazed by the sheer number of people. "It's bigger than most weddings," he told her, and she had responded, "Oh, if this was Nikhil's wedding, Vic would fly in his entire family *and* invite everyone he has ever met. And the celebration would probably last all day, not just a quick dinner."

"This is a small party," Vic shook his head. "Only 150 people. Nikhil did not want more than a hundred, but I told him that was impossible. You see, he had to invite his friends. He knows many people in Newport Beach because he studied here from elementary school right up to high school. There are also some people from MIT who live in the area, and then the boys he used to swim with. I wanted him to invite *anyone* he wanted to. Then I had to call all my friends, and also my workers. These days, I am a member of the Indian Chamber of Commerce and some other organizations, so those people, too, I invited. But, as you can see, I made sure to invite many, many Americans. Most of them I am knowing through work, and some are working for me. Ah, I see one of them there. He is an interesting fellow who has visited India. He is working in my PR department and is useful because he knows Spanish and is also knowing a little about our culture. Let me call him here so you can meet him. Ricardo!" Vic shouted.

"We can meet him later," Jay said. He wanted to spend time with the gang, not incorporate a new face. He had been relieved that the Frenchmen hadn't intruded into their group. At another time, he would have wanted to chat with the bikers, hear some stories about this new Vic who rode a bike, but not today.

"No, no, he has asked especially to meet you. When I was telling him that you had lived near Delhi, he was most interested that I arrange an introduction. He spent some time in that area and does not get many chances to talk about that. Ricardo! Ricardo!"

This time the gray head turned, and nodded, before starting toward them.

Lali and Frances exchanged glances. Vic was so inept socially. Lali wondered if he had Asperger's—he definitely did not pick up clues. Priya, poor thing, was just standing by, a smile on her face.

"Ricardo, you wanted to meet my good friends from UCLA. This is Jay, the one I told you studied in Delhi."

"*Namaste*," Ricardo said.

Lali sighed. This man was probably going to stick around, forcing them to listen to details of his India trip, the anecdotes punctuated with the few Hindi words he remembered, like his badly pronounced "*namaste*." She was tired of meeting people who had traveled to India and who assumed she would be riveted by the experiences that had fascinated them. As she told Jonathan one day after listening to a long account of a train ride, "I've lived there and know the place. I'd much rather hear about Hungary or Sweden or Alaska."

Jay was just about to pick up the social baton that clueless Vic had dropped and introduce the others when Priya smoothly took over and said, "Ricardo, this is Jonathan, who is married to Lali," she indicated Lali, "and the lady next to Lali is Jay's wife, Frances."

"Frances?" Ricardo peered, shaking his head sideways as if brushing away strands of hair. "Fran Dias?" Then he said, "Oh, my God, I don't believe it. It's you. Wow! Oh my God, I have to get my wife. Wait a minute. Don't move. Stay right there. She's going to be blown away. I'll be right back."

FRANCES STARED AT his retreating back. Her own back was clammy, and her heart had accelerated so quickly that the sound blanketed out the music and loud conversations all around her. She had been so concerned that people would poke their noses into Jay's job, Mandy's grades, the upcoming trip to India. She had never thought to worry that her past would be standing before her.

Ricardo was Rich, the man who had proposed to her, who had sung that stupid song about Nixon, who had abandoned her. She had thought about him only a few hours ago, and here he was, gray and pudgy and rushing off to get his wife.

"You know him?" Jay and Vic asked together.

She was saved, temporarily, from answering, because Rich had already returned, dragging a woman who looked Indian—and annoyed.

"Carmen, this is Frances," Rich explained to his wife.

"Hello." Carmen extended her hand, her voice evenly civil, though her face hadn't lost its tight, "Why have I been dragged here?" expression.

Frances was limply shaking the other woman's fingers when Rich said, "Carmen, it's Frances—you know, Frances from India."

"Oh my gooooosh!" Carmen exclaimed, and kept on shaking Frances's hand.

Jay had no idea what was going on. He thought he knew everyone Frances knew.

Lali watched the tableau with amusement, a little puzzled that Frances was not delighted to meet an old friend.

"Ricardo told me so much about you," Carmen said. "He said your family was related to that famous explorer—what was his name, sweetheart?" she asked her husband.

"Bartolomeu Dias. Fran's father told me he was their first known ancestor."

"I remember. I was so jealous, because my family has no one famous. We don't even know if we are Spanish or Indian. So when Ricardo told me you are Indian, and Portuguese, I was, oh, very jealous. But now enough time has passed that we can all be friends."

"Isn't it amazing?" Ricardo spread out his hands. "Vic was telling me that he was going to be meeting all of you who are his old friends, and I never thought I'd meet an old flame."

Frances heard the words that slipped out of his mouth so easily. At one time she had been completely enamored of his accent, dazzled by the way he strung sentences together. After meeting Rich, Mama had decided she preferred an American accent over a British one. "Americans let their words marry each other," she said. "The British keep their syllables separate, and it sounds so divorced," she used to laugh.

Now Rich's smoothly flowing words flung open the door to

a room no one knew about in America. She did not need to turn her head to know that everyone was staring—Vic with surprise, Lali with another sort of "why, you dark horse you" surprise, and Jay with the worst surprise: "You never told me this."

If only she had seen Rich first. Then she could have avoided him.

But would she have recognized this gray-haired man who called himself Ricardo? He had been bright blond when she last saw him. Now his blue eyes were behind glasses, and the wide torso he had kept exposed to get a tan was sunken. He even seemed much shorter than the man she had looked up to with such admiration and love.

He had told her that his family was Irish Catholic, like President Kennedy, except that they weren't rich. "Another thing we have in common," Frances had marveled. It was the Catholic connection that had pushed aside her Indian fear when he started opening the buttons of her blouse the night before he was to leave. She had wanted to make him happy, and she convinced herself that a Catholic man would marry the woman he had slept with outside the bounds of marriage. So she allowed him to undress her, rejoiced in hearing him repeat how much he loved her. Years later, after she had learned about STDs and ovulation, she realized how lucky it was that Rich hadn't given her a disease or left her pregnant. He didn't have a condom, and when he told her he would pull out, she had automatically said, "Sure"—the same answer she had given to his earlier, "Can we spend my final evening in India together?"

Frances had assumed their link was greater than any engagement band around her finger. The small diamond had cost him money; what she had given up on the beach had cost her the way she had been brought up. When he didn't write, she didn't know what to think. Had he not enjoyed that time together? Or did he think that since he had already had her, he didn't need to marry her? She had never told Mama or her sisters.

Then Mama told her he had written that his family didn't want their son marrying a non-American. He still loved Frances, but he could not go against his parents' wishes. That's what Mama told the curious townspeople.

Frances had somehow managed to live through those empty, desperate days. But Mama had lied. His family hadn't objected to a nonwhite daughter-in-law. Carmen was as brown as Frances, and spoke with a Spanish accent. He had even taken a Spanish name.

Old flame? Jay felt as if he were at the edge of the beach, with the waves pulling the sand from under his feet. He knew he was standing in one place, but it was as if he were moving, about to fall down.

When they started dating, he had asked Frances if she had had other boyfriends. "You're the first Indian man I've ever gone out with," she had told him.

"Are you telling me that Goans don't count as Indian?" he had teased.

"I never went out with a Goan," she had responded.

He had worried that precisely because she *was* Goan, she had been kissed, touched, caressed by other men who might even have asked her to marry them. So when she told him that he was her first boyfriend, he had been relieved. He was more modern than Vic, but, like his friend, he still wanted to be the first and only man for his wife. It was the right of every Indian man, and he was not going to be left out because he had chosen his own wife.

Lali scrutinized the gray-haired man. She didn't recall meeting him at UCLA. Had Frances gone out with him before she met Jay? She was sure that Jay and Frances had started dating in the very beginning, right after the orientation party where they had all met.

"Did you go to UCLA?" Lali thought she'd end the silence and assuage her curiosity.

"I went to Berkeley," Ricardo replied. "Why didn't you tell me you were at UCLA?" he asked Frances.

"Sweetheart, sweetheart," Carmen said, clasping his hand in hers. "Do you want me to get jealous again?" She turned to the others and said, "We met when he was studying at Berkeley. He came into the restaurant where I was a waitress, and six months later we were married."

So he had even married quickly, Frances thought. All the reasons she had invented crumbled. He hadn't married a blonde woman, or someone he had known for years. He just hadn't wanted *her*.

Frances wanted to turn her back and walk away from this man who had done the same thing to her so long ago. How could *he*, the one who had promised to send her his new address in America, ask why *she* hadn't kept in touch? The humiliating wait of those days and weeks and months knocked down her teetering self-esteem.

She had come to this party in her best dress to cover up their present circumstances. Now Rich was exposing the past she had thought was behind her. All her life she had concealed things. When they were young, Mama made sure they dressed nicely, even though there were days when they ate only rice and dal. In Hyderabad, she told the other rich girls that her house was on the beach. It was even easier to pretend in America. No one could check up on her stories.

Now Rich, with his big mouth, could tell everyone the things she had so desperately hoped would never become public.

She wished she could send him away with some well-chosen words. But anything she said to show that he had been a boor could boomerang and hit her in the face. For the first time in her life, Frances had nowhere to hide.

Frances grappled to find an answer that would close him down. Finally she said, trying to coat her words with lightness, "I met quite a few Americans who were traveling through Goa. I didn't tell *any* of them that I was coming to study at UCLA."

"Oh, come on, Fran," Rich said. "I wasn't one of those smelly hippies we used to laugh at. Remember? We had something going."

"It's okay," Carmen said, "you don't have to worry about hurting my feelings. I am no longer jealous that Ricardo was engaged to you before he married me."

"Oh, man, that was such a trip," Rich said. "I loved India, and meeting Fran's parents. I tell everyone about that Christmas I spent at your house. It was so old-fashioned. We sang carols, and ate, and your neighbors kept coming by to wish you . . . it wasn't Merry Christmas, it was something else," Rich paused, then said triumphantly, "Happy Christmas, that's it, Happy Christmas. It was all so quaint to me."

Vic said, "You never told me that you had gone to Goa, Ricardo. I thought you would want to talk to Jay because you were working in a place that was near Delhi. If you had told me you were in Goa, I could have arranged for you to meet Frances a long time ago."

Just then Rajesh came up and told Vic that the caterer wanted to know whether he should put the meat items on a separate table.

"I must go and check on it," Vic said and took off, followed by Priya.

Vic's departure left them without someone to direct the conversation.

Lali kept staring at Ricardo but seeing Aakash. Thank God

Aakash wasn't at the party. Then *she* would be like Frances, standing still amid the debris of her past indiscretion. Something about that stillness alerted Lali. Frances used to say that when things went wrong, she just wanted to crawl back into her mother's womb, and since she could not do so, she would just stay quiet and hope the moment passed by quickly.

"My knuckles get white," she had told Lali years ago. "Jay can say that my tongue is white, but the only thing white about me are my knuckles when I get anxious."

Lali glanced down at her friend's clenched hands. The fingers were curved into the palms, and the knuckles were large, protrudant, and very white.

Until Ricardo spilled the news of their engagement, Lali had been amused, especially by the ridiculous idea that Frances could have been related to Bartolomeu Dias. Such a story would never work with an Indian.

Then she remembered the story Frances told her the day she confessed that Jay might not marry her.

"It's the curse of being the youngest of five," she explained. "My sisters got all the good stuff. One's the beauty, another's the brains. It's as if my parents ran out of things to give me. Now I won't even have a husband."

Lali turned to Jay. He looked as though he had just seen an alien life form. For the first time since Lali had known him, he was quiet—no quip, no joke leavening the situation. Then Lali swung back to the tightly held fists that Frances was holding close to her sides. She recalled Frances banging on her apartment door, demanding to be let in. Frances had listened so patiently while she told her about Aakash. She had not asked many questions, had simply wanted to send some *gundas* after Aakash. Lali had been very grateful that Frances was not being the typical inquisitive Indian. Now, years later, she understood why. Frances had gone through the same experience. Instead of poking away at Lali, she had turned her fury on the person who deserved it. It had given Lali comfort to know she wasn't the only person who wanted to get rid of Aakash.

Lali realized she could do the same now.

"It's nice to meet you," Lali told Ricardo, "but do you mind very much if I steal Frances and Jay away? We were just about to find a table so we can sit down and eat. I'm famished, and since I haven't seen my friends in a while, we have a lot of catching-up to do."

"Hey, that's cool," Rich said. "We're about ready for dinner too. Maybe I'll see you around later?" he asked Frances.

Frances could not believe she was still standing. Thank God the children hadn't heard this. Thank God Lali had gotten rid of Rich.

What was she going to tell Jay? Would he understand?

Jay watched Rich walk away. That dirty-looking fellow had been engaged to Frances? Knew her so well that he had a pet name for her? Fran. He remembered once when he had called her Frannie. Frances had told him to please use her full name. He tried to recall that first month at UCLA when they had started going out. He had been surprised when she said, 'Yes.' The few Goans he knew always made much of their Western connections, and he assumed that she would prefer to be with an American.

"You mean you chose Jay when you could have had Tom, Dick, or Harry?" one of his college friends had asked Frances when they were visiting in Delhi.

"I had no competition, man," Jay had laughed. "She didn't want a Great American Nope."

Jay now looked at the Great American Nope that Frances had met before him. Had she given her virginity to this bozo? Was that why she was so keen, so desperate to get married? One time they had been kissing, and Jay had put his hand under her skirt. Frances had reacted very strongly, pulling away immediately, telling him that was only allowed after marriage. She had finally slept with him after they became man and wife. There had been no blood on the sheets, and he hadn't planned to say anything, but Frances had quickly explained that her gynecologist had suggested she switch to using tampons six months ago.

He needed to talk to Frances. Now.

"Lali, Jonathan, can you save a spot for us?" Jay asked. "I'm going to get us a drink," he lied. He took hold of *Fran*'s hand and pulled her to the side of the house. It was dark, no one was there, and they could talk. Music still poured onto the lawn, and people were laughing, chatting with each other in Hindi, English, loudly, softly. No one would miss them or know they were here.

"What else haven't you told me?" he demanded.

Frances just wanted to go home. The headache that had started when Rich said, "Fran?" had become a steady, excruciating pain in both temples. As always when she had headaches, her stomach, too, was upset. Her mouth was dry, and it felt as if she were going to throw up. She knew from past experience that though the sensation would remain, nothing would come up.

But she was feeling bad enough to legitimately say that she was unwell. They could collect the children and get away from here.

Instead, Jay—the man whose favorite Hindi word was *bindaas*, who told her to give Mandy some space and time, who kept suggesting she "relax, be *bindaas*," when they put money in the meter for an hour and were late, because, as he claimed, things always work out—Jay was making a spectacle of them.

He had also lied to Lali. It was clear that they weren't going to get drinks. Lali would also know *exactly* what they were talking about.

Or would she?

Frances ignored the raging blood vessels in her head and met Jay's accusing eyes. "And you have told *me* everything?"

"Of course I have. I never had another girlfriend. I even told you that my parents expected me to marry Geet, their best friends' daughter, though we haven't spent five minutes alone together. I am not the one who was engaged," he reminded her.

"I'm not talking about that," Frances said. "I know about UCLA."

"I never had another girl when I was a student. That was Vic."

For a brief moment, the pounding stopped. Frances felt the—release—of being sidetracked from her own anxiety. "Vic had women?"

"Lots," Jay said, "but we're not here to talk about him. This is about you."

"Before we talk about Rich, I need to know why you lied that you got your degree from UCLA."

The angry words Jay had been formulating in his mind evaporated. He had never discussed his classes with her, so of course he hadn't mentioned the one incomplete paper. How had she found out about it? Had she known all these years that he could never exchange the blank piece of paper everyone received at graduation for the real thing? Yet she hadn't said a word when he told her he didn't want to pay money to pick up his degree, that he would rather celebrate by going out to dinner.

"You see, Jay, I'm not the only one with secrets."

"I can easily fix mine," Jay said brazenly. "I just need to finish one lousy paper. How can you fix your past? You were engaged, practically married to another man, but you never thought to tell me?"

"Because I knew how you would react," Frances said, starting to cry. She tried to control the tears, but they kept gushing out.

Jay had never been able to stand tears. His school had taught him early on that no one cried, no matter what the circumstances. Any boy who showed moist eyes was immediately dubbed a sissy, a moniker that would follow him the rest of his school life. His own mother was stoic, and he had never known her to weep, or raise her voice. Even when he had called to say he was going to marry Frances, she had sighed and said, "Geet's parents will be so disappointed." It was Papa who had yelled, and Jay had imagined the Adam's apple bobbing up and down, the large eyes. He'd been relieved there was an ocean between them. He didn't have sisters who might have prepared him to deal with tears. Mandy had learned of his weakness when she was very little. All she needed to do was *pretend* to cry, and Jay would give her whatever she wanted.

Frances wasn't a crier. When they argued, she grew quiet and retreated into herself, her face hard, her voice cold. It was usually Jay who had to seek her out, say the first word.

But now Frances was sobbing, her body trembling, the tears leaving black lines on her cheeks as the mascara came off her eyelashes.

"Don't cry," Jay said. Then he added, "People will see."

People had already seen so much of her life, Frances thought. What did a few tears matter?

But as much as she had just been frantic that the past had come before her, now she was terrified of the future. She had never before seen that bewildered, devastated look on Jay's face. He had crushed her hand so hard it still hurt.

Was Jay going to divorce her because she had been engaged to another man? His family was modern in many ways, but not when it came to marriage. He was the only person in his extended family to have made a love marriage. It had infuriated his parents so much that they had quickly arranged a girl for his younger brother.

Would he now feel that he should never have gone against his parents?

She had lost Rich years ago. Was she about to lose Jay? The thought of getting a divorce, of having to tell Mama, the women at the office that she was going to be like them, a single mother, paralyzed her.

"So I didn't tell you about Rich," Frances admitted, hiccupping a little. "It happened a long time ago. We were only engaged for ten days."

"Ten days is a long time," Jay reminded her. "Vic got married in less time than that."

Frances took a long breath, her body shuddering. Jay had lived a rather Western life, but she instinctively knew that, like every other Indian man, he preferred an unsullied wife. She had heard about Indian men who slept with prostitutes yet demanded their bride be a virgin. Since Jay himself had never had a girlfriend, his purity had rendered her youthful mistake a catastrophe.

She had come to America with the idea of meeting someone. Mama had advised her to concentrate on boys more than on her studies. Everything had been new to her at UCLA—except Jay and the idea of getting a husband. His brown face had been familiar; his Western manner, reassuring. She had not so much fallen in love with him as fallen *in* with him. He was just like her, an Indian who fit into America.

But since he was Indian, she knew that he knew they could not simply date; they would need to marry. This time, she made sure she did everything correctly. Chaste kisses, plenty of handholding, but no sex. In anticipation of their becoming husband and wife, she had switched to using tampons.

Everything had gone well, and when they went to India, she

asked Mama to meet them up north. She allowed Jay to believe she was doing him a favor by letting him spend all his time in India with his family. Mama knew, without being told, never to mention Rich. Frances never did take Jay to Goa. Years went by, and her fear that Jay would somehow find out about Rich faded. Even this morning, at the dining room table, her fear had been a flicker, a moment, not an avalanche. The episode in the car had confirmed that her secret was safe.

"Well?" Jay asked.

Frances looked at his face. She had never wanted him this much, not even during those weeks right before graduation when it seemed that he was not going to propose.

This is it, she thought, I'm going to lose everything. He will leave me. Jay was a Hindu. She had been engaged. And never told him. Two very bad things. There was no Catholic guilt to keep him with her.

"I was ashamed," Frances said honestly. If she was going to lose everything, she might as well speak the truth.

Jay hadn't expected that. He didn't know how to respond.

"I met him, he asked me to marry him, and then he went back to America."

"Did you come here to look for him?"

"I came here almost two years after he had left. I came because I was so tired of people in my town asking me when I was going to America. You know how people love to gossip, love to make you more sad than you are already."

Rich hadn't written or sent for her, but he had left behind the idea that she should plan for her future. He had not gotten into Berkeley on his first attempt and knew that universities paid special attention to Peace Corps applicants. She did some of her own research and discovered that universities like applicants who are focused and have things in place. She had gone to church all her life. She knew the priest, knew the country, and so she put down her dissertation idea in her application.

"So you *wanted* to marry him?"

"What did I really know about marriage at that time?" Frances shook her head. "My mother told me he was a good man. Dada was excited that I was finally going to get married. I was the only one of my sisters who didn't have a boyfriend. I didn't lie when I told you that I hadn't had an Indian boyfriend."

"Did you sleep with him?" Jay asked the question that bothered him the most. He had been a virgin when he married. He didn't know what he would do if Frances said she had given up the most sacred part of herself to that dirty scumbag. First he needed to hear her answer.

"I didn't." Frances did not hesitate to lie, but as soon as the words left her mouth, her tongue grew dry. What if Rich told everyone at the party about that night? He was so unpredictable. He might even have told his wife, and she might confess that she wasn't jealous that they had been intimate.

Jay closed his eyes and put his head back. He breathed out. Opened his eyes. A few stars speckled the smoggy sky. Virgo was up there. Frances had been born in late August.

"You're a virgin," he used to tease her, and Lali would make a face and say, "Only *you* would keep saying virgin instead of Virgo."

"Okay," he said.

Frances felt the lie tickle her throat. She coughed and then could not stop.

"Are you all right?" Jay asked, suddenly alarmed. "Do you need water?"

Frances managed to shake her head. When she turned her back to him, he realized she needed him to pound the dip between her shoulders. One, two, three—he counted just to occupy his mind. She stopped when he got to twenty-three. It was the number of years they had been married.

"Thanks," Frances said shyly, as if this was their first date.

"I guess we should go back," Jay suggested.

Neither of them moved.

Of all the unknowns in her life—Mandy, her job—this particular one was something she could not live with, or fix on her own. She needed to know what Jay was going to do.

But before she could ask him, Jay spoke. "You should have been honest with me. I felt like an idiot out there."

And just like that, she was furious at him. He was thinking about himself.

"I've felt like an idiot all these years when I've told people you had an MBA," she said.

She had supported his every change of job; she had never told him that he would have more confidence if he did get his MBA. She knew he was afraid that someone would uncover the truth and kick him out of the company. That was why he never minded switching jobs, never lobbied for better pay. When she began doing well during the boom years of real estate, she hadn't flung her bigger paycheck in his face. She hadn't told him that *she* felt like an idiot for marrying a man who had studied at UCLA but who could not provide her with an upper-class life. Never once, during all their squabbles, did she compare him to their neighbor Jason, who had gotten his MBA from Northridge but whose wife didn't need to work because he did so well.

Jay remembered putting off writing that stupid paper. Next week, he had told himself. Then he walked across the stage at graduation, moved the tassel on his cap, and started the job. Slowly the need to finish faded. He had gotten the job based on having an MBA, and for a while he didn't feel bad, because he kept thinking he would write the paper. He even called the department to see how much time he had before they would not accept late work. Years passed, and though he kept telling everyone he had the degree, the knowledge that he did not, that anytime someone could out him, began to bother him almost on a daily basis. America was a forgiving country, but companies don't forgive liars. He had made his bed and now had to lie about it.

He grew ashamed, felt unworthy, didn't try for better and bigger jobs.

His father would never understand such stupidity. Papa had always done everything correctly. Thank God Papa hadn't asked to see his transcripts.

Frances had known, and she had kept the lie.

He had never felt so vulnerable in his life.

"Frances?" Lali came into view, her voice hesitant, her step tentative. "Your younger daughter is looking for you."

"Is everything all right?" Frances switched immediately to being a worried mother. When Lily was five years old, she had been running around at a birthday party and tripped over an exposed tree root, fracturing her arm. They had gone from waiting to hit the piñata to waiting in the ER.

"Yes, yes," Lali said. "She wants to know if you will allow her to play some game on the Wii. I didn't feel that I could give her permission."

"I'll go," Jay said, and walked away quickly, making sure to smile at Lali as he strode past her.

Frances saw the eagerness with which Jay took off. It was clear that he wanted to get away from her. Did that mean he always wanted to distance himself from her? But he was leaving her to take care of Lily. It gave her hope, made her think that perhaps he would want to continue being part of a family with her.

LALI APPROACHED FRANCES. She was standing in the strip of land that divided Vic's house from his neighbor's. The neighbor must have been invited to the party, because the house was dark. There was just enough light from the strings of bulbs out front for Lali to see the debris left from Frances's crying jag. Mascara encircled her eyes, her quivering mouth was bare of lipstick, and even her hair was disheveled, as if she had pulled at strands.

She had known that Jay and Frances were "talking" and hadn't wanted to disturb them, but Lily really wanted her mother. She was glad she hadn't sent Lily herself to find her mother.

Frances was too distraught to do anything, so Lali took charge. She started walking toward the back of the house to see whether she could sneak Frances inside that way and find a bathroom. She tripped over something and looked down to see the undulating length of a hose. Jonathan always called it the garden hose. She sometimes referred to it as a hosepipe, which made him laugh. This hosepipe was reassuringly attached to a tap. They did not need to find a bathroom after all.

"Frances, come here," Lali called softly as she turned on the faucet.

She didn't say a word the entire time Frances was washing her face. Lali found a packet of tissues in her purse and handed them over.

Frances wiped her face and put on some lipstick, her fingers trembling as she outlined her lips.

"There's something under your right eye," Lali said and wiped it off.

"Thanks," Frances sniffed, then blew her nose into a tissue.

"You want me to send some *gundas* after that *harami*?"

Frances wished she could laugh. "Just keep him away from me," she said.

"I was already planning to do that. Now let me look at you." Lali took a step back and surveyed her friend. "You look fine. You're lucky your eyes don't get small when you cry." She recalled her own face, and how she had worried that Jonathan would see her scrunched-up eyes and figure out something had happened while he was giving his paper.

"I'm lucky I have you for a friend," Frances said.

Lali felt like a hypocrite. What would Frances think if she knew that Lali had initially found the Ricardo encounter quite amusing? It was only when she noticed Frances's knuckles that she realized her friend was suffering.

"Let's go. We need to make sure Jay has taken good care of Lily. Men," she said, shaking her head, then thought, belatedly, that this time Frances would not find the put-down funny. They stepped onto the lighted, warm, canopied lawn and were taken aback by the bustle. "Dinner must be served." Lali pointed in the direction of the buffet, which was crowded with people.

"Mom, I've been looking all over for you." Mandy hurried up to them. "What happened to you?" she asked.

"I—" Frances struggled to come up with a response and then stopped as Lali took over. "I wanted to spend some alone time with your mom, so I spirited her away to the side of the house. But she tripped over the garden hose and her hands got dirty, and then her face got dirty, so we ended up turning on the hose to get her clean."

"Oh." Mandy accepted the long explanation, then turned her attention to why she had been looking for her mother in the first place. "Can we go to Delhi when we go to India?"

"Yes, of course," Frances said, not sure why her daughter was suddenly asking questions about their itinerary, instead of screaming that she was never going to India.

"Good. Nikhil and I were talking, and he said that if we go to Delhi, he'll give us a culinary tour. He says they have the most amazing street food. I'll go tell him that we'll see him there."

"When are you going to India?" Lali asked, hoping that the new topic would give Frances something else to think about.

"I'm taking Mandy there next month," Frances answered.

"Oh, a nice mother-and-daughter trip," Lali said. While she was pregnant with Aaron, she had read a newspaper article about mothers and daughters traveling together and had decided that if she had a girl, she would at the very least take her to India and show her where she had gone to school, buy *kulfi* at her favorite ice-cream stand in Bangalore.

"Mom," Mandy rushed back, "Nikhil wants to know if we can go to Delhi in October. That's when he'll be done with his classes in Europe."

"I guess," Frances shrugged, eyes scanning the crowd for Jay. At this point, she would agree to anything.

"Thanks, Mom, I'll go tell him." Mandy ran back.

"You're staying that long?" Lali asked. "Won't Mandy miss a lot of school?"

Frances was too empty to come up with an angle for their trip. Mandy's failures were already out there. So be it.

"Mandy hasn't been doing well in her classes here, and I'm taking her to Bangalore to finish high school."

"Really?" Lali thought back to the letters about Mandy's grades, her piano recitals, her swimming cups. When she had met Mandy, she had assumed she was seeing the class valedictorian, a female version of Nikhil.

Frances kept looking at the groups of people but did not see Jay or Lily. Then she realized that he must have gone to the game room Vic had told them about.

Lali felt a jolt of guilt. Frances was being so honest about her daughter. She opened her mouth to tell Frances about Aaron, then closed it. They were two different problems. Aaron was doing well academically. He simply didn't like Harvard. Mandy was not cutting it in high school. She remembered Aaron's tenth-grade report card. "You know, Aaron went through a rebellious phase in high school, but it passed by pretty quickly," Lali said, wanting to help Frances. The poor woman was coping with so much this evening. If Aakash had showed up at the party, and if Jonathan and she hadn't sorted things out, *she* would have been the one with the sad face.

"I can handle a phase," Frances said. "Mandy needs to do well in her last year, and there's nothing to do in India except study."

"Are you nuts?" Lali looked at Frances in astonishment. "When was the last time you were there? Now they have all the same distractions—TV, computers, everything electronic. And the games are much cheaper because they are pirated. India's not like it used to be in our days."

"I'm going to be putting Mandy in a *Catholic* school."

"I went to one of those too, you know. But even those types of schools have changed. My mom keeps telling me about ten-year-olds checking porn on the computer, and girls as young as twelve going on dates. She says that these days parents work and the servants don't monitor the children. From what I gather, the electronic world is so new over there that they don't have any rules. Kids are going crazy."

"That may be, but I think they study harder."

"That's probably true," Lali agreed, "but you need to consider the effect on Mandy. If someone like Mandy had come to my school when I was young, everyone would have wanted to be her friend. But India's opened up and people travel outside the country easily, which means foreign-returned folk aren't exciting anymore. I've heard horror stories of children being mean to those who return from abroad. They might even figure out why she needed to return and tease her."

"Look, I can't talk about this anymore," Frances shook her head.

"Sorry. I didn't mean to overload you." Lali wished she hadn't gone on about the new India. Who was she to tell Frances what to do? "Let's get something to eat."

"I'm not hungry."

"It smells great," Lali cajoled. "Let's go find our table and then hit the buffet. Remember that Vic went to check on the meat items. They might be serving pork vindaloo."

"I'm not hungry."

That morning years ago, Frances had made tea for Lali, joking that while the British had created many problems in India, they had also given them a pot filled with an all-powerful palliative. She had cleaned the kitchen, waited until Lali had a shower, and insisted she fill her stomach—first with the tea and then with a sandwich.

"Look at me, Frances." Lali stood squarely in front of her friend. "Don't let that man have such power over you. He's nothing. He's less than nothing. Forget about him. That's what you told me about Aakash, remember? Now, you are going to eat and enjoy yourself and act as though he doesn't exist."

Frances sighed. It wasn't just Rich she was worried about. It was Jay. She still hadn't seen his gray-and-black-haired head anywhere.

"The children," Frances brought up as a last-minute strategy to keep away from the food. "I should check on them."

"They're probably playing inside. You just saw Mandy. She seems to be managing nicely on her own. Come on, let's go."

JAY SETTLED LILY in front of the Wii and looked around the game room. It was much bigger than their own living room—the sectional couch, large-screen TV, and various games still leaving a lot of space. Lily and Sam were playing Halo, a game that Frances had refused to let them buy. But, as both children had told him, they had played it many times in their friends' homes. Jay had almost given Lily the same, Frances-inspired, "We do things differently in our house" answer, then thought, why not? Someone had to have a good time at the party.

It had been a while since the kids had begged him to play with them. These days, they viewed him as an interruption, perhaps because by the time he came home, they were often in the middle of a game and didn't want to stop and let him join in.

Jay sat down on the couch, and the plush cushions pulled him in. He had no desire to go outside. He wanted to leave the party but knew that Vic would be hurt. Vic was an odd bloke. Did he even understand what had transpired after he made those introductions? He had blithely gone off to see about the dinner.

Jay could smell fried onions, ginger, garlic, and chili, the definitive aromas of Indian cuisine. He usually assuaged anxiety with food, but not this time. The pakoras seemed to be drowning in a sea of oil in his stomach. He thought of his mother, who used to give him bicarbonate of soda any time he complained of a tummy ache. He was now a father of three and yet he felt young—unprepared for an ex-fiancé, a daughter not doing well in school, children asking if they can play certain games. He felt as if he were still in college, waiting to finish that paper.

How had Frances known about that bloody paper? He had never told anyone. Even if she had gone through his desk one day when he wasn't there, she would not have found any information about it. American professors don't pressure students to do their work. It was the reason Frances was taking Mandy back to India.

Maybe this was the best time for her to go. They could, as the Americans say, take a break from each other, see what happened.

The idea was terrifying. He was Indian. He had always assumed they would leave this earth still married to each other.

Why hadn't Frances told him about her American fiancé? Was it really shame? Back home, a broken engagement was hardest on the girl. No matter why the engagement ended, it was always the girl who suffered. He recalled Mummy telling him about her cousin's daughter. Her parents had found a nice Indian man living in America. He had returned, as Vic had done, and they had gotten engaged. But once he went back to finish his PhD at Rutgers, he phoned his parents with the news that he had married his German girlfriend. It had taken Mummy's cousin three more years before she was able to find her daughter a suitable husband.

Goans might claim they are different from Indians, but a broken engagement is a broken engagement. Even in America, land of the free to divorce and home of the bravely divorced, it evoked some shame. He wasn't surprised that Frances had come here to get away from the nosey parkers in her town.

Had she married him on the rebound? He had never planned to marry her. Guilt, along with love, had prompted his proposal. That final semester had been an obstacle course of finishing classes, going for interviews, getting a job—and, for him, dealing with Frances's asking face. He had even talked to Vic about his ambivalence, had envied his friend's clean life. In the end, he had asked Frances, a little shocked that he was going against his parents' wishes yet at the same time pleased that he was doing something so different.

"Dad?"

The word invaded his inner torment.

"What?"

"I'm hungry."

"You're in the right place," Jay recovered, and smiled. "I think I can smell dinner."

"I know," Lily said. "I can see the men with the food." She pointed to the doorway that led farther into the house. Just then, a waiter passed by holding a large platter.

"That's tandoori chicken," Jay said, surprised to see the mounds of meat. Then he remembered Rajesh asking Vic whether the meat should be on a separate table.

"It's my favorite Indian food," Sam said with satisfaction.

"It's the *only* Indian food you eat," Jay reminded him. "Why do you think Mom and I haven't taken you back to visit?" When their neighbor Lucy once asked them why they didn't visit India, Jay had explained that it was difficult with the children, because they missed American food too much. Sam had been standing beside him and nodded, saying, "It's too spicy."

Now Sam said, "Let's go tell Mom she was wrong. She told me Uncle Vic doesn't eat meat, so there would only be vegetables. I bet she's gonna love eating the chicken."

Jay knew they couldn't hide out forever.

He had reluctantly stepped outside, hyperaware that Rich and Frances were among all these guests, when someone shouted, "Speech, Nikhil, speech!"

"What's going on, Dad?" Lily asked.

"Someone wants Nikhil to make a speech."

"That's because he's a vad-e-lic-to-ri-an," Lily said the big word slowly, with grave importance.

"You're right, Lily," Jay said, "which means he'll make a short speech."

"Speech, speech." The refrain was picked up by other groups.

"Oh, God, these Indians will never learn," Lali groaned. "If they wanted to hear a speech, they should have attended his graduation. I hope it's short, at least."

Frances wanted to tell Lali that's what Nikhil had said about being a valedictorian, but the words stuck in her throat. She had heard them an hour ago, when her family was intact, Jay standing beside her, their plans certain even if their future wasn't so great.

She looked toward the house—and saw Jay. Her heart lifted. He hadn't left the party. She knew he wouldn't, but she was so insecure that she wasn't convinced he was still here until she saw him. Lily and Sam were standing next to him. Their glances interlocked. Jay broke away, and Frances, feeling the long-distance slight, turned her head. Mandy was standing by herself. She didn't look caged, just a girl taking in all the noise around her.

Right behind Mandy was Rich.

Her heart dove to her toes. She took a step toward Mandy to pull her away, then realized that Rich hadn't met her daughter. Even *he* wouldn't talk to a total stranger. As she watched, Mandy met her gaze and started walking toward her.

"Speech! Speech!" The word sounded like rounders, as it was shouted by group after group.

• • •

Vic wished his friends weren't so—traditional. How could he tell them that Nikhil didn't want to give a speech? They expected it. They would also be shocked to learn that Nikhil hadn't wanted a big party in his honor.

Priya looked at him and raised her eyebrows. Once again, he had to do something, fix the situation.

He finished his glass of whiskey and handed it to her. "Go stop the music," he instructed.

He walked toward the buffet tables, a little hot from the bodies around him as well as the golden liquid that had just coursed down his throat. He waved his hands over his head to gain everyone's attention. The music stopped, and slowly, the insistent chant also ended.

Everyone stood still, including those serving themselves food from the buffet.

"You are asking for my son to give you a speech, so I am going to ask him to come here. I hope everybody can hear him. Nikhil, *beta*, come say a few words."

As he said that, Vic suddenly realized that this was exactly what he had been planning to do if Priya hadn't created such a fuss about Nikhil not wanting to join the company. He wouldn't have had Nikhil give a speech, but he would have ensured everyone's attention as he presented the key to his son.

He could give Nikhil his present as soon as the speech was over.

"Nikhil?" Vic called again.

"He's here," a tall American boy shouted.

"Come out, come out," the crowd now intoned.

Nikhil's shoulders were bowed as he reluctantly made his

way toward his father. "My son, the MIT graduate, Nikhil," announced Vic, clapping his hands.

Nikhil looked down. Then, as if he had gained inspiration from the earth, he raised his head and started speaking.

"Gosh, well, first of all, thank you for coming here this evening. It means a lot to my family and me that you took the trouble to come. I'm afraid I didn't take the trouble to write a speech. Truth to tell, I didn't expect to say anything today." Nikhil paused and then continued: "I'd also like to thank my parents, especially my dad. Most people finish college with huge debts. My dad and mom were very generous, and Dad insisted that I never take out a single loan. My degree from MIT in some ways is really *his* degree."

Everyone started clapping boisterously. Vic felt as if someone had swaddled him in a warm blanket. It was so nice of Nikhil to show his appreciation. This was what fathers do for their children, he wanted to say. He didn't want Nikhil to feel indebted to him. He fingered the box in his pocket. All evening long, it had knocked against his leg with every step he took. Now he curled his palm around it and moved closer to Nikhil.

But Nikhil wasn't done yet. He waited till the crowd was quiet and said, "In fact, I not only took my father's money to go to MIT, I even took his suggestion to study computer science. As you all know, my father studied computers at UCLA and started a company. My own trajectory is going to be different from that."

Vic rushed up to Nikhil. He would have grabbed the microphone if Nikhil were holding one. What was Nikhil about to do? Tell everyone here that he was going to peel cucumbers in the kitchen?

"My son is too good," Vic interrupted Nikhil. "I was more than happy to send him to MIT. I only went to MIT one time for his graduation, so I don't know why he is saying that the degree is mine. I never took a single test or anything." Vic paused to let the people laugh, as he knew they would. "But because he has done so well, I would like to give him a present that I had made some months ago. It is very small, but I hope my son will accept it."

"No, Dad," Nikhil said, moving away. "You've done enough."

Priya joined them. "Vic, let it be. Nikhil is correct. You have done more than enough."

He wasn't in the bedroom, worried whether they would join him downstairs. They were here, with people all around them. If he didn't do it now, then when?

Vic retrieved the box that had felt so heavy all evening long.

"For my son, Nikhil." Vic held up the square golden box so everyone could see it. He had taken it from Priya's jewelry case, pleased that it would give people the wrong idea.

Sibilants swirled around the crowd. A few spoke, their voices high with excitement. They expected Nikhil to open it and find something gold inside.

Only Priya and Nikhil knew what it contained.

"Oh, Dad, you've done enough." Nikhil resisted taking the box.

"It's for you," Vic insisted.

The box remained suspended between his fingers. He felt foolish. Nikhil was supposed to accept it.

He was just about to force it into Nikhil's hand when Priya reached out and grabbed it.

Lali bent closer to Frances. "Any idea what this is about?"

Frances shook her head. She lived within driving distance of Vic and Priya, but she didn't know them any better than Lali did.

"I think Vic's drunk," Lali said.

"He isn't slurring his words," Frances answered without thinking. She didn't know what exactly was going on, but it was evident that everything wasn't as happy and joyful as she had imagined all these past weeks leading up to the party. If Vic continued acting this way, it might eclipse the Rich disaster.

"But he's being so pushy, not listening to his son or to Priya."

"Oh, he's being a typical Indian male," Frances said, the words accompanied by her knee-jerk thought that Jay was so different from Vic. Then she recalled Jay's face, his stern voice. Jay, who prided himself on being more open than Indian men, had acted like a typical Indian male about Rich. What had happened to the man who said his daughter could date? The man who made dinner on the evenings he arrived home earlier than Frances, and who clearly didn't object when his wife earned more money? The similarity she now saw between Jay and Vic hardened Frances. Jay had no business being so mean to her for something that had happened long before they met.

"Priya, let me give it to my son." Vic held out his hand for the box.

Priya shook her head.

Now Nikhil took his place in the arena. "Hey, you two, loosen up. Let's go get dinner. I'm sure our guests are starving. Come on, everyone, eat before the food gets cold. There's nothing worse than cold dal."

Jay marveled at Nikhil's composure. He knew Vic was up to something, and so did Nikhil. But instead of cowering in his father's presence, Nikhil was tackling it head-on. He himself had made sure there was an ocean between them when he anticipated his father's anger.

"I am only wanting to give you my present," Vic said as he tried to wrestle the box out of Priya's hand.

Priya stepped away from Vic and, in front of everyone, slipped the box into her blouse. Lali had seen her servant do this every month when Amma paid her. The servant woman didn't have a purse, and the saree blouse was the safest place to hide something valuable. She herself had tucked her apartment key into her bra when she went to her graduation. But she had done that in the privacy of her apartment, aware that it was not something upper-class women do. Now Priya was displaying her village origins to everyone.

Vic was furious. First Priya had threatened him with a no-show at the party, now she was making sure he did not give Nikhil the key to the office.

"Give it to me." He walked toward her, clenching his hands tightly to stifle the urge to strangle her.

"Dad, let's go eat," Nikhil said.

"You step aside." Vic pushed Nikhil. The boy was such a sissy. He had a good degree, yet he wanted to take on a woman's job.

"*Aree, aree*," Rajesh said soothingly as he approached the trio. "Listen to your *beta*, Vic. He is an MIT graduate and so he is knowing what to do."

The simpering words infuriated Vic. Rajesh had given Nikhil a wok. He was encouraging his son to become a cook. Only a fool would do that. Or a man who wanted to make a fool of another man. He imagined Rajesh returning to India and telling people that Nikhil was dicing onions in the kitchen and crying like a woman.

"You shut up," Vic hissed. "Don't come near my family."

"*Aree*, this is my family also."

"Keep away!" Vic rushed at Rajesh, but before he got to him, Nikhil stepped between them.

"This is getting way out of hand," Nikhil said. "Dad, calm down. Uncle Rajesh, why don't you check the situation with the caterers?"

"Come with me, Rajesh," Priya called out.

"Always looking after your cousin," Vic jeered. "Why didn't you stop him from drinking too much? Look at him."

"*Aree*, I am only drinking one-two beers," Rajesh said, wiping the sweat from his brow with a large handkerchief.

"*He's* not the drunk in the family," Priya said archly.

"Hey, you two, cut it out. Mom, just give me Dad's gift." Nikhil held out his hand.

"Rajesh, let's go." Priya ignored Nikhil.

"Did you hear my son?" Vic asked. "Give him the box."

"Why are you doing all this?" Rajesh asked Vic. "Let it be, no?"

"Why isn't someone stopping this?" Jonathan whispered in Lali's ear. She hadn't heard him come up beside her, so riveted was she by what was going on. This was more dramatic than a Bollywood film.

"And take on Vic?" she whispered back. She didn't want to tell Jonathan that most of the Indian guests were probably enjoying this open-heart surgery of a family that was rich and successful. Other people's problems invariably made one feel better about oneself.

"His cousin's sweating an awful lot," Jonathan noted.

"He drank an awful lot," Lali said.

Rajesh leaned over, held his stomach, and opened his mouth. A gush of liquid fell to the ground.

"Yeeuch," someone said, while others groaned.

Lali watched the watery mess pool around Rajesh's feet. Rajesh tried to move away, but was too unbalanced and fell down. "See, I told you he drank too—," Lali started to tell Jonathan, but he had rushed past her.

"Someone call 911," Jonathan called out as he bent over Rajesh and checked to see whether he was still breathing.

"They don't come because a drunk puked," a voice pointed out.

"I guess Americans have no idea how much we Indians enjoy our drink," another sniggered. "We would be calling 911 at *all* our parties."

"He's having a heart attack," Jonathan stated, as he started doing CPR.

"This chap doesn't know the difference between a heart attack and a drunk?" another voice asked plaintively.

Lali wondered whether Jonathan had misjudged the situation. He had been pointing out Rajesh all evening. Had that initial worry prompted him to make the wrong call? It would be so embarrassing, especially in this group. Indian parties invariably had lots of doctors. She also knew they would like nothing better than to best an American doctor.

"Call 911, dammit," Jonathan said as began to give him artificial respiration.

"Is he okay?" Priya's voice was barely audible.

"What's wrong with my uncle?" Nikhil asked, squatting beside Jonathan.

Jonathan didn't respond, and suddenly everyone realized, at the same time, that Rajesh wasn't drunk.

"I'm a doctor," an Indian man said.

"I'm also a doctor," said another.

"Step aside," an Indian with a goatee ordered Jonathan, "I'm a cardiologist. Let me handle this."

"Don't push him away," Jay shouted. "He's a cardiologist from Harvard."

The Indian cardiologist knelt down, and Jonathan stood up. He mopped his forehead with a handkerchief and slowly walked back to Lali.

"He's okay, right?" Lali asked him, sure of the answer. This was a party. They were supposed to be having a good time. People got drunk at parties. Nothing worse happened.

Jonathan didn't answer.

"Is Rajesh okay?" Jay asked, with Lily and Sam beside him.

"He's not," Jonathan said. "You should get the kids away," he recommended.

"You mean he's—" Frances could not say the word.

She looked at Jay. They had both thought that Rajesh was a village idiot. They had wanted to get as far away from him as possible. It was people like Rajesh whom they routinely laughed at. Priya's insurance-selling scam of a cousin would become the next story they told everyone.

Jay felt the business card in his pocket. He had slipped it in there just to shut up Rajesh. He had meant to throw it away but had been sidetracked with other things.

Mandy's face was small, frightened. "Mom, what did Uncle Jonathan mean?"

"Come here," Frances said, pulling Mandy against her. "The doctors are taking care of him," she murmured. She looked down at Lily and Sam. For once she was pleased by their distraction. They weren't paying attention to the events around them. Sam had found a red stone and was telling his sister that it was a ruby.

Priya was crying, tears falling at her feet.

Nikhil was asking all the guests to please go inside. The ambulance was on its way, he explained, and they would need to get to Rajesh easily.

Jonathan joined Nikhil in herding people away from Rajesh. "Let's move, everyone, let's keep going," he kept saying.

"We'll lead the way," Jay said, ushering the children ahead of him. He didn't want the younger ones to see Rajesh. They hadn't realized what had happened. Only Mandy knew, but he figured she was old enough to handle this. His own cousin had been fifteen years old when he lit his father's funeral pyre.

Lali noticed that the doctors who had shoved Jonathan aside were whispering to each other. Their bodies hid the one lying on the ground. Rajesh had not been moved. The siren sounded, the noise confirming that something bad had happened.

Lali had heard the blaring, undulating sound of a siren many times, was used to pulling over to the side of the street to allow the ambulance to keep going.

This time, they were the destination.

"Let's go inside," Jonathan started toward the house.

"Don't you want to be there when the ambulance arrives? Tell them what happened?" Lali asked.

"The others will do that," he said.

She quickened her footsteps, reached him, and took hold of his hand.

"I couldn't save him," Jonathan shook his head. "I couldn't save him. I knew he was sick, I saw the signs, and I couldn't save him."

"You were the only one who tried," Lali comforted him. "I should have called 911 when you first said it," she said, guilt shaming her. Like the others, she, too, had thought that Rajesh was drunk.

"I'm a doctor," Jonathan said. "I should have been able to save him. But it was too late by the time I realized what had happened."

"Honey, you tried your best." It was what she always told him when he lost a patient.

"I wonder if things would have turned out differently had I checked him out earlier."

"He wouldn't have let you. Vic told us he was working too hard, remember?"

"I saw his color, the sweat on his face. I should have insisted."

"He wouldn't have let you, honey. Just accept that."

"I suppose you're right. Boy, Indians sure close in on their own. Those doctors shoved me aside pretty damn quick."

"I saw that. I hated that they did that to you."

"It was already too late. That's why I let them take over."

She pressed his palm tighter and wished she could give him a hug. Until now, she had always been the outsider in their marriage. She had the brown skin, the accent, the different religion.

He had always included her, always made her feel that she was the right partner for him.

This was the first time that he had been treated as the odd one. When they visited India, her parents and relatives had done their best to make him feel like family, but this evening the other doctors had refused to let him be part of their fraternity. She felt his hurt, both from their shunting him aside as well as his inability to save Rajesh.

"I love you," she whispered.

"Same here." Jonathan unclasped his hand and put his arm around her shoulder. Their steps grew unified, their bodies so close she could feel the hard edges of his belt.

A walkie-talkie crackled behind them as two men carried a stretcher. The body was covered with a sheet.

Priya watched the men take Rajesh away. Her cousin, her only relative in America, was gone. And it was all Vic's fault.

"You did this," she told Vic.

"How did I do that? I never asked him to come early to help us."

"You didn't give him a nice job. That's why he took that stupid insurance job."

Vic started to speak, then closed his mouth.

Priya stood in front of him, her face right under his nose. "He would still be alive if you had let him work at your company. But he was forced to take that job and then his wife left to go back, and so he ate badly. This is all your fault."

The shock of Rajesh's death at his feet was still reverberating through Vic's body. Pitaji had died by the time he returned. No one had ever given up their life right in front of his eyes.

Now Priya was telling him that he was responsible. Her words were dripping with sadness—and truth.

Vic hung his head. He remembered his American reaction

to Rajesh. "I can't give you this office just because you're my relative," he'd said. "You have to earn it." He had known the fellow would never be good enough to have a nice, big office. He had been so relieved when Rajesh had left the company. Then Rajesh had found a job on his own. He had been so proud. He hadn't cared about the long hours. He only complained about the difficulty of finding vegetarian fast food. The man had worked and eaten himself to death.

"And now you are going to do the same thing to Nikhil," Priya said, wiping her nose with the edge of her saree pallao. "You will force Nikhil to work in your company and he will hate it so much it will kill him. But we won't burn his body. We can just bury it in that swimming pool you made for him. Do you ever see him swimming? Do you?" she shouted. "He hated it, but he did it to make you happy. He went to MIT and studied hard to make you happy. But you are not happy. You just want him to work in your stupid company. Here," she said, removing the small box from her blouse, "give it to him."

Vic didn't reach out his hand.

Priya threw the box on the ground.

It lay there, almost on the same spot where Rajesh had so recently fallen.

Vic picked it up.

Nikhil, who had followed Rajesh to the ambulance, returned.

"They're going to do an autopsy," Nikhil said. "I think we should go to the hospital in about half an hour, after we send everyone away."

Vic thought of how his son had never wanted the party, had only wanted to follow his heart to a chopping board, the way he had followed his own heart to the motherboard of a computer.

"Nikhil, I am never going to give you this present," Vic promised, his voice shaking.

Nikhil stared at his father.

"Never," Vic repeated.

Nikhil walked up and clasped his father in a long hug. Vic had never hugged his own father. The first time he saw a lot of hugging was at Nikhil's graduation. Nikhil had walked beside him, had introduced him to his friends and professors, but, unlike the other boys, he had never hugged him.

Vic put his arms around this body he had helped create. Uncomfortable at such closeness, he patted his son's back. Then he felt the strength and warmth of the two long arms across his own back. He stopped the halfhearted pats and slowly tightened his grip on his son, drawing him closer. He vowed that his son would never be unhappy, that he would allow him to be a chef. Nothing mattered, so long as Nikhil lived.

Frances, Jay, and the children huddled together in the hallway. The other guests were in the living room, the dining room, many peering out the windows. A few mothers were feeding their children. It was past dinnertime, and the little ones were tired and hungry. Frances could not believe there had been a dead body outside. She moved closer to Jay. Thank God he was alive, they were alive. They still had a chance. Rajesh's wife would never be able to talk to him again.

She wanted to tell Jay all this. "I'm so—" she started, and then she remembered the pack of cigarettes she had found on the dashboard of his car. "Please stop smoking," she implored, hoping that he would realize it was her way of keeping him alive longer.

Jonathan and Lali walked up just as Frances finished saying the word *smoking*. "Oh, God, Jay, don't tell me you're still smoking," Lali joined in. "It's terrible for you. You've got to stop."

Jay straightened his lips.

"Is that a yes?" Lali pushed.

"Honey, I think he knows," Jonathan said. "Let him be."

Frances wanted to cry. They had just witnessed something awful, and instead of coming together, Jay was standing apart from her, the children between them. He wasn't going to listen to her. He was going to do what he wanted.

"Some party, eh?" Jay said, trying to get the conversation away from the nagging duo. He could see Rich's gray hair in the corner. The man hadn't left. Was he waiting to talk to Frances?

"I think this party is over," Jonathan said. "We should tell the people they ought to go home."

"Honey, let Vic do that," Lali said.

"He's too busy coping with what just happened," Jonathan said, and then raised his voice. "Listen up, everyone. Please go home. Give Vic and his family their privacy."

Nobody moved.

"Look, look," someone near the window said, and bodies rushed to find out what was going on outside.

"May I have your attention, please?" Jonathan tried again. "The party's ended. You can all go home now."

"Who is he to tell us what to do?" a man in a dark blue suit asked challengingly.

"I'm just trying to help Vic," Jonathan said.

"We don't have to listen to you," the man insisted.

Lali wished she could go up to the man and hit him. This was the second time they were being mean to Jonathan. They had laughed off his initial diagnosis, but as soon as they realized he was right, they had thought nothing of taking over, as if brown hands alone could minister to brown patients. Now another brown face was refusing to listen to Jonathan's logic.

She was just about to say something when Jay spoke. "What do you want to do? You want to eat dinner after what just happened? You want to sit and talk to Vic? What exactly do you want to do?"

"There is no need to get all angry, anyway," the man responded.

"Jonathan here is being sensible. He thinks we should go, and let Vic and his family deal with this tragedy."

"We are going." Pierre's French accent rang out. "All of us who are in his motorbiking club will leave now."

"Thank you," Jay said.

"What about you?" the blue-suited man goaded Jay. "You are staying?"

"Why don't you worry about yourself, huh?" Jay suggested. "We're Vic's oldest friends. We know better than to bother him now."

"Fran?" Rich approached them. "I guess we never had a chance to talk."

"I was hoping to get to know you," Carmen said. "Now, of course, it is . . ."

Frances didn't respond. She hoped that both Rich and Jay would read her signal correctly.

"I know this must be hard on you," Rich said. "Anyway, I'll ask Vic for your phone number in a few weeks."

"Yes, you can come to our home for dinner," Carmen added. "I won't have to worry about using chilies because Indians also like spicy food."

"Frances doesn't eat spicy food," Lali spoke up. She could not believe this couple's insensitivity.

"Of course, I forgot, you are Portuguese," Carmen said. "Good-bye."

"See ya," Rich said, and they left.

"Looks like we're the last ones here," Jonathan said. "We should get going as well." They walked past the tables, the flowers, the grass that was now flattened. The buffet tables were loaded with food. Vic, Priya, Nikhil, and Nandan were standing there, a linked group, oblivious to the departing guests.

Frances had wanted to leave from the moment they arrived. Now she was frightened to leave. She was going with Jay, but going where?

"I'm hungry," Sam announced as soon as they stepped beyond the canopy.

"I can't believe you can eat at such a time." Mandy shook her head.

"I can always eat," Sam said.

"Did the man die?" Lily asked.

Frances didn't want to lie, but she also didn't want to tell the truth. She looked at Jay. He had sung and laughed the whole way to the party. It was unimaginable that it had ended like this.

Before she could come up with an answer, Jonathan said, "He's gone to the hospital."

"But I thought you were a doctor."

"You're right, I am," Jonathan said, "but I didn't bring my bag with me."

"You should do that next time," Lily said.

"You're right," Jonathan agreed.

"Shall we go somewhere together to eat?" Frances asked, not looking at Jay.

"I can't eat a thing," Lali said, "but if you're hungry, honey," she told Jonathan, "I'll go."

"I'm done for the night. It's been a long day. I'm ready for bed," he said.

"Are you sure?" Frances asked.

"We left our house at five thirty this morning," Lali said. That hour was an eternity away. She could not remember the woman who had dressed in the newly bought blouse. "We're really tired."

"Can we go to In-n-Out burger?" Sam begged.

"Yes, yes," Lily said. "I want the animal fries."

"Maybe we'll see Mr. Billy-ant when we get to the car," Frances said, and caught her breath.

"Let's say our good-byes, then." Jay held out his hand to Jonathan. "See you in better circumstances. Lali, you two drive safely."

"You two drive carefully as well." Lali hugged Frances.

"Thanks," Frances whispered.

"Friendship means never having to say, 'Thank you,'" Lali said, repeating the *Love Story* phrase that Jay had readjusted and taught them all years ago.

"Thanks just the same," Frances insisted as she drew away.

"See you up in the Bay Area?" Jonathan asked.

Frances looked at Jay. "Sounds like a good idea," he said.

"See you there, then," Frances said, holding out her hand toward Jay. They weren't a demonstrative couple in public, but Lali and Jonathan were holding hands, and, after all that had happened, she needed to feel his touch.

Jay looked at the proffered palm, the long fingers that all his children had inherited.

"Dad, Dad," Lily said excitedly, "come quick! I see a cat! Maybe it's Mr. Billyant."

Jay held Frances's gaze for a moment, then turned and followed their daughter.

"*Chalo*, you all. Let's go see if it indeed is Mr. Billyant, or if he is sitting on the wall, waiting for us."

The Invitation

It is with great pleasure that we invite you

to share our happiness when our son

AARON

is called to the Torah

as a Bar Mitzvah on

July 31, 2012

Reception
immediately following the ceremony
in our backyard

RSVP:

Lalijonathan@yahoo.com

The Responses

Send | Save | Close | Check Names

To... Lalijonathan@yahoo.com [remove]

Cc...

Bcc...

Subject: Bar Mitzvah RSVP

Attachments...

Dear Lali and Jonathan,

Congratulations on your son's great accomplishment. Unfortunately our whole family will be unable to attend as we will be in Spain. Nikhil is taking some classes on tapas. They are not at all delicious.

Please expect our gift via UPS.

Vic

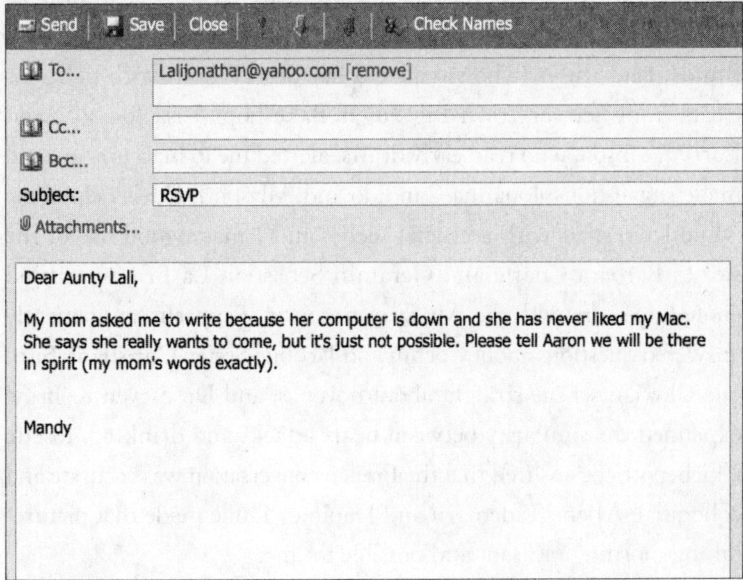

Send | Save | Close | Check Names

To... Lalijonathan@yahoo.com [remove]

Cc...

Bcc...

Subject: RSVP

Attachments...

Dear Aunty Lali,

My mom asked me to write because her computer is down and she has never liked my Mac. She says she really wants to come, but it's just not possible. Please tell Aaron we will be there in spirit (my mom's words exactly).

Mandy

Acknowledgments

THIS NOVEL STARTED as a conversation with my agent, Bonnie Nadell, and ended when she said it was fine. I continue to marvel that she took me on. Maria Guarnaschelli, my editor, and Melanie Tortoroli, her assistant at W. W. Norton, were unfailingly supportive and responsive. I could not ask for better backing. Kathy Brandes cleaned up the manuscript and caught mistakes.

I reserve my greatest thanks for Ellie Miller, who started my weekdays with a walk, during which she offered wonderful insights into the characters I was creating. I'd also like to thank Barbara Bundy, Lisa Ritter (who sweetened her observations with delicious treats from her very own Big Sugar Bakeshop), Lisa Jonsson, and Larry Jacobson, who read early drafts, alerted me to inaccuracies, and made suggestions. Johanna Candido and Allyson J. Davis helped me while I wrestled with a crucial scene, and I made good use of the stories Barbara Chaffe and Geramin Sebastian La Brie were kind enough to share with me. My favorite cousin, Pappachayan, patiently answered questions about Cochin and Jacobite Syrian Christians; Simone Cherian set me straight about novenas; and Dr. Steven Kobrine explained the similarity between heart attacks and drinking. Josette Chicheportiche ensured that the French conversation was accurate and colloquial. Arlene Tademaru and Daphney Duke made that picture-taking morning pleasant and possible for me.